HEARTS, MINDS, AND COFFEE

A Vietnam Peace Odyssey

Kent Hinckley

Publisher's Note
This is a work of fiction. Names, characters, places, and incidents are the product of the author's imagination or are used fictitiously, and any resemblance to actual persons, living or dead, events, locales, or business establishments is entirely coincidental.

Copyright © 2014 by Kent Hinckley
ISBN-10: 0991545303
ISBN-13: 9780991545308
ISBN-978-0-9915453-1-5 (ebook)
Library of Congress — pending

Published by: Reyall Corporation
5666 La Jolla Blvd. #200
La Jolla, CA 92037

Printed in the United States of America
Cover by: Alexander von Ness, www.nessgraphica.com
See also www.kenthinckley.com

Dedicated to: Buck Kingman, Fred Abramson, and Jim Cannon

– I miss you –

1

January 13, 1970

From a remote valley in the highlands near Pleiku, Second Lieutenant Slater Marshall and three enlisted men took cover behind an earthen rampart. Lying prone on the cool ground one hour before sunrise, the Special Forces quartet, alone with their thoughts, waited to face a company of North Vietnamese regulars. Holding rifles loaded with blanks gave them little comfort.

Two weeks ago, the world welcomed a new year. Six months before, America put two men on the moon. None of these events impressed Slater because the government forced him into a war that he thought was wrong.

Two administrations proclaimed that our country was fighting for democracy, so families would send their sons to kill. The military proposed a goal of winning the hearts and minds of the Vietnamese. This propaganda and other programs were aimed at Congress to obtain the war's funding.

The hearts and minds campaign sounded feasible in the States, but it didn't work in the jungle. Each foot soldier on patrol literally fought to stay alive against a determined foe. No one was able to pause and talk about civics or international relations especially when both sides carried weapons with hair triggers.

Despite the program's deficiencies, Slater carried the spirit of the operation and tried to reason with the enemy. His men thought he was nuts, but the tactic succeeded for a while until he realized that the village had won over his mind and his heart.

Risking their lives, he and his men set up an ambush against the North Vietnamese to protect both sides: the American soldiers to the east and the village and its coffee crop to the west. Being this brave or foolish depending on the point of view went outside the bounds of Slater's quiet nature.

For most of his young life, he avoided confrontation and followed society's dictates of being seen and not heard. Given his shyness, he wondered how he got into this mess. Maybe he shouldn't have vocalized his anti-war stance during infantry training in Georgia. Maybe he should have escaped to Canada. He definitely should not have enrolled in the ROTC program at the University of Iowa.

These thoughts added to the stress of the impending battle, but he couldn't dislodge them.

The more he reflected, the more he returned to Fort Benning where he constantly stood at attention and received verbal abuse from his commanding officer. Captain Gray stuck with him like a bad case of VD. No matter how much penicillin he took, the CO wouldn't go away.

2

NOVEMBER 1968

" Eugene McCarthy?"

The disgust of Captain Delaney Gray III could not be greater than if he wore white sweat socks with his formal dress blue uniform.

As commanding officer of this infantry training company, he was charged to produce gung-ho, combat ready officers for assignment to Vietnam. He did not tolerate goof-offs, and in his mind Second Lieutenant Marshall was a smart-ass. The CO believed his subordinate did not take the training seriously, didn't respect authority or chain of command.

Discipline made a man of Captain Gray at the United States Military Academy, so he would apply the same indoctrination to Slater. Gray would not tolerate any deviations from army regimen.

"You maggot. How dare you say that?"

Slater saw the captain's face redden as hot air spurt from his throat against the cool air of the afternoon.

Dressed in tailored, starched fatigues that clung to the contour of his muscular torso, the captain despised the trainee's nonchalant attitude. The lieutenant's baggy fatigues and lightly polished boots did not help his cause.

3

"Brave men fight for your freedom, and you disrespect them."

Second Lieutenant Marshall braced while his irate CO thundered inches from his face.

"Of all the brave men to admire, you chose Eugene McCarthy?" The captain's jugular bulged in rhythm with every word. "That pussy, that yellow belly? He undermined the war effort."

Slater saw from the corners of his eyes that the platoon cringed with every decibel. They were grateful that the CO was not upbraiding them. Slater tried to look intimidated so as not to encourage further tirades, but in reality he didn't care. He hated the army, the war, and had only himself to blame. Still his answer of "Eugene McCarthy" seemed innocent enough.

The moment had started when the class congregated in an open field, preparing for a march. The CO walked among his men and asked a simple question, "Whom do you admire?"

"George Washington," "Robert E. Lee," "Stonewall Jackson," came the shouts. Captain Gray looked to his right and focused on Second Lieutenant Marshall who, the CO thought, should demonstrate more enthusiasm.

Slater glanced away, hoping Captain Gray would pick someone else.

"I didn't hear anything from you, Lieutenant," said Gray in a bellowing voice that intimidated those around him. "Whom do you admire?"

"Eugene McCarthy." The answer came easily. Slater thought it better not to say Dietrich Bonhoeffer, his real hero, whom Gray wouldn't know. He would think Slater too pretentious if he mentioned an obscure German pastor. Eugene McCarthy, whom Slater highly regarded, seemed less controversial. Upon hearing his choice, Captain Gray fulminated.

What was so infuriating about choosing Eugene McCarthy? The senator from Minnesota displayed courage of conviction by following a principle in which he believed. He went against his own ruling party by disagreeing with Lyndon Johnson in 1968 over Vietnam. He took a political risk and ran for President against the incumbent to give Americans another option. McCarthy wanted to end the war, bring peace to America, and get the troops home. His candidacy tapped into a groundswell of support that three months later caused President Johnson to remove himself as a candidate for re-election.

Slater thought the CO's explosion served no purpose. Why would a sane man behave this way? He knew military decorum demanded it, so he didn't take the scolding personally. In fact, he felt he deserved this treatment. He sold himself to the devil when he accepted an ROTC scholarship. He wanted to attend college, the first in his farming family. He had no money, so accepting a military commitment of four years after graduation seemed simple enough. Then President Johnson escalated the fighting in Vietnam. Slater couldn't bear to shoot a rabbit. Now the army was training him to kill people.

Thoughts of the past vanished, and he returned to the verbal bombardment in the present. He became impressed with his CO's strong vocal cords. How can he erupt for such a long time? Keeping a straight face now became his primary concern.

As Captain Gray fired verbal missiles, Slater reflected on his cavalier attitude toward the military and authority. Others in his training platoon described it as rebellious. They did not describe him as a rebel. Definitely not a rebel. Not here in Fort Benning, Georgia, where the South still fought the Civil War. Slater's aloof attitude encouraged more screaming. Did Captain Gray believe he could motivate this lieutenant by raising his voice and increasing the invective?

"Honor the traditions. Honor country. I want you to be a disciplined soldier that follows orders and contributes to the unit and to the country. Are you trying to provoke me by saying that traitor's name?"

Captain Gray made an imposing presence. After receiving his parachutist badge that said "Airborne" signifying his proficiency at jumping out of airplanes, he next attended the combat leadership course or Ranger school. Upon completion he earned his Ranger tab. Appointed as head of Fort Benning's company for graduates of the Reserve Officer Training Corps, Gray was tapped for the fast track. All the trainees respected his Airborne and Ranger patches.

They knew Captain Gray would go to Vietnam after finishing this class. He would lead an infantry company, a sought-after position for Academy graduates. He would get his "command" ticket punched on what he anticipated would be a stellar career. What an opportunity. He felt so lucky: a chance to lead men, get medals, and receive promotions. His father and grandfather commanded. No peacenik was going to derail his future.

Gray said, "I'm going to turn you into a 'strack' soldier." Slater had never heard this term before. The army defined it as a soldier being competent, gung-ho, and carrying out orders crisply without question. Slater defined it as a person who had a frontal lobotomy.

Captain Gray was an army brat mainly growing up around Fort Campbell, Kentucky, near the border of Tennessee. He upheld the family tradition of fealty to one's country and served as the poster child for straight arrow. He didn't tolerate anyone who went against God, the government, and the armed services. Those in the community took pride in his accomplishments: a role model for youth, for America, and for the values of the status quo.

Questioning the rules did not penetrate his thoughts. He did not appreciate Slater's disregard for esprit de corps and planned to ride this second lieutenant for the remaining weeks of the class.

When Gray stopped his shouting, no one interrupted the awkward silence that followed. The burn in the captain's cheeks lingered in the air. After a brief respite, the CO turned and yelled to the platoon, "All right men. Saddle up and move out."

As the squads pulled together, many glanced at Slater in disapproval. Others muttered, "Who's Eugene McCarthy?"

Slater and the platoon marched for three hours through Georgia thickets. At night, Gray put Slater on guard duty one hundred yards outside the campsite. After setting up his position and pretending to protect the platoon from enemy raccoons, he fell asleep, awakening four hours later to the snores from a nearby sentry. He couldn't go back to sleep and faced two hours before the morning exercises. During this time he wondered if he would survive infantry training.

No way could he be the mechanical trooper that Captain Gray prized. Slater learned to question everything in his life. He believed one of America's attributes was to search for the truth and not accept the status quo.

He thought about his hero, Dietrich Bonhoeffer, a Lutheran priest who questioned the Nazis from day one. Many in the German Protestant churches welcomed Hitler as a strong leader that Germany needed to replace the chaos of the Weimar Republic. Slater tried to emulate his hero's example. He questioned the merits of his father's beatings and questioned the Vietnam War. In his mind, the lack of obedience to authority seemed justified since those in power led the country into this futile conflict.

After the field exercise ended two days later, Captain Gray felt duty bound to inform higher echelons about his incorrigible trainee. Placing a scathing assessment in Slater's personnel file, he described 2Lt. Marshall's behavior as snobbish, trying to get by in his army obligation, and protesting against the war, against discipline, and against the military. The only way Captain Gray could have inflamed the message with greater poison was to write it on red paper and affix neon lights to the manila folder.

3

1947-1965

Slater was a lanky, towheaded farm boy with a tanned face, blue eyes, and strong arms. He grew up in rural Sigourney, Iowa, population 2,031. It was isolated from other towns, and his family's farm was located far from its nearest neighbor. Working the fields to grow corn and soy plus tending to the pigs occupied most of his waking hours. The house had no heat, and they only listened to the radio for the weather and crop reports.

His parents spoke few words that seldom strung their way into sentences. His father objected to legislation requiring children to attend school. He wanted his boy full time. When the harvest loomed, he got his son back. The schools shut down so everyone including the kids worked the fields. They cared less that Slater earned excellent grades, so he stopped mentioning his high scores.

Slater's day started at 4:30 AM when he strode to the hen-house to get fresh eggs for breakfast. Even during winter at twenty below with frost on top of his quilt, he didn't delay rising. His mother's voice reminded him that his father wanted break-fast at a certain time. Slater knew the consequences if he didn't accomplish this task.

The major force in the community in tandem with farming was religion. God rewarded his flock with harvests and punished sinners with storms, floods, and draught. Slater attended the Lutheran Church with his mother. His father never joined them.

Slater couldn't reconcile the love of God and the fear of God that the minister preached along with the rule that one had to respect one's parents. If God were so loving, why was Slater supposed to accept the beatings? The fear of God paled against the fear he held for his father.

From the rector's sermons, Slater learned about Dietrich Bonhoeffer. He was a German Lutheran pastor, theologian, reformer, and martyr. His letters and books influenced Christians throughout the world even after his death.

During World War II and in conflict with the German religions, he spoke against Hitler and the killing of Jews. Bonhoeffer was eventually imprisoned and later executed in 1945. Slater venerated the man and his principles. He especially admired Bonhoeffer's courage to stand up for the disadvantaged even as he faced staggering adversity.

At Lutheran socials he met the Sun family and their son, Albert. They were Chinese immigrants who owned a farm not far from his parents' spread. Iowa at different times welcomed Asian refugees. Slater and Albert were the same age and attended school and church together. They talked, laughed, and soon became pals. Many of the townsfolk shunned the Chinese family because they were different. Slater saw their humanness.

On rare occasions, he visited the Suns' farm and stayed for dinner and an overnight. He saw television for the first time. He thought "Leave It to Beaver" was a fantasy since Ward Cleaver never beat his sons.

When Slater started to return to his farm, Mr. Sun gave him a small pocketknife. "Thanks for being friends with my son."

Slater treasured the gift and always kept it with him, even in college and in the military. It reminded him of the affection the Sun family held for him.

When Slater grew taller than his father, he resisted the poundings and fought back. The old man backed down but kept his meanness. It was the beginning of Slater's independence.

Once in a while, the family would listen to news broadcasts on the radio. Being the only window to the outside world, it aroused his curiosity to learn more about other cities like Chicago, New York, and Washington, D.C. Traveling to a new country never entered the realm of possibility.

He labored hard with the raising and harvesting of the crops, but farming didn't appeal to him. The backbreaking effort yielded few rewards. He admired the inner strength and optimism farmers possessed, but Slater wanted more control over his life. Many variables governed the success of crops like weather, sun, and rain. All these factors happened outside of his control and occurred by the grace of God.

As the only son, he was expected to take over the operation. Since he didn't care to remain on the farm, Slater wondered how he could buck the traditions of a small town and his family. The answer seemed obvious. Graduate from college and get a job, preferably in another state.

Since his family did not have any money for higher education and since his father thought books were overrated, Slater kept his own counsel and researched alternatives. At a meeting with the seniors, the high school principal recommended getting grants from colleges or accepting scholarships through the Reserved Officer Training Corps. Slater never saw himself as a soldier, but the free education seduced him.

The University of Iowa at Iowa City with its business program provided a way out. The college was considered liberal at the time, although Slater didn't know what that label meant.

He overcame the objections of his father by explaining that he would enter the military and do his duty. He added that the education would not cost the family anything. Joining the armed services was considered honorable for any farm family. Slater knew that his father valued the cost-free feature more.

When Slater started classes in the fall, he thought he landed in Oz without the green horses. Culture shock set in, but he didn't let his awkwardness stop him. Everything was different, from clothes to an urban way of doing things. His poverty was the only constant. He coped by taking three part-time jobs during the week to pay for expenses. He returned home every weekend to work on the farm and studied with enthusiasm in the evenings. He was excited about his future.

Christian principles governed his behavior, so he was jolted when college put life in terms other than God. He studied different philosophies, religions, and other forms of government. He learned the term "secular" and started to question. Maybe the Earth wasn't four thousand years old. He dug into the business curriculum and avoided agriculture classes.

While his business and liberal arts courses took God out of the equation, the tedious military lectures put Him back in. Slater never understood how a partnership between the military and God evolved. Everyone accepted the incongruity between a peaceful God on one side and a killing deity on the other. Questioning this orthodoxy was not socially acceptable in the ROTC or Iowa.

Nevertheless, he liked the idea that he could travel to other parts of the country at the army's expense. That appeal disappeared in February 1965 when President Johnson escalated the war effort. After this decision, Slater's world cratered.

4

1965-1968

Knowing Vietnam loomed in his future, Slater's attitude in the ROTC slackened. Prior to the escalation, he could ignore the propaganda, but now going to fight what he thought was an unjustified war grated on his sensibilities. Because he sold out for a free education, he felt like an indentured servant. He had three more years until graduation, three more years to confront his mortality.

He thought about becoming a conscientious objector, but since he volunteered for ROTC without mentioning pacifism, his claim would be denied. He decided not to pursue it.

Frustration increased every day that he attended military classes. With his frustration growing he mounted a form of protest. He complained, criticized, and argued.

The ROTC instructors recognized Slater as a double-edged sword. He excelled in his courses but lacked dedication to military doctrine. Not wanting a disrupting influence among the other students, they allowed him to skip certain seminars to study the Vietnamese language and still gain credits toward his commission. Slater did not miss the boring lectures covering marching formations and discipline; he preferred the challenge of learning a new tongue.

Outside of ROTC he kept sane by concentrating on his business major and by pursuing a minor in history. Late night talks with his dormitory roommate encouraged him to become more social, and he even dated a few co-eds. Slater gained confidence in his classes, in interacting with professors, and in handling himself in social situations. Of his past patterns, he still retained a distrust of authority. In his senior year, he had completed the transition from a bumpkin to an idealistic collegian ready to make his mark in the world.

Upon graduation, he received his bachelor of arts degree and a commission as second lieutenant. Because of his grades, the ROTC administrators honored Slater's choice of branch. He chose the Adjutant General Corps which focused on personnel work. He vetoed the Infantry Branch that the army preferred because it led to combat assignments. The following day, as instructed, he reported to the ROTC office and picked up his orders. They directed him to attend a three-month infantry training class at Fort Benning, Georgia, followed by two months of personnel training at Fort Benjamin Harrison, Indiana. After these classes he would go to Vietnam. Upon seeing the word "Vietnam" in the formal document with his name on top brought a flood of anxiety.

At his request the reporting date to Fort Benning was delayed until November. His father demanded that Slater return to the farm and help for four months.

When he returned to Sigourney from Iowa City, it seemed as though he never left. His parents did not acknowledge that he was a college graduate nor notice the self-assurance in his manner.

Gaining new perspectives by being away from home, Slater saw his parents in a different light. They looked like hicks. His father dressed in blanched denims, and his mother wore old-fashioned printed dresses. Both were short in height. His father was wiry with calloused hands and heart, thin white hair with a bald spot in back, and a permanent scowl on his crooked mouth. His mom was stocky and had gray hair tightly knotted in a bun. Her wrinkled face and tiny faded blue eyes reflected her strenuous life.

When he visited the Sun family, they observed the changes immediately. Albert was home for the summer and would return in the fall for a master's degree in agronomy from Iowa State University. Albert's father was prospering and had quietly bought troubled small farms in the area.

In Slater's absence, his father let the upkeep of the farm slip, which required the new college graduate to labor long hours. His parents seldom spoke except at dinner and then only a few words.

His mother said, "Everyone is so proud of you for going to Vietnam." His father snorted.

"But I don't want to go," he said.

"Of course you do. You're fighting for freedom," said his father.

When Slater attended church, his words also went unheard. Not wanting to go to war didn't register.

At one dinner, Slater wanted to relate his concerns to his parents so they could understand his rationale.

"Vietnam doesn't affect our freedom. We're just killing people for some general's power trip. Didn't Jesus say something against killing?"

"When did you become a Commie lover and what did those pansy-assed professors teach you?" was all his father could growl. End of subject.

In his room that evening, Slater reflected on his university experience. His horizons expanded at college, and his talks with fellow students and protestors gave him deeper insights, but two courses during his senior year shook up his ordered world.

He didn't plan to enroll in History of Communist China for the fall semester. He preferred European history. Since many classes were filled, he registered for the early morning China class. His professor, Dr. Klaus, encouraged his students to read books that described both sides of issues. The reading showed the inadequacies of American foreign policy which caused him to question the government. Outside of the Vietnam conflict, he never doubted the government before. The more he studied, the more blunders he saw.

For spring semester, Slater continued with Dr. Klaus in History of Southeast Asia and learned about bigger mistakes the various administrations made in Vietnam starting in 1945.

Dr. Klaus said, "Since the 1920s in France, Ho Chi Minh was striving for independence. He became a Communist as a reaction to imperialism and believed its philosophy would help achieve his goals. During World War II, Ho was our ally against Japan and an admirer of Franklin Roosevelt. Ho appreciated FDR's commitment to allow self-determination for former colonies at the end of the war.

"Events changed when Truman became president and the Cold War started," said Dr. Klaus. "The United States reneged on promises to Ho Chi Minh and supported France to reclaim her colony."

*   *   *

Realizing he wouldn't make any headway with his parents, Slater gave up arguing his cause. He decided to hear more about their lives and points of view, even if he differed. He saw their foibles certainly but after a few weeks saw their struggles and efforts to cope.

Arranging flowers on the dining table or over the sink provided Slater's mother with her only creative outlet. Cleaning, washing, cooking, and many other chores eroded her spirit. She looked at her husband before saying or doing anything as though she needed his approval. Her Sunday attendance at church enabled her to interact in a quiet way with the other townsfolk away from her spouse's reproach.

His father seemed imprisoned with his lot in life, and his resentment showed as meanness. Slater concluded that his father's distorted outlook resulted from his inability to look at where he went wrong and how to change it.

If only Slater could storm their fortress of misery and improve their outlook, he thought they might become a family. He agonized about their plight but quit trying to change them since he found no openings. Instead he focused on a bigger frustration: going to war. What would be his assignment? How would he perform in training and in war? Would he lead men? Would he die?

* * *

A soldier's departure from home usually provided the town with an occasion to celebrate. Church socials and picnics along with speeches bestowed affection on the individual and his family. The citizens of Sigourney learned about Slater's dissent against the war, and this attitude disheartened them. His parents did not receive the accolades from their neighbors as was normally accorded when a son went off to battle. Instead their friends looked the other way.

With farm chores demanding his parents' attention, Slater asked Albert Sun, who was home for the weekend, to drive him to the bus station.

Farewells proved difficult. Slater's father didn't want to show his soft side and used work to avoid a lengthy good-bye. He gazed at his boy with a less-than-stern look and extended his hand before going to the barn. "Good luck, son."

Slater was warmed by this brief encounter of affection.

After his dad left, he had time alone with his mother. Albert was expected to arrive at any minute, and he told her, "I'll be fine. I'm not in the infantry branch."

Though she tried to be composed, he sensed that she wanted to express her motherly love, but her lips quivered. She started to clean up the table in hopes that it would distract her mind, but the effort failed.

When Albert showed up, Slater grabbed his bag. His mother looked at him before he went out the door and tried to smile. She hugged him and said, "Hurry back."

Twenty years later she said it was the saddest day of her life.

5

MAY 1969

After completing the two training courses in Georgia and Indiana, Slater was granted a thirty-day leave. Since he'd endured enough torture from his family at his send-off, he elected to forsake the vacation and go directly to Southeast Asia.

Dressed in army khaki and carrying a duffel bag, he made it to Travis Air Force Base near Sacramento, California. He went through the paperwork lines and sat for hours in the air force terminal feeling alone in the midst of hundreds of soldiers. After an interminable wait, he boarded the airplane wondering if he would experience a return flight.

The twenty-hour journey made brief layovers in Honolulu and Okinawa's Kadena Air Force Base. At each location Slater disembarked and stood in the airport lounge until refueling was complete. Even though the stops were short, he marveled at these exotic places.

On the last leg, his anxieties resurfaced. The pilot announced that they were approaching the Vietnam coast. Slater's throat tightened, and his lungs hyperventilated. A few minutes later, he looked out the window and saw the ocean, the coast, and the green forest that looked like masses of broccoli. Vietnam looked innocent from thirty-six thousand feet.

Twenty minutes later, the plane started its descent. Slater tried to show his cool without much success. When he looked around the cabin, fear showed on many of the faces. The soldiers tried to control their nerves and prepare for survival. They were so young and yet answered their country's call at the risk of death. Despite his anti-war posture, Slater respected the courage of these Americans.

The plane approached Tan Son Nhut Airport, the world's third busiest, located near Saigon. As the wheels touched down, a bomb exploded at the end of the runway. Slater stiffened, but as he looked out the window, no one near the terminal seemed concerned. As the black plume reached to the sky, a bus drove up to the airplane and picked up the exhausted passengers.

A soldier next to him upon seeing the smoke from the explosion said in a sarcastic voice to those around him, "Welcome to Vietnam, suckers." The comment broke the tension for a moment.

The hot temperature of Southeast Asia melted Slater as though he were in a steam bath. The heat and humidity differed from Iowa heat. The air in Vietnam contained caustic odors mixed with humidity, dust, and pollution. The stink plus the uncertainty of Slater's assignment caused him to assess his life once again. "What have I done?"

After he grabbed his duffel bag, the bus drove them to an army depot at Long Binh. During the trip Slater looked out the open windows that had bars across them and saw Vietnamese men and women scurrying along the side of the road. Wearing conical straw hats and conveying two baskets on a yoke full of goods or food, the peasants meandered down dirt paths like ants. To Slater, it seemed as though he was watching this new country through a television screen. Maybe he wasn't really here. Inhaling the acrid fragrances from food stalls brought him back to reality. After being in Vietnam for forty minutes, he concluded he should have escaped to Canada as many draft dodgers had done.

At Long Binh, the army processed the new arrivals to their in-country destinations. Some soldiers already had assignments prior to departure from the United States. Most, like Slater, had to wait until administrators filled unit requisitions. Names were then placed on a bulletin board and orders were issued. His body tensed every morning and afternoon when the assignments were posted. For two days his name did not appear.

Slater did not like this idleness. He stayed near his bunk and fought bugs and spiders by day only to be assaulted by mosquitoes at night. He figured that the army should award a medal for valor against enemy insects. He also endured the stench of burning human waste that permeated the base. The army incinerated the sewage with diesel and insecticide. Fighting the Viet Cong should be a leisurely stroll after enduring these noxious fumes.

To prepare him for his assignment, Slater received new attire for the war zone and favored the color army olive drab or dark olive. Supply at Long Binh issued him three sets of olive drab fatigues, one olive drab baseball cap plus t-shirts, socks, underwear, all in olive drab. Even his light-weight jungle boots were olive drab. Khaki uniforms were not worn in Vietnam.

The suspense about obtaining his orders was worse than the bomb explosion at the runway. He didn't know if the anxieties would lessen each day without an assignment or if they would increase once he knew it. He expected a non-combat duty, but this assumption provided little comfort.

On the third day he saw his name and destination: Special Forces, Nha Trang. Two hours later, a C-130 army transport plane flew him and other passengers two hundred miles north where the 5th Special Forces Group was headquartered.

Slater thought someone had made a mistake. One volunteered for Special Forces, not get assigned. Slater thought his Adjutant General Corps designation would keep him in a cushy job away from the fighting, maybe even in Saigon. He guessed that even Special Forces required paper pushers, so they must have recruited someone with his skills.

Sitting next to Slater on the flight was First Lieutenant Bruce Hendrickson from Dayton, Ohio, who was returning to his base. He had short reddish hair, a red face, a broad smile, and a beefy frame. He had been in-country for eight months and loved to regale rookies about his knowledge of Vietnam. Bruce had difficulty enunciating as his mouth sloshed words from having too much saliva. In his rush to speak, he forgot about swallowing. He struggled to talk over the roar of the engines and the rattling of equipment. Slater leaned over to hear more clearly, wishing he had a towel to wipe off the spray.

"You will love Nha Trang. It's headquarters for the military zone called II Corps. Vietnam has four corps, and ours has the best weather, especially in the highlands."

"Is Nha Trang safe or under attack?" asked Slater as he mopped his face.

Bruce laughed. "It is a safe haven. We don't bother them; they don't bother us. The airport is used to train the South Vietnamese pilots, so the city has plenty of protection."

"Couldn't they attack the airport?"

"If they did, Charlie would ruin the black market which they use to help finance their war effort."

"What's the black market?"

Bruce smiled at Slater's innocence. "If you have American dollars, you can convert them to Piasters, Vietnam's currency, for twice the bank rate. Once the Vietnamese have dollars, they can buy anything. The Piaster is weak and not convertible.

"GIs make money by selling consumer goods, such as tape recorders, amplifiers, and other electronics, at a greater price than they paid for them at the PX. These products aren't on the neighborhood market. The locals in turn make big profits selling them to other Vietnamese. Some locals are VC."

"And the army allows it to operate?"

"Don't apply logic to Vietnam. There's big money to be made during a war, and many people have figured out how to prosper. Uncle Sam allows it because he doesn't want to offend his ally."

"This place is scary enough with the fighting. Now I have to worry about a black market?"

"Forget the black market. You'll love the climate, the beaches, turquoise ocean, and friendly people. Not to mention the delicious French Vietnamese restaurants downtown."

After more banter about Nha Trang, Bruce said, "Hey, you might enjoy the briefing I attend every day. Want to join me?"

"What time?"

"Ten, er I mean ten hundred at II Corps Headquarters. If you can swing it, be at the front at 9:45 AM."

6

MAY 1969

A dilapidated complex of corroded structures comprised the headquarters for the 5th Special Forces Group. The tattered buildings and temporary huts sprawled over barren soil. Dust pervaded everywhere except for thirty minutes during the afternoon when torrential rains drenched individuals in five seconds. Weathered Quonset huts, idle jeeps, and rusty equipment endured the daily downpours, humidity, and constant heat. Soldiers adjusted to the climate by walking in slow motion.

When Slater passed enlisted men on his way to the personnel section, they saluted without meaning it. Not many extended military courtesy to a second lieutenant clad in new green fatigues. They gave him no respect.

The gold bar on his collar brought muffled ridicule. His junior status despite its officer designation occupied a low rung in the military hierarchy. Enlisted men had to salute officers but did so reluctantly when it came to second lieutenants.

Most "second lewies" didn't realize their precarious standing. They carried themselves with self-importance similar to a major-domo in charge of a valet crew. This hazing lasted until they were promoted to first lieutenant, one year after receiving their commission. Slater accepted his lowly status and didn't care what people thought as long as he made it home.

Rounding the corner, he noticed a brown and gray Quonset hut with the insignia of Special Forces Adjutant's Office on the door. He entered and faced Sergeant First Class Eddie Doyle sitting on a metal chair in front of a typewriter. Doyle, a wiry, twelve-year lifer with a butch haircut, kept a low profile by following orders. He wanted the security of a paycheck, a place to sleep, and a desire to suppress any ambition.

Even though he didn't graduate from high school, he could recite the regulations backward and forward. The officers trusted him to process reports they dreaded. He hated greeting new arrivals and didn't want to answer their insufferable questions. Today he paid attention to the second lieutenant in front of him and the three enlisted men sitting nearby. He knew their assignment.

"Lt. Slater Marshall reporting for duty."

Doyle looked up quickly and ran his hand through his short hair. "Sit over there with your team. You can introduce yourselves later. Major Pemberton will see you within the hour."

Slater took a seat away from the desk and noticed the three soldiers and their ranks of "Specialist Four" or "Spec 4." That rank was the same as corporal but the army favored the "specialist" distinction over the more traditional rank for some unknown reason. It implied that the soldier acquired a certain skill and did not have leadership abilities. A corporal rank is used in infantry squads and assumes leadership ability.

The three Spec 4s looked at Slater with impassive faces. He didn't notice that they cringed when they heard that a second lieutenant would lead them. Slater gave a nod as he sat down.

He put on an air of confidence but inside questioned his competency to lead this group. Could he reconcile his position as an army officer yet sympathize with anti-war protesters? He convinced himself that he could do his job, take care of the men, and follow military dictates for one year. He would force himself to last twelve months until his return to stateside. Thank goodness he wasn't assigned to an infantry unit and exposed to combat. His reverie ended when Sergeant Doyle called his name and directed the group to the adjutant's office.

Major Kirby Pemberton from Mississippi sat at his desk with a look of disgust. He had just reviewed these men's 201 files which contained negative information about their soldiering abilities. His tanned, pockmarked face and riveting blue gray eyes frightened new arrivals. He was on his third tour of duty and relished every moment in a war zone.

Slater didn't know proper protocol. This was his first assignment. So he stood at attention along with the others. The team saluted without much crispness. Major Pemberton didn't say to stand at ease. So the four sweated.

"You turkeys are a disgrace to the army, your country, and yourselves."

Slater wondered what happened to the welcome committee. The major exercised the same blood vessels that Captain Gray did in Georgia.

"I have looked at reports from your units, and they did not paint a complimentary picture. Apparently you don't appreciate our mission here. You prefer Commie protesters to the brave servicemen defending our freedom. You make me sick."

Slater did not expect a happy ending to this outburst. He let the major rant. Of all the alternatives available to address an upset, the military employed two: yelling and screaming. A person was guilty until proven innocent. Slater was losing patience. To himself he proclaimed, "I'm an American. An Iowan. Screw you. What ever happened to military solidarity?"

Major Aorta did not have the durability of Captain Gray's arteries. He stopped after a minute of venting. What Slater heard next made him realize that perhaps he should jettison his cavalier attitude. With a mischievous glint in the adjutant's eyes, he gave the troops their assignment.

"You will serve as a reconnaissance team."

Each man knew this assignment had combat embossed on the orders. They would be exposed to the Viet Cong.

The adjutant then referred the men to the assistant S-3, ("S" standing for staff at battalion or brigade level, "3" signifying operations). The group saluted Pemberton with alacrity and departed in a bigger sweat oblivious to the humidity.

Sergeant Doyle escorted the team to the Assistant S-3 who confirmed their suspicions. His desk was located in a corner of the sweltering Quonset hut. Seven enlisted men in the room turned their heads when the four soldiers entered. Air conditioners clattered, so one could barely hear. The A/Cs seemed to be out of Freon as they recycled the hot air. The gray metal desks appeared to be rejects from goodwill. The papers on top of them were held down by various weights so they wouldn't fly away with the gusts from the air conditioners.

The assistant S-3, a captain, didn't introduce himself but said "at ease." He had cropped hair, a big paunch, faded fatigues, and glasses showing his bookish demeanor. He kept looking at the far door.

"You are assigned to the Phan Lac area and will support the 187th Infantry Regiment by providing surveillance of the enemy."

"Surveillance?" asked Slater.

"It is your job to monitor the VC and watch for North Vietnamese units coming from the Ho Chi Minh Trail."

He then pointed to a dot on a map showing the village and the Ho Chi Minh Trail thirty miles away. He waved the stick to show the boundary with Cambodia. Slater knew where they would find his body.

"Sir," he said. "I'm with the Adjutant General Corps."

The captain looked at him with a stern face and said, "I have little patience with second lieutenants. You are an officer and had Vietnamese language training. Any other questions?"

"I thought Special Forces required its ranks to be volunteers." Slater asked.

"Staffing needs. You were volunteered."

He realized that Captain Gray put a scathing memo into his personnel file that motivated the powers-that-be to give him this posting. Slater learned his lesson. Don't upset the army during wartime.

The far door opened, and Commanding Officer Colonel Erastus Wilberforce strutted in. Later the group learned his nickname was "Bull Dog" or "BD" because he hailed from Georgia, with "Bull Dog" being the mascot of the University of Georgia. He probably gave himself the name, Slater thought. His squat physique moved like an awkward linebacker which he was at a small religious school. Others on his staff quietly referred to him as "Highpockets" emphasizing his large hips. His shaved head seemed out of proportion to his body. He kept biting his lower lip which distracted subordinates when they spoke to him.

Everyone stood at attention. He kept the team in this pose to show his power. Slater recognized a mean man who recruited "yes men" for his staff.

"You are the lucky ones. I'm going to make soldiers out of you even if it kills you." No one doubted it. "Stow your gear, pick up your kits, I'll have some men get you rifles and ammo. Personnel processing should take one day, and then a chopper will transport you to your new base. I expect you to secure the area and assist the 187th in its operations. Now let's say a prayer."

Slater's crew and the men in the Quonset hut stood and closed their eyes while Wilberforce spoke what they thought were their "Last Rites."

"Bless these men while they defend our great country from Communism and kill the heathen who want to deprive us of democracy. In Christ's name, Amen."

Slater was dumbfounded. What kind of prayer was that?

Wilberforce then said, "Dismissed."

7

After departing the Quonset hut, Slater and company found a shady spot by the motor pool. Having never been a leader, he didn't know how to speak to or gain the confidence of his men.

"Looks like we drew the short end of the stick." This comment was thin, but he trudged forward. "So if we're on the same team, let's introduce ourselves. I'll start."

Being nervous in front of the group, he stumbled with his words at first and gave his name, age, schooling, and mentioned the forts where he trained adding that he spoke some Vietnamese. The longer he talked, the more self-assurance he gathered. He decided to keep his anti-war sentiments to himself.

"It appears that we have upset the army, and that's how we got this assignment. My commanding officer in infantry school chewed me out because I liked Senator Eugene McCarthy. Maybe that's why I'm here."

The three raised their eyebrows and looked at each other seeming to say, "How can liking Eugene McCarthy, an obscure politician, warrant a death sentence, and what dumb ass would mention him in the first place?"

Slater finished and waited for the next man to speak.

Spec 4 Ernie Alvarez, aged twenty, Armor Branch, glanced at the group and waited for someone to volunteer. When no one did, he decided to take his turn and get it over with. He raised his arm halfway, and Slater called on him.

With his constant habit of pushing his black locks back where cowlicks kept shoving them forward, Ernie said, "I've always been tall for my age, so my friends called me 'Baby Bull.' I have big feet as you can tell from my boots."

Everyone looked at them and acknowledged their generous size.

Slater noticed that Ernie had a slight accent and probably was born in Mexico. He also had the whitest teeth he had seen. He showed his ivories often since he smiled every time he finished a sentence.

"I grew up in Albuquerque and like mechanical things especially cars. I can jerry-rig anything. They trained me in electronics but assigned me to tank maintenance. I'm married and prefer being home than with you guys."

"Why did you get assigned here?" asked Slater.

"I had a run-in with my CO."

"What was the problem?"

"He didn't like Mexicans."

Patrols and listening posts were equipped with radios, and Slater needed a dependable person to operate one.

"Can you repair radios?"

"Sure."

"Do you have any problems if I make you the radio operator?"

"Sir, I can fix them, but talking? I dunno. And I'm not used to working for officers especially talking to them."

"Do you have a problem with me?"

"Oh, no sir. It's just that, well, people don't give me big jobs like this."

"Ernie, I'm relying on you, okay?"

31

He looked at the others and in an uncertain voice said, "Yes, sir."

Spec 4 Jesse DeWitt, twenty, spoke next. "I come from a place called Vermont Square. Bet you've never heard of it."

The three shook their heads.

"It's a dump. Poor part of Los Angeles. Whitey doesn't come here. Cops patrol in threes and fours if they come."

The white guy next to Slater said, "You're from the ghetto?"

"You gotta problem with that?"

"Naw, we got plenty of ghettos in Newark. I just don't know anybody from one."

With a broad face that showed a permanent frown, Jesse said, "Figures. They wouldn't want to know you anyway."

"You look like a construction worker. Is that what you did before Uncle Sam grabbed you?" asked Ernie.

"Nothing like that, but I did odd jobs." Jesse changed the subject. "I received training in the Signal Corps and was assigned to a Signal battalion in Bien Hoa for two months. My commander didn't like brothers, and I got tired of getting all the crap duties. Blacks were given the hardest jobs. Whites got the easy ones. Am I clear, Lieutenant?"

Slater asked, "What about schooling?"

"You mean did I graduate from high school?" Jesse acted as though education was no big deal, but the others noticed that this subject was sensitive. "I dropped out after my sophomore year. Someone in our family needed to work."

Slater didn't want to raise any touchy issues. He'd find out more about Jesse later. The lieutenant turned to the last member of his team.

Stocky torso, thin brown hair, furrows in his forehead, Spec 4 Vico Fortino, who looked ten years older than his twenty-one years, said, "I'm from Newark, New Jersey, love pasta, and hate officers. After getting a diploma, me and my buddies drove trucks in Newark. Weekends were cool. We went to Monmouth Park and bet on the ponies. After getting drafted and finishing boot camp, I can truthfully say that I'm not cut out to be a soldier."

Slater asked, "Why is the Army mad at you?"

"You mean how did I get this cushy assignment? They wanted to put me into Officer Candidate School because I scored well on their tests. Make me an officer? Who wants to be with those bozos? They take the army too serious. Told them they're nuts, and so here I am."

"I can't imagine they'd send you here just because you didn't want to be an officer."

"Apparently they didn't like the way I rejected their offer."

After the introductions ended, Vico asked, "Lieutenant, if this is your first assignment, why should we follow you?"

"Who would you choose, Vico?"

"Maybe me. You're from Iowa. I've been on the streets of Jersey. Who would these guys want to follow?"

"So you'll run roughshod over the Viet Cong?

"Damn right."

"Would that attitude endanger the team? Might it expose us to a fire fight that a cooler head might avoid?"

Vico said, "We're going to die anyway. What odds do you give us for surviving in Viet Cong territory? Why not go out in style?"

"I had plenty of experience in LA," Jesse interrupted. "I can show you guys how to stomp 'em."

Ernie said, "I want to return home and be with my wife. Why should we go along with the army? Let's hitch a ride to Bangkok and stay there for twelve months? No one will know we're missing."

Vico reasserted himself. "Well, Lieutenant? I'm still waiting for your answer."

"Forget it, sir. He's trying to pick a fight." Vico eyed Ernie with contempt.

Slater said, "It's a legit question. You ready for the answer?"

"Give it to me."

"My goal is to return home. I don't want to wander around the hills and kill everything I see or be killed. I don't want to be cannon fodder for some uppity general. We've been set up. Highpockets and others expect us to die. I plan on waging peace with the VC."

Vico said, "Making peace with Charlie?"

"At least reach an understanding that he doesn't kill us, and we won't kill him."

"Sounds like a stupid idea to me," said Vico.

"Probably so. Yet the alternative means more killing, and we're prime targets. So I say we look out for ourselves, not rely on anyone, and come back alive. If I screw up, we can try new leadership. In the meantime, we need to help each other."

Vico couldn't resist a final comment. "Trouble is that if you make a mistake, none of us will be around to try new leadership."

"Any other discussion?" Not waiting for any responses, Slater said, "So it's settled. Clear?"

"Yes, sir," Vico said with a bit of sarcasm.

"Oh and by the way. My name is Slater, not sir."

"Yes, sir," Vico said loudly and they all laughed.

8

MAY 1969

That afternoon, Slater's team returned to the adjutant's office and met with Sergeant Doyle to complete their in-country processing. He gave them papers to sign and pointed to an important box on the form showing the date of departure from Vietnam to return to the USA. He called it DEROS – Date of Eligible Return from Overseas. Everyone knew their DEROS because they wanted to go home. Some soldiers planned to name their kids "Deros." Slater had accumulated four days of time in Vietnam, so he had 361 days until his DEROS.

Sergeant Doyle mentioned that Slater's group would leave at 1400 hours the next day. He would have plenty of time to attend the II Corps briefing with Bruce and find out more about his area of operations. No one in Special Forces informed him about his duties. They treated his assignment as on the job training.

Next, the group went to the Supply Office to receive their gear. They were issued minimum provisions, equipment, and a map showing their new highland domicile. Rifles came first, and everyone was surprised when M-14s were passed out instead of M-16 rifles that were standard for infantrymen.

Vico said, "Wilberforce screwed us again."

Jesse said, "Even I received an M-16 in my last post, and I wasn't in a combat zone. You guys would like the M-16. It's lighter, sleeker, can hold 30 round magazines not the 20 of the M-14, and it hardly has any recoil. Even the ammo is lighter."

Vico said, "Slater, you need to go to Pemberton and object."

"And he of course would listen to me," said Slater. "Let's make sure we get bullets first."

Ernie said, "Maybe we can swipe M-16s from the 187th Regiment. We ain't getting any here."

The next round of supplies included food, web belts, water purification pills, malaria pills, first aid kits, and little else. The Supply Office provided green berets, but no one wanted them. They kept their olive drab baseball caps. Ernie picked up a radio that had outlived its life in World War II. He would fix it although he could not guarantee that it would work beyond one week.

Subdued or darkened arm patches showing they belonged to the 5th Special Forces Group were sewn onto their fatigues by two mama-sans, Vietnamese women who did laundry and cleaning. Afterward, Slater's group split up agreeing to meet the next day after lunch.

That evening, Slater went to the Officer's Club. He ordered a burger and coke and ate at a side table while viewing a show put on by a Vietnamese rock and roll band. They copied the songs and sounds of American rock groups. All the officers enjoyed the entertainment in their alcoholic stupor. At the end of the show, the band sang the Animals' 1965 hit which was the most popular song in Vietnam, "We Gotta Get Out of This Place." All the officers including Slater stood up and shouted in unison. The last stanza remained imbedded in his mind:

We gotta get out of this place
If it's the last thing we ever do.

We gotta get out of this place,
Girl, there's a better life for me and you.

* * *

The building that housed the II Corps Tactical Zone Headquarters could have functioned as a large hotel before the Vietnam War or a large government administrative building. The U.S. Army appropriated it for offices to govern twelve provinces. The military said they were partnering with the South Vietnamese army, but in reality the local forces carried no weight and were housed in another building. Uncle Sam was paying the bills and wanted everything his way. The headquarters was located two miles from the Special Forces camp.

Morning briefings for the top brass were given at 8:30 AM followed by a second briefing for the lesser ranks. It started at 10:00 AM. Approximately twenty men attended each session.

Slater greeted Lt. Bruce Hendrickson at the front door. Apparently mornings reduce the amount of saliva in Bruce's mouth, so spraying was kept to a minimum.

As they walked toward the briefing room, Bruce said, "The army uses lots of abbreviations, and I'll try to keep you abreast of the discussion. The bad guys are the VC, which you already know means Viet Cong and NVA means North Vietnamese Army. The good guys who are on our side are called ARVN, and that stands for the Army of the Republic of Vietnam, the South Vietnamese forces. You won't hear their name much since they aren't trained well enough yet to fight their brethren in the north.

"The brass might mention the 'Hearts and Minds' program."

"I heard about it in the States, but that's all."

"It's an extra duty that LBJ put on the army. We're supposed to win the hearts and minds of the villagers, so they'll show allegiance to the South Vietnam government. It's just a slogan, propaganda."

"Why?"

"The South Vietnam government is nowhere near the villages, and the ARVN are afraid to fight. They leave everything to us. The army comes during the day, and Charlie comes at night. We pray that snipers don't shoot us. It's an impossible situation."

"Then what are we doing here?" asked Slater.

"If you find out, tell me because our mission doesn't make any sense. Someone sold Washington a bill of goods, and we risk our necks."

They stopped talking as they drifted into the briefing room.

It consisted of enough space to host a reception for sixty people. The aroma of coffee and the scent of cigars permeated the space. The twelve-foot ceilings and the white crown molding had seen better days decades ago. Thirty metal folding chairs were configured in three rows on scuffed hardwood floors. A podium was placed in front, and behind it was an array of large maps. Bruce and Slater sat in the last row.

Major Amos Hardy and Major Herman Laurel strutted onto the podium and presided. These dark-haired, bespectacled, presenters acted as though they were the famous news team, Huntley and Brinkley, of the NBC evening newscasts.

The first briefing, given to colonels and a brigadier general, went smoothly, so the two presenters appeared relaxed in the informal second briefing where most of the audience had a rank of major. A few captains and lieutenants were allowed to attend.

Major Hardy and Major Laurel used large sliding panels that had various maps attached. On each map were colored stickers, arrows, and symbols marking the positions of Viet Cong and the North Vietnamese Army as well as U.S. forces.

Each officer digested the intelligence in rapt attention except Bruce. He said quietly to Slater that the briefings were compiled by self-promoting field officers and had no semblance to reality. Few in the U.S. military knew what locations the VC occupied let alone the larger North Vietnamese forces.

"Why attend the briefings then?" Slater whispered.

"I compile the information for my commander and his staff. They treat it as gospel and can't imagine that someone in the army would issue misleading reports."

"How do you know the information is tainted?"

"Because I've been in the field where the reports were prepared. I've seen the men and their biases. Some officers want to look good to their higher-ups, so they make up anything especially killed in action or KIAs. I don't trust any of the dispatches."

Bruce leaned over and said, "Charlie knows how to gather accurate intelligence about us. Many local Vietnamese work on the base in maintenance, laundry, cleaning, and office jobs. At night, the army allows Vietnamese prostitutes to enter the base from 7:00 PM to 10:00 PM. The young girls hawk themselves by saying, 'Twenty dollars for love, thirty for true love.' The locals collect information, forward it to the villages who carry it to Viet Cong."

Ten minutes into the briefing, Major Hardy extended his pointer to an area near the Cambodian border referring to the 187th Regiment. Slater straightened in the chair.

"That's where I'm headed," he muttered to Bruce.

"Watch out. Charlie roams at will around there."

"Doesn't the 187th engage him?"

"Too much territory to cover. Their mission is to secure a small piece of land near the border and protect roads."

Major Laurel spoke next and stated that recent intelligence suggested that a large NVA force is expected to attack in the coming months.

A captain on the front row asked, "Where will they enter Vietnam?"

"North of LZ 42," Major Laurel said. Everyone except Slater knew where LZ 42 was located. "Most of the 187th are mobilized northward and doing search and destroy."

To Bruce, Slater said, "What's an LZ?"

"Landing Zone, bare ground so helicopters can land."

"Can I ask any questions?"

"Sure. Go ahead."

Slater caught Major Hardy's attention. "What about the Phan Lac area?"

He looked at Slater's green fatigues and gold bar, gave an audible snort and said, "Since the skirmish six weeks ago, the 187th set up a defensive perimeter and stopped search and destroy around Phan Lac. Colonel Nguyen inflicted damage, but G-2 felt that his goal was to distract the 187th away from the Cambodian border. They moved Company B south four klicks away from their camp to protect the southern end."

Slater asked Bruce, "What skirmish? What's a G-2? Who's Colonel Nguyen? What's a klick?"

"No one's told you? A Special Forces team was ambushed. All killed. The army nicknamed the man in charge as 'Colonel Nguyen.' He leads the VC and gives us fits. We don't know who he is or anything about the locals, but he knows everything. He might as well attend this briefing. Hell, he could give the briefing. G-2 means Regimental Intelligence Section, and a klick is a kilometer or six tenths of a mile. You'll get used to it."

The meeting ended fifteen minutes later, and everyone filed out. Walking down the hallway Slater saw a large water bottle that contained yellow liquid.

"What's that?"

"Water laced with chorine. It tastes awful, but it's all the army can do to make the water drinkable."

"It looks like piss. Don't they have anything else?" asked Slater.

"Warm soda for breakfast. You'll adjust and eventually prefer it warm."

"Encouraging. What color is the meat?"

"What's meat?" They laughed.

"You really going to Phan Lac?" Slater nodded and Bruce added, "The 187th has admitted defeat around Phan Lac and concentrated in other areas. You going there doesn't make any sense."

*   *   *

Slater finished his processing at the adjutant's office and left to rejoin his team. From a block away he saw his troops organize their packs except Spec 4 Jesse DeWitt who struggled with his gear. Two captains walked near the group, saw Jesse, stopped, and lit into him.

"What'cha doin', boy?" Both captains rained abuse at him. "You're not supposed to be here. Trying to get out of work?"

Jesse tried to swallow their insults and act passively unless you focused on his eyes. Vico and Ernie felt for their comrade, but they couldn't say anything. Hadn't this team received enough harassment? Then they saw Slater walking toward the captains and wondered what their fearless leader would do in his confrontation against the enemy.

Seeing his man tormented by two captains offended his moral sense of fair play. He was also gripped by panic. The captains outranked him and could crucify him in front of the men whose respect he tried to win. Should he remain silent or speak out against this injustice?

Remembering Dietrich Bonhoeffer, Slater said to himself, "What the hell. What more can they do to me? Send me to Vietnam?"

Armed with shaky knees, Slater approached the officers and spoke in a firm voice. "Sirs, if you have anything to say to my man, say it to me. He is following my orders." He looked them in the eye. The captains stopped. They were having fun at Jesse's expense.

Despite the captains' combined seven years of experience in the army and two combat tours, this measly second lieutenant caught them.

"Lieutenant, he was sandbagging and didn't display any military courtesy toward us."

"He's with my team. Colonel Wilberforce is sending us on a special mission."

They were ready to slam into Slater being a second lieutenant with new fatigues and because the insignia on his collar indicated he belonged to the Adjutant General Corps. Upon hearing Colonel Wilberforce's name, they kept silent but did not apologize for their bullying. As they departed in a chastened state, Slater did not salute them. Watching them leave, he gave a big exhale of relief. It was his first action as a leader, and he felt light-headed from the exchange. Bonhoeffer would be proud.

As everyone organized the supplies and waited for their transportation, Slater noticed that his team paid more attention when he spoke. Vico didn't challenge Slater's authority.

Their gear was loaded into a pickup truck including four medium-sized cardboard boxes of ammunition that they had just received from Supply.

When Vico saw them, he said, "One for each, eh?"

"How long do you think they will last?" asked Ernie.

Jesse said, "For Vico, about five minutes."

Slater said, "We shouldn't waste the ammo since we're not a part of the regiment's supply line, but I'm sure they will give us plenty of bullets if we run low."

"How sure are you? No one has shown support for us so far."

"Is there time to ditch to Bangkok?" said Ernie.

When the pickup stopped at the airport, all four watched their supplies being loaded on the plane especially the boxes of ammunition.

9

MAY 1969

S later and team flew on the dependable yet clattering, prop driven C-130 transport plane traveling from Nha Trang to Pleiku. Upon arrival they boarded a HU-1 helicopter known to the troops as a Huey. It flew them to the regimental compound. After landing at the 187th, the pilot pointed to another Huey at an adjacent helipad.

"It will take you to Second Battalion, Company B." After a three-mile flight, the whirlybird dropped them and returned to base.

Securing their gear, Slater's team walked to the nearest soldier and asked where the command post was. He was anxious to meet with a platoon leader and get a proper briefing. The Spec 4 gave directions and said the officers were busy with the battalion commander who came down from headquarters to bestow medals on five soldiers.

Slater and the group continued on the path to the command post and walked by the Company B formation which comprised four platoons. Each platoon approximated fifty men. The soldiers faced straight ahead during the ceremony and ignored the new arrivals in their new green fatigues. They in turn ignored the company except Slater who spotted a captain at the front leading the award presentations. He looked familiar but was so far away, Slater couldn't be sure about the man's identity.

When the team reached the command post of the First Platoon, a black staff sergeant named Herb Boydston approached them. "We received your paperwork. The company commander ordered that your group proceed to your post right away."

"What's the name of the CO?" asked Slater.

"Captain Delaney Gray."

If Slater could ask how a lethal assignment could get worse, he found the answer: Captain Gray, his Fort Benning training CO, who rode his butt during most of the course. He shook his head in disgust and then lowered it in despair.

Ernie noticed the change in his leader. "Everything all right?"

"I'll fill you in later. Let's head out."

The gear including the four heavy boxes of ammunition was loaded on the helicopter. Sergeant Boydston instructed Slater and Ernie about using the proper radio channel.

"I haven't seen a radio this old before."

"How can I contact you?" asked Ernie.

"This is easy. Just select the channel and press this button to talk and this button to listen."

"Will it hold together for a week or two?" Slater asked.

The sergeant continued, "You actually goin' to Phan Lac?"

"Yeah. What about it?"

"Did anybody tell you?"

"A little."

"Charlie runs the place especially the village. He fires weapons all the time. They show up at night and leave during the day. They have your Landing Zone gauged for mortars, so set up your camp away from it and use lots of sandbags for shelter. I put in plenty for you. You get food and supplies from us by chopper but radio us first. The LZ is two miles west of here."

"Anything else?"

"Who'd you piss off?" asked Herb.

Slater appreciated Herb's civility. "Where're you from?"

"Phoenix. You take care."

"You're the friendliest person I've met in Vietnam," said Slater.

They shook hands. Herb released a big smile and nodded in appreciation of the compliment.

* * *

ROTC orientation, language classes, and Fort Benning prepared him somewhat for the mission. Slater trembled knowing that his survival instincts would be tested. Four men primed themselves for a camping expedition in enemy territory.

The chopper ride broke their depression and provided temporary relief from all the bad news they had received that day. It glided over lush trees and beautiful hills. The mountains received plenty of rain, so they sparkled in a verdant green.

Slater's trance was interrupted when a crewman said, "Watch out for snipers. Some are armed with anti-chopper rockets."

"Wonderful," thought Slater.

Slater worried about his new quarters in the middle of nowhere. In his heart he felt he was a civilian. Wearing a uniform felt foreign, and developing a mindset for killing seemed blasphemous. He wanted peace. He couldn't imagine killing any Vietnamese. He didn't think they would accept or offer any olive branches, and his proficiency with the Vietnamese language was yet to be tested.

The pilot, First Lieutenant Derrick Williamson, wore semifaded fatigues. The subdued Aviator badge sewn above the left pocket signified his expertise. Handsome, smart, strong, from Palo Alto, California, with a crew cut, he had flown choppers in the area for two months. He loved flying and supporting the men. Everyone loved Derrick and felt luck resided in any helicopter he flew. When troops were extracted from the jungle or medevaced, they took comfort when his whirling chariot came into view. Last month, Derrick earned a Silver Star for extricating men from a VC ambush while dodging a hail of bullets.

Over the weeks when Slater's group received supplies, the chopper pilot usually was Derrick. Soon he and Slater became friends.

"See the flat area next to the hill?" Derrick said and pointed straight ahead. "That's the landing zone. We'll hover for thirty seconds and then depart, so hustle."

Slater understood. He didn't need any reminder about the danger. His group had no support units and no artillery. The landing of the aircraft alerted the VC in the area which put his group at an immediate disadvantage. He never felt more vulnerable.

The ground was hammered from previous shelling. How could one call it a Landing Zone? It looked like an ordnance test range. Derrick hovered the chopper two feet above the ground. He wouldn't risk damage to his landing skids. Everyone dumped the supplies and kicked off the bulky ammo boxes.

After Slater's team disembarked, Derrick yelled down to them, "Good luck. See you soon." He gave a big smile and a thumbs-up. Then he elevated his aircraft and headed for the safety of the 187th Regiment's compound.

Slater looked over the jetsam of gear strewn over the red clay. The team sorted the packages, found the shovels, food, medicine, and ammo boxes. The open area exposed the group to sniper fire and possible attack, so they moved out of sight to a better location.

The four chose a protected part of the mountain nearby and set up camp so they could watch the LZ. They took shifts to dig a shelter and fill sandbags. Two men started to dig, one unpacked the boxes, and one was posted as a sentry. Opening the first box, Spec 4 Ernie Alvarez said, "Hey. Highpockets screwed us again. We have blanks for ammo."

10

E rnie opened the other boxes with the same result and said, "They're also blanks."

"All of the boxes?" asked Vico.

"All four," said Ernie. "Three of the boxes are blanks for M-16s. Only one box is for M-14s, and I thought I had problems in Albuquerque."

Vico swore, "I'll get that bastard."

"Me first," said Jesse.

"How do blanks make us soldiers?" Ernie asked in anger.

"What do we do now? Charlie will slaughter us," said Jesse.

"We have a few bullets available in our clips, but I'm planning to use them all on Wilberforce," said Vico.

In the face of this setback, Slater said, "We need to forget the good colonel for the moment and rely on support of the 187th." Slater hoped to settle everyone down and reassure his men. "For tonight we will assume a defensive position. If the VC attack, we can fire blanks and pray they won't come any closer. Tomorrow morning, we'll hike to the 187th and get bullets."

At 2:30 AM, Slater's Rangers received a welcoming salvo from Charlie. One mortar shell exploded in the middle of the landing zone. Everyone but Ernie who was on guard duty woke up, grabbed rifles, and waited. Sixty seconds elapsed. A second shell exploded and then silence. The four readied their rifles with blanks and bayonets. No one came. Not a sound. The shift for the next guard duty started, and the rest tried to sleep.

The guard at First Platoon's perimeter also heard the two explosions. He relayed the information the next morning to Sergeant Boydston who wondered if his new friends survived.

* * *

At daybreak around 6:00 AM, Slater's warriors began the journey to Company B. With limited light in the spring morning sky, they had difficulty seeing the ground ahead of them. Vico took the point because he lost in rock, paper, scissors. Jesse followed Vico, and Slater and Ernie with the radio comprised the rear. Ernie tied down the aerial so Charlie wouldn't see it over the foliage.

Because this patrol was their first, they put themselves on alert with every step except Jesse who had been in country for two months and was more relaxed. Trails were hard to find, so they forged ahead encountering thickets, branches, and insect noises. Progress was slow. Slater tried to envision what he would do if they bumped into Viet Cong. What orders would he give? His training did not include a four-person recon unit.

After one hour of stomping on the rough ground, everyone tired of the hike and wanted to return to the camp. The hot sun contributed to the agony. Two miles seemed to be five miles. Where were they on the map? Where was 187th? Did Company B return to Pleiku or advance to Cambodia?

Slater knew that they didn't go to Cambodia because the Army was not allowed to cross the border since it would violate international law. He never understood why the North

Vietnamese troops could travel along the Ho Chi Minh Trail, part of it in Cambodia, and US forces could not.

To combat the monotony when Slater took his turn at the point, Vico started a conversation with Ernie and Jesse. "Isn't that radio heavy?"

"Be thankful you're not carrying it."

"Does it work?"

"I'm not sure."

"But you're the expert," said Jesse.

"Sometimes the components work, sometimes they don't. That's all I can guarantee."

Vico decided to carry the talk further. "How is it in Albuquerque? Must be hot."

Ernie said, "It's like a little Mexico. We work for the rich guys to make a living. When Vietnam comes around, their kids get off, and we get to carry radios in the jungle."

Vico said, "Yeah, same in New Jersey. I got sent to the jungle too."

Jesse chimed in. "Double standard. Uncle Sam makes the rules and forces the poor to fight for him. When we come back, they forget all about us. 'Tell me again what you did for us?'"

Slater, as point, turned around and said, "I can hear you guys way up here. Quiet. We have one more hill. Vico, it's your turn at the point."

The group climbed a large hill that had a high angle to the crest. As Slater struggled up the pebbly incline, he saw Vico come back toward him in a crouched position motioning for silence.

"Vietnamese are marching in the valley on the other side of the mountain. They're moving toward the First Platoon."

11

E veryone wanted to see if Vico's sighting was accurate, so they crept to the ridge. Slater knelt next to Vico, and looked into the valley below. Vico estimated thirty VC advancing along the makeshift dirt road preparing for an ambush. He assumed the First Platoon, Company B, was located on the east side of the hill north of their position. They saw the curved magazine clips which meant that Charlie carried AK-47 rifles that were manufactured in Russia. It appeared that three men had mortar tubes. Slater focused on one man who seemed to act as leader. He directed the guerillas into their formation.

Ernie untied the aerial. "I'll radio the platoon."

Slater got nervous. "Can they hear us? Let's get away from here so they can't see the aerial."

Ernie went ten yards down the path and fumbled with the buttons. Jesse and Vico watched him start up the radio wondering if it would work. It sputtered for ten seconds, but Ernie got some static and kept the volume low while he talked into the speaker. After getting a corporal, Ernie gave Slater the mike.

"Is this the First Platoon, Company B, 187th Regiment?"

"Who's this?" responded the voice.

"This is Lt. Slater Marshall of Special Forces. We have spotted VC coming your way. We are on the top of a ridge, two klicks from you." He didn't know if he was two or twenty klicks, but the words sounded professional.

"Charlie doesn't come near us."

"He's near you now, and you had better alert your guys. They're moving along the valley and carrying AK-47s and mortars."

"I need a password."

"We were not given a password."

"I can't acknowledge without one. We don't have any patrols out there, so I don't know who you are."

Slater tried to withhold his frustration. "Get me your CO."

"He's away at a meeting."

"Your sergeant then."

"He's at the same meeting."

Slater took a deep breath trying to resolve this impasse. A name came into his mind, and his eyes opened more widely.

"Get me Herb. Herb Boydston. He knows me."

"Hold on."

After one minute, Slater heard a voice. "This is Sergeant Boydston."

"Herb. Herb. This is Lt. Marshall. We talked yesterday. Do you remember? Phan Lac?"

"Lieutenant. You survived last night's mortar? How're you doin'?" Herb said with his friendly manner.

"Get your men ready. About twenty-five to thirty VC with mortar are coming your way, and I think they are close to your camp. Your radio operator doesn't know who I am. I don't have any codes. Just be prepared for an attack."

Yelling into the radio, Herb said, "Holy crap. We're screwed. We don't have many men here. We're sitting ducks."

Slater said, "Are other men nearby?"

"Many pulled back and are at least twenty minutes away. Everyone thought Charlie wouldn't attack us in the daytime."

Not knowing what options lay in front of the First Platoon, Slater wanted to help. "We're too far away to reach you. Do you have machine guns? Will they help?"

Herb said, "I can radio for the choppers. They can get here in ten or fifteen minutes, but we need a diversion to slow them down."

Slater thought for a moment. "I'll see what I can do. Out."

Ernie gave Slater a funny look. "We're sitting ducks too if they spot us. Don't risk it."

"I want to go home too, remember?"

Slater gathered his team. "We need to fire against the VC and then scramble for cover. Let's look for protection around here."

"We're going to fire with blanks?" asked Jesse.

"That's all we have. Enough to surprise and distract them for ten or fifteen minutes."

Vico said, "When did John Wayne join our unit?"

After three minutes, Jesse found a recess in the hill that provided cover except a direct hit. Everyone checked it out and agreed with the find.

They walked to the crest, and Slater positioned them so each had two places from which to fire before rushing for cover. On Slater's signal, they fired their clips and then clambered to another position on the side of the mountain. They then fired the second magazine. The Viet Cong returned the rifle fire as the four Americans scrambled to their safe hiding place.

While the others ran, Slater looked down in the valley and saw the older Vietnamese man order his troops to mobilize. Then Slater hustled to the next hill since he knew mortars would shortly rain down. All four clung to each other in the recess as mortar shells landed all around them. Some came close, some exploded far away. After ten minutes of blasts, the group heard the sound of helicopters, and they smiled in relief. The mortars stopped.

Climbing out of their hiding, the group saw two choppers spraying bullets in the valley. Their gunfire put Charlie on the defensive, and they retreated. Some mortar units hid behind trees and fired at the First Platoon's camp. Some enemy soldiers fired at the helicopters without success. In fact, nothing happened against either side except the expenditure of bullets. The VC leader ordered them to withdraw, and they disappeared into the foliage.

"Those guys are good," said Vico.

Ernie commented, "Why can't we do that?"

"It's not our country," said Jesse. "They have motivation. I'd learn to disappear too if choppers fired at me."

"Careful, you guys. Don't let them see us," Slater whispered.

After fifteen minutes, all quieted. Ernie asked to proceed, but Slater shook his head. "I don't want any hidden VC to attack us when all we have are blanks."

Finally the group skirted the side of the hill and went toward a valley road that would take them to the platoon's camp. The trek took longer than anticipated. The group stopped for one breather. Slater realized that the team needed to get into better shape.

Ernie radioed that their four-man team was approaching and not to shoot.

The group passed through an opening in the concertina wire and paraded into the camp where they received cheers from the platoon members. Some of the men with dirty faces, wearing their helmets and green t-shirts, passed out warm cans of beer to celebrate.

Herb came out, shook hands with the four, and introduced the team to the men of the First Platoon.

"Where's the brass?" asked Slater.

"They're at HQ. Charlie knew we only had a few soldiers. Amazing," said Herb.

Others in the platoon returned from sweeping the valley under the protection from the choppers overhead. They did not locate any enemy.

Shortly after the choppers left, 1Lt. Dale Whitney, platoon leader, arrived and introduced himself. "Thanks, man."

12

S later's team meshed well with Lt. Whitney's unit. No barriers existed especially when a sergeant broke out more beer.

Relaxing and chatting in their seedy fatigues while listening to rock and roll in the background, the troops acted as though the war zone were thousands of miles away. They came from all over America and seemed so young. The soldiers of the First advised about little things to make life easier in the bush like shaving and washing their clothes.

"Just leave them out in the afternoon, and the rains will clean everything. After the rain, the sun will dry them. Pretty simple. After two weeks they will stand at attention without any support." Everyone laughed.

A sergeant gave Slater the First Platoon's mailing address so his crew could receive letters from home. All four wrote to their families. No stamps were needed when mailed in Vietnam. Over the course of their tour, Ernie received letters from his wife every two weeks, Vico from his family every month, and Jesse and Slater did not receive any correspondence.

Lt. Whitney from Oklahoma City had eleven months in country and didn't want to take unnecessary risks to spoil his DEROS next month. Slight of build, brown hair, slow in talking, small mouth, big teeth, he went to Officer Candidate School after two years of college and became a gung-ho infantry lieutenant. During his eleven months in the highlands, much of his enthusiasm for the war eroded. He accepted his duty and performed it efficiently but questioned more and more why he and his men had to tramp through the hills.

The military's motto is "mission first, men second," and Whitney complied, but he cheated against the first principle in favor of the second toward the end of his tour. He made decisions based on the safety of his compatriots. The men appreciated his concern and followed him everywhere. Slater and Whitney became friends immediately.

Slater watched his team interact with young men who had little in common with each other except that they served on the same side. They teased each other, talked about army screw ups, and told stories about home. First Platoon's troops were rough around the edges, naïve, and pro-Vietnam. They believed in their government, Jesus, and apple pie. They thought they made America free.

Somehow the two groups appreciated the similarities such as being American, adventurous, and the fact they needed each other. One Spec 4 noticed Ernie's radio and without a word brought back a new one from a nearby tent.

"Supply gave us too many. Take this."

Ernie thanked his new friend.

"What's your mission?" asked Slater.

"We patrol the area and search for the enemy although we avoid Phan Lac," said Lt. Whitney.

"How do you know the enemy when you see him?"

"They're all VC."

"So what do you do?"

"We shoot them," said a corporal from Arkansas.

Jesse said, "And the villages?"

"We search for VC and guns. If we find anything, we shoot them," said a private first class from Colorado.

"The Vietnamese hate us, so we are careful," said a squad leader, a sergeant from Pennsylvania.

"I can see why they hate you. You kill them," said Slater.

"We're giving them democracy and they fight us. We have no choice," said another corporal.

"How do you feel about the killing?" asked Ernie.

"It's them or us."

Slater asked, "What about the 'Hearts and Minds' program?"

A nearby sergeant said, "Only Charlie is here."

A private yelled, "Someone said, if you grab 'em by the balls, their hearts and minds will follow." Everyone laughed except Slater.

Lt. Whitney said, "The South Vietnam government does not have a presence here."

"Then why should we be here?"

"I'm not smart enough to understand the military's master plan, and I don't know what we're accomplishing. Nothing's changed since I arrived in Vietnam."

"How often do you patrol?" asked Jesse.

Whitney said, "We patrol or what is called search and destroy one week on and one week off. Sometimes we coordinate with other units, but for the past month we have guarded the company's south flank which is also the battalion's southern area of operations."

"Where are the other platoons?"

"North and northwest of us. If you want, I can introduce you to them as well as Captain Gray."

Slater could hardly wait.

* * *

Late afternoon, a chopper landed within the platoon's perimeter and out charged Captain Delaney Gray with his top sergeant. Gray wore a scowl along with resolute eyes. He approached Lt. Whitney and said, "Fill me in."

He informed Gray in typical military monotone about the surprise attack. "The Special Forces reconnaissance team spotted the VC, alerted us, and exposed themselves to enemy fire in order to divert them. The Special Forces unit received incoming fire until our choppers took over and repelled them."

Seeing Captain Gray listen to the report, Slater thought he might earn brownie points with his former CO by foiling the VC attack.

As Gray viewed the recon team, his eyes landed on a familiar lieutenant.

"Oh my God. He's leading the recon? We're in big trouble."

Hearing the captain's sarcasm disappointed Slater. He thought his team conducted themselves in a competent manner, worthy of acknowledgment. During the silence that followed, Slater noticed the Combat Infantryman's Badge sewn on Gray's fatigues.

"You got your CIB. Congratulations."

"I didn't hear 'sir' in your address, Lieutenant. Did you forget your protocol?"

Slater was still sore at Gray from his treatment at Fort Benning, but feigning respect he yelled, "Sir, yes sir."

Lt. Whitney interrupted. "Captain Gray has already won an Army Commendation Medal and a recommendation has been submitted for a Bronze Star with a V device for valor."

Slater thought Whitney was a kiss ass but understood that he still needed Gray's support because his date of departure was so close.

Slater said with an undertone of resentment, "Too bad you missed out on today's action, sir. You might have earned a Silver Star."

Not picking up Slater's irony, Gray said, "I'll have plenty of opportunities. The VC operate all over. How did you spot them? Luck?"

"They stepped on me while I was asleep."

"So you are assigned as our listening post? Why me? Why do I get the morons?"

Slater needed to reel in his anger. Gray was a higher ranking officer, a company commander, and Slater unfortunately needed his cooperation. Venting his frustration would not end happily. He decided to change the subject.

"Who do I see about getting a briefing and how do we coordinate? Plus our team needs a few things."

"Like what?"

"Bullets, food, drink," said Slater.

"Bullets?"

"Colonel Wilberforce issued us blanks?"

"Must be a mistake. I can't imagine he would do anything like that."

Slater removed a bullet from his webbing and showed it to Gray. "We fired at Charlie today with blanks. We bluffed our way in order to keep them away from the First Platoon."

Gray focused on the blank cartridge and didn't know what to say.

"So can we get some bullets?"

Gray noticed Slater's M-14 rifle. "You don't have M-16s?"

"Wilberforce issued them to us instead of the M-16. Thanks for the recommendation, sir."

Gray thought something didn't smell right, but he wasn't going to give Slater any satisfaction. Gray said without any apology, "You earned it."

"Do you have some ammunition for us, sir?" Slater put an emphasis on "sir."

"We don't have any bullets for M-14s, only M-16s. You'll have to get them from Special Forces since they issued the rifles to you."

This exchange was not going well for Slater who was getting more enraged by the minute.

Whitney intervened to the relief of all, and led the CO away from the group. Slater's team looked at him in disbelief.

"Don't we have trouble enough with the VC without having the friendlies mad at us?" said Vico.

"So much for cooperation between units," said Jesse.

"What did you do to him?" said Ernie.

"He was my CO at training camp and didn't like my attitude especially since I scored so well in all the exercises."

When Whitney returned, he said, "You and I will coordinate since my platoon will be guarding the south end of the perimeter. Gray is not in our line of communication."

"That works for me."

"Slater, I'm sorry that we don't have any bullets for you. We're even in short supply ourselves for M-16 ammo."

"Not what I wanted to hear," said Slater.

Whitney said, "The attack caught us unprepared. It didn't make sense. Intelligence indicated that the enemy would enter the theater from the north. This area has not experienced any unfriendlies since the VC overran the previous crew who manned the listening post six weeks ago."

Whitney saw Slater cringe at the thought of Americans dying in Phan Lac. Whitney would be careful in his choice of words in the future. He didn't want to discourage a group assigned to support his unit.

Slater recovered. "How did the previous Special Forces listening post do?"

Lt. Whitney said, "To be frank they were a strange bunch. They loved being Special Forces and wearing the green beret. They thought that made them special. Hey. Why aren't you wearing them?"

They didn't have our sizes," said Vico.

Whitney continued. "They were gruff and saw too many war movies. Thought they would win the war by themselves and took lots of chances. No one was surprised when they got killed."

Slater said, "We plan to be plenty cautious."

"Sorry you and the captain don't get along. You saved our butts today."

"We came because we needed bullets. That's why we hiked over the mountains. By coincidence we happened to bump into the VC. Nothing special."

"But you fired at them exposing your position. That's special."

"We also got tired. We're not in any shape."

"Don't overdo it. Phan Lac has many hills. They're not too rough to climb. Go on short hikes at first to adjust to the climate."

His suggestion was welcomed since no one wanted to take long hikes.

Whitney's point man, Corporal Pete Sanchez, warned the team about the enemy's booby traps and informed them about the use of Claymores, an anti-personnel mine similar to a an explosive device placed for defensive purposes. He gave one to the group and told them to handle it with care.

The group ate dinner and slept with the platoon. They felt more secure within the concertina wire than out in Charlie's jungle. Slater didn't agree with Whitney's words that enemy activity declined in his area. The attack this morning told a different story.

*　*　*

II Corps briefing: the next day

Major Hardy aimed his pointer at the highlands although it wasn't near Phan Lac. He focused on an area six miles east of the attack and said, "The 187th Regiment overran a VC company killing twenty, wounding fifteen, and capturing two. Their search and destroy mission resulted from the intelligence report from our G-2. No casualties on our side."

13

For the next five days, the team patrolled in the vicinity of Phan Lac without incident. They hiked to become familiar with the local terrain. Since the men were scared that a Viet Cong hid behind every bush, they remained vigilant and didn't take any risks. They focused on the immediate shrub or the nearby rocks and ignored the hills, valleys, and creeks. The daily treks annoyed them. They hated being in the middle of VC territory especially since they only had blanks.

Vico and Jesse trudged the hillsides next to each other. Jesse hardly spoke during most of the day, so Vico asked, "What's in LA that isn't in my town?"

Just thinking about his hometown brought Jesse's neighborhood accent back that he and his friends spoke. "I don't know nuttin' about Newark, man."

"So tell me about LA."

"You want to know about LA? So here goes. People read about the Hollywood glitz, but it's hard to make a living there. Not many jobs, man, so we work for ourselves. Get all we can.

"Remember the Watts riots in '65? That's where I got my start with my friends. Everything exploded, and we took what we wanted. Newark had a riot too, didn't it?"

Vico said, "They rioted in '67. Everyone was mad at each other."

"Anything changed?"

"Nothing. The city got worse. No one came into downtown any more. Any changes in LA?"

Jesse thought a moment and said, "It scared the rich folks real bad, so they ponied up more jobs and threw more money in our area. It helped, but I was still mad. We got no respect, and I didn't get no jobs. So I continued to take until I got caught. The cops gave me a choice of jail or army. Imagine? If we are such a moral country, why put crooks in the military?"

Vico didn't know how to respond. He thought Jesse was a good guy and didn't want to get on his bad side.

Jesse didn't care if the others thought he was a criminal. His people didn't get many breaks, so he created them. And he didn't regret his decisions. He needed to survive.

Silence ruled for twenty minutes until Vico tripped over a branch. He kicked the offending limb away and unleashed his anger about the war and the army, and soon Ernie and Jesse joined the gripe-fest. They groused about their assignment in Phan Lac and railed their frustration against any officer in Special Forces Headquarters.

The next day followed the same routine: walk around trees, straddle underbrush, slog over hills in and out of downpours. Their feet were soaked, and their skin chaffed against drenched fatigues.

"Humping in this crap makes me sick."

"Cranky again, Vico?" said Jesse.

"What're you complaining for? Try carrying this radio," said Ernie.

"How do you do it?" said Vico. "Carrying this fake ammo is bad enough, but a radio?"

Jesse said, "We sweat in this hell hole, not sure what we're doin', and for what? What's the military importance of these mountains? I need to pound on somebody for putting me here."

"Then pound," said Ernie.

"Let's find Charlie, and we can wail."

"If we find Charlie, he'll wail on us," said Slater. "He has real bullets, remember?"

"You guys are pussies. We're supposed to kill him, so let's go," said Vico.

"I don't want to be killed in the process. Slow down," said Ernie.

"Charlie will attack us when we sleep, so why not go after him now?" said Jesse.

"With what?" asked Ernie.

As they climbed up a steep incline, no one spoke because all drew upon their reserves of energy to make it to the next level. As they arrived at the crest of the hill, Vico as point motioned for quiet. The others sat down while he inched forward to look over the top.

"No one here."

"Thank goodness. I'm too tired to pull a trigger," said Ernie.

"I'll shoot your rifle for you, blanks and all," said Jesse.

"I don't need your help," said Ernie, looking at Jesse with an edge to his words.

"You talk a good game," said Jesse. "How will you perform in combat?"

"You been in combat?" said Ernie.

"In the states, yeah."

"Hey. Knock it off. Remember who the enemy is," said Slater.

"Who is the enemy?" said Ernie. "What's Uncle Sam done for me? He's taken me away from my wife. I don't want to be here, but in many ways it's no different being at home under the thumb of some stupid-ass rich guy."

"At least Uncle Sam give us blanks. We get nothing at home." said Jesse.

"I see we're in great form today. No chance we'll run into Charlie. We make too much noise," said Slater. "We need these hikes to get in shape. Look at us. We complain after two hours."

Vico said, "We're in a remote area. Charlie doesn't operate here anyway. Why don't we return and rest up for tomorrow?"

Slater said, "We need to prepare in case we meet up with Charlie."

"What do we do if we meet him?" asked Jesse.

"We throw rocks at him," said Ernie.

They stopped in a shady area, sat down against a tree, drank water, and ate a snack.

Slater knew how easily the complaining could demoralize his group. He didn't blame them because he agreed with their comments, but the grumbling had to stop.

Impatient with their situation, Slater raised his voice and tore into his crew.

"I'm tired of your griping. I don't care about the army either. I don't care about Vietnam. I care about returning home with all of you. We need to shape up. Your bitching gets us nowhere. This recon is for our safety. We need to know the lay of the land. So saddle up and move for one more hour and then we'll head back."

The team knew they deserved the scolding. Grouching did not improve their predicament.

When they resumed the march, Jesse went to the front as point and Vico went to the rear. All agreed to improve their attitudes and pay more attention to the geography. They exercised caution by using hand signals and silence. They weren't in Kansas any more.

After forty-five minutes, they edged up a knoll surrounded by tall trees. Jesse motioned with his hand for the group to stop. He looked over the area and returned quickly.

"I spotted a Vietnamese guy and girl. They are holding hands. I didn't see any guns."

Slater crept to the hilltop and after ten minutes returned. He developed a plan whereby they would surround the two. He slowly went to the top and waited until Vico and Jesse moved to each flank. When the Vietnamese couple neared the lieutenant's position, Slater stood up and spoke in Vietnamese, "Hello. Can we talk?"

The surprised Vietnamese turned to run only to see Vico aim his rifle at them from the left. When they went the other way, Jesse showed himself. Ernie came to Slater's right side. The Vietnamese stopped and raised their hands. Slater walked over to them determined to communicate despite his rusty language skills. He motioned for them to put their arms down.

"Can you understand my Vietnamese?"

At first, the couple experienced shock. They didn't recognize the Vietnamese words because they didn't expect an American in the jungle to speak their language.

The three Spec 4s had never heard the lieutenant speak the native language. The words sounded weird with so many strange sounds. How can anyone communicate this way? They held their ground and remained motionless while staring at the two foes who stood in silence.

Slater repeated his words more slowly. "Can you understand my Vietnamese? I won't hurt you. Do you understand me?"

They looked so young, thought Slater. He felt badly that he interrupted a moment where they could enjoy privacy together in the highlands. They never expected that U.S. soldiers would come here. The young girl looked at her companion and turned to Slater.

She said in Vietnamese, "I understand you, a little." The young man nodded slightly.

"I need you to listen to me. Okay?"

They both acknowledged.

"I know you are Viet Cong." They both tensed when Slater said he knew they were the enemy. "We come in peace. I don't want to kill you. Can we have peace?"

The two teenage VC didn't reply. They didn't know what to say.

"Did you understand my message?"

The girl said in a soft voice, "Yes."

"Can we live in peace?"

She glanced at her boyfriend, then at Slater. She looked at the soldiers who had rifles and returned to face Slater. She nodded again, but her eyes remained cautious. The soldiers became restless at not knowing what was discussed.

"Can you talk?" Slater asked the girl.

"I'm afraid. I don't know why you want peace. Your men have rifles. Will they kill us?"

"Killing is stupid. I want you to live and me too." He then said, "War is dinky dow." Every American who was exposed to the Vietnamese, north and south, knew that "dinky dow" meant "crazy." Jesse's ears perked up. He knew its meaning; the other two did not. Vietnamese referred to Americans as "dinky dow," and Americans used it back at the locals. A game. Here in the highlands, the girl understood Lt. Marshall's message.

In English, Slater said, "Men, I am releasing these people. Be careful but let them leave."

"They're our prisoners. Why are you releasing them?" asked Vico.

"They're VC. Anyone over sixteen serves in the South Vietnamese Army. Anyone else is VC," said Jesse. "We might be releasing people who will kill us."

"Or save us," said Slater. "The killing stops here. With us, with them, understood?"

"Understood, and you're nuts," said Vico. "We're trained to capture the enemy."

"Anyone pleased with army training?" asked Slater.

"Okay, but Slater, the enemy? We're at war," said Vico.

"Do you want to kill them?"

"No, but . . ."

"Let them go. They will think we're crazy and avoid us," said Ernie.

"How will I reach DEROS if I'm court-martialed? I thought we fought for the USA," said Vico.

"Any other comments?" Slater looked around, felt the frustration, and saw his men reluctantly acquiesce.

The two Vietnamese saw the Americans object to the officer and hoped that he prevailed.

Slater looked at the two prisoners. "Now you can go but go slowly. I wish you peace."

They looked at each other, not knowing what to do. Then the teenage boy grabbed her hand, turned, and walked away but kept his eyes on the soldiers. As they rounded the far hill, they ran.

"We better return to camp. They might alert a regiment to come after us," said Ernie.

"Where's our white flag? It's never around when I need it," said Vico. "We just lost the war and our lives."

The team wheeled toward camp. Jesse walked up to Slater and said, "I hope you're right. Releasing them is a big gamble."

Slater took a big breath and said, "I know. My bargaining position is pretty weak when our rifles are loaded with blanks."

*   *   *

Resting at camp, Vico could not let the subject go. "We almost had a good day. We got some prisoners, not an everyday happening, and then we throw a good catch away. Can you explain to me your reasoning?

Ernie looked beyond Vico and saw something in the middle of the LZ. "I'll be right back."

"How are we going to impress Colonel Highpockets if we surrender without firing our blanks?" asked Vico.

Slater finished his water, and began his defense. "How can we win in Vietnam? It's a vicious circle. You heard Whitney. They go out and kill Vietnamese. Then they retaliate against the Americans. The pattern goes on until someone decides to stop.

"In order to win, are we supposed to kill all the Vietnamese we see? Doesn't anyone see the stupidity of this policy? This strategy is insane."

Slater paused and then said in an exasperating voice, "What chance do we have? Four soldiers against thousands? We don't belong here. The previous team was overrun, no survivors. My goal is to experience a DEROS, and I'll do whatever it takes. Right now, I trust my own instincts. If I'm wrong, we'll be over-run anyway. If I'm right, we have a chance."

After a prolonged period of silence, Vico said, "What the hell. They're only two people."

Ernie returned with a basket. "I found this at the LZ. No note, just a basket of fruit. Maybe you did it, Slater."

"It's poisoned," said Vico.

"I'll try it. I'm sick of C rations," said Jesse. He grabbed two pieces. The others joined in. Slater could not stop smiling.

14

JUNE 1969

The Americans continued to scout the surrounding area. They avoided the village since they needed to become more proficient at patrolling, to establish better coordination as a group, and to build more endurance on hikes.

Three days after their run-in with the teenage Vietnamese, Slater planned to reconnoiter the village. He couldn't help feeling like a goldfish in a shark tank. Was he entering an ambush against a swarm of VC? But he couldn't ignore Phan Lac any longer.

He understood that members of the 187th burned the village after the previous listening post was overrun, so the locals would not throw a parade when his gang arrived.

Vico questioned Slater's sanity for approaching Phan Lac in the first place. The others agreed with Vico, but they begrudgingly knew that at some point they needed to observe the village and face the Vietnamese.

The men took longer to eat breakfast and even delayed gearing up. No one spoke. They had similar fears as Slater. The moment of truth couldn't linger any longer. The group picked up their kits and moved out. Jesse assumed the point backed up by Vico. Ernie held the rear.

Twenty minutes later, they reached the entrance. The village consisted of eleven small huts made of palm leaves with thatched roofs nestled in the forest. Each hut had one entrance, one makeshift window, and bamboo stocks on the ground lying against the side of each hut.

The path curved its way into the middle of the village placing six huts on the left and five on the right. A gentle slope behind the huts on the right led downward to a creek. The ground was swept and neat. Clotheslines were erected behind each hut, and five women either tended the laundry or brushed the front walkways. Kids wore very little clothing and played in the dirt.

Slater wasn't sure what to do. His group presented an excellent target to any snipers if they were positioned in the trees. What if his group was attacked?

Jesse and Vico upon Slater's direction moved to each side, and the group entered with rifles at the ready at least to present an appearance of being armed. The Americans looked imposing despite having blanks in their magazines.

Slater led. Each man walked with a deliberate stride. They passed the first two huts when suddenly two small kids burst out of the third hut, stopped within five yards, and stared at them. A mother followed. She raised her middle finger and said, "Dinky dow."

Other kids from a fourth hut ran out raising their middle fingers and laughed. A second woman exited the hut with a scowl. She also said, "Dinky dow," and raised her middle finger. The women knew the meaning. The kids thought these strangers were funny.

Vico said, "Slater, what's dinky dow?"

"It means crazy. They're saying we're crazy. GIs also use it to describe the Vietnamese."

Slater approached the first woman who flashed her angry eyes. In Vietnamese he said, "Good morning. I am sorry to disturb you. I come in peace."

The woman's face held her scorn of these foreigners. Besides she didn't like his measly effort to speak Vietnamese. His accent applied to the area around Hue, not the highlands. Slater could see a lack of progress and wondered what to try next. He understood the skepticism. He wouldn't trust U.S. soldiers either.

As he contemplated various options, a little girl aged five ran from her hut much to the worry of the women and went to Jesse. She stopped, smiled, and waved. She had never seen a black man before, and she liked Jesse.

He tried to remain cool but surrendered to her enchanting antics. He smiled back and waved. The girl giggled and spoke to her two friends. They came over and grinned. Jesse looked at Slater and contorted his face asking what should he do next? Slater laughed and shrugged his shoulders.

A third young woman dressed in a white long-sleeved shirt and baggy black pants came out of the hut to herd two of the children back. She had long black hair, a soft face with smooth skin, penetrating eyes, and was absolutely beautiful. She looked at the soldiers with hatred.

Slater stared at her in awe. The Earth's rotation stopped for a moment. He was struck by her charms despite her apparent contempt for him and his men. Slater's troops noticed the effect she had on their leader as did the Vietnamese women. He just stood motionless watching her as she traipsed in front of him leading two kids to her hut.

When she turned to enter it, Slater said, "You have cute kids."

Jesse asked, "What did you say to her?"

He translated and then told his men to walk through the village and leave. The women's eyes followed their departure with resentment. As they disappeared from sight, one woman uttered, "Dinky dow."

Vico said after they departed, "Slater, this isn't the 'Dating Game.' They hate us. We don't need to complicate our presence further."

Ernie said, "At least get a better line." They all laughed including Slater.

The group's routine over the next few weeks consisted of hikes to the village and plenty of downtime. In the recent food package from the supply helicopter, Sergeant Boydston added a load of paperbacks discarded by Company B. Everyone except Jesse was overjoyed. They could relax yet keep their minds engaged and avoid boredom. They ignored the romance stories, horror, and religion.

Ernie preferred Western stories, James Bond, and then tore into "The Scarlett Pimpernel" when Vico finished it. Vico also liked James Bond. After reading "Catch-22," he concluded that its author, Joseph Heller, did not write a comedy but described Special Forces.

Slater selected "The Chosen" and the thick "War and Peace." He saw "Soul on Ice" and "The Autobiography of Malcolm X" in the batch. When he mentioned them to Jesse, he said he wasn't interested.

Slater asked Jesse, "What interests you?"

"Nothing. I don't like reading."

Slater suspected Jesse wasn't giving him the full answer. Debating in his mind whether to pursue the topic, Slater said, "I've read 'Malcolm X' and I think you would enjoy it."

Jesse shot him an angry look and spoke in a subdued voice. "I'm not interested, okay? Leave me alone."

That evening, while Jesse served as sentry, Slater left Ernie and Vico to their own devises and approached his man.

"I don't mean to be forward, but can you read?"

Jesse's outward appearance of pride sagged. "I read slowly. It's not easy for me. No one really helped me when I needed it, so I stopped."

"I can help if you wish."

Jesse looked at the others and turned to his lieutenant. "I will look like a fool. A grown-up studying like a grammar school kid."

"No one will say anything. Besides you'll grasp it quickly. And you can help me with better pickup lines."

Jesse felt conflicted. He didn't want people to know he was dumb and didn't want a white man to help him. But reluctantly he accepted. He reasoned that he wouldn't see these guys after the war, so why not take a chance. Besides Slater was a college graduate, so he must be smart.

Ernie and Vico did not criticize Jesse but encouraged him. They also admitted to their own reading problems but never had time to improve. Now they did.

Slater had Jesse read out loud. The progress was slow, but Jesse gained confidence the more he practiced. The art of reading became less challenging as he finished more books.

At the end of the day, each man summarized his progress, and why he liked or disliked his novel. They enjoyed expressing their opinions and hearing those of the others.

15

O nce or twice per week, Slater's team would drift through the village. He would offer polite conversation, but the women continued to spurn him. They did not raise their middle fingers but only muttered, "Dinky dow."

The young woman who beguiled Slater was present at each visit watching the children. She wore the same clothes and in the manner as before radiated hostility.

The children persisted in projecting their middle fingers followed by laughter. Each time the little girl would stop in front of Jesse and wave. Jesse asked her name in an awkward Vietnamese phrase that Slater taught him. She giggled and ran away. The women overheard Jesse's question and appreciated that he learned a little of their language. One woman said the little girl's name was Lan. Slater said it meant "Orchid."

On the fourth trip, Slater brought back the basket Ernie found at the LZ and gave it to a woman filled with fruit. He asked the chopper when they dropped off supplies the next time to bring fruit. When she accepted the basket, he thought she almost unfurled a little smile.

On the fifth trip, the children remained in the huts. Only the young woman came out, glared at Slater, and said, "Get out of here. Why talk peace? You kill us."

"I don't kill. I hate war." Slater noticed Lan was not present. Where is Lan?"

"Sick. Big sick. Need medicine."

"Can I see her?" asked Jesse after Slater informed him about her condition.

Jesse and Slater entered the hut and saw the little girl in pain. Lan looked at her swollen hand and then switched her eyes to Jesse imploring him for help.

"Can we do anything?" said Jesse.

"I think she has an infection or else a poisonous bite from some insect," said Slater. Turning to the woman, "What happened?"

After a few minutes, Slater learned that Lan scraped her hand against a sharp piece of wood when she fell. Slater saw the infected gash.

The next morning Slater's team arrived at the village with medicine they obtained from the 187th. Ernie radioed the regimental doctor and asked for help. He said Vico had injured his hand. After the diagnosis, the doctor put the pills on the chopper along with ointment and bandages.

Slater took the pills and salve into the hut and showed the mother how to administer them. Jesse entered and gave Lan a makeshift doll he made from a green towel. Lan gave a slight smile and held the doll close to her. As they departed the village, Slater's girlfriend continued to show her displeasure.

*　*　*

Three days later they returned to find Lan improved and smiling. She walked over to Jesse, showed him her doll, and hugged his leg. The troops and women recognized the bond, but the women remained impassive. From a far hut, Slater noticed a man walking toward them. Slater recognized him as the leader from the ambush attempt weeks earlier. He seemed unarmed, and Slater said, "Careful. A man is coming."

They didn't raise their rifles but remained alert. Slater shouldered his rifle indicating a peaceful gesture. The Vietnamese man was older, confident, and unsmiling. He knew he presented a good target to the Americans. Slater admired his guts and wondered if other VC hid outside in the trees ready to shoot them. What could the man want?

As he came closer, the women disappeared into the huts taking the children with them. Jesse took his focus off Lan, Vico tensed, and Ernie didn't budge because the unwieldy radio on his back inhibited quick movement.

Slater told Vico, "Relax. Let the man talk."

"Maybe he doesn't want to talk."

"He wants to talk."

The VC leader stopped ten yards away and said in Vietnamese, "Who wants peace? Army kill. Army don't want peace."

Slater said in his ablest Vietnamese, "I want peace. Do you want peace?"

The VC looked at Slater and eyed the other soldiers who tried to look tough.

"Army dinky dow."

"My name is Slater."

"My name is Nguyen but people call me Tram." Slater mostly understood his Vietnamese.

"Can we have peace?" asked Slater.

"I don't believe anything you say. I don't like Special Forces." Tram recognized the subdued Special Forces patch on their arms.

"What can I do to convince you?"

The Vietnamese man stared again at the other soldiers and then focused on Slater. "You have two prisoners. Bring them to me."

"Who are they?"

"My cousins. They don't like the South Vietnamese government. They not spies."

"Where are they?"

"At 187th Headquarters."

"They may not want to come with me. Why should they trust me?"

"Tell them that Uncle Tram has nuoc mam for them."

"What is nuoc mam?"

"Fish sauce. Vietnamese love. Americans hate smell."

"If I get you the prisoners, what do I get?" asked Slater.

"I will get you six American prisoners. Then we talk more."

Slater said, "Get the prisoners ready."

Tram turned and strutted back on the path toward the last hut and disappeared. Slater informed his men about the discussion.

"Now what?" Ernie said.

"The army won't release those guys," said Vico.

"We have to try."

16

Securing prisoner releases posed red tape problems only a shady bureaucrat could surmount. Getting top secret information was easier. Lt. Whitney informed Slater that the regiment did indeed hold two prisoners. They endured preliminary questioning without revealing anything.

"Slater, no one gets to see those guys," said Lt. Whitney.

"What about a prisoner exchange?"

"The whole thing could be a setup. No one wants to risk more casualties," said Whitney.

Slater asked, "Did the 187th lose any soldiers?"

"A Lurp was captured five weeks ago.

"What's a Lurp and how many men?"

"Lurp or LRRP means Long Range Reconnaissance Patrol which is comprised of six men."

"Can't we send out some men and get them back?"

"They were captured in Cambodia, and no one admits that the army went into that country. They're goners."

* * *

Back at camp, Jesse said to a depressed Slater, "Give it up. It's impossible. Tram will have to understand."

"Tram won't understand. He will see that we failed, and then what will become of us?"

Ernie said, "What would you do if you could get the prisoners?"

"I'd have a letter authorizing the guards to turn over the prisoners to me. We'd go to headquarters and show the jailer the letter. He would release them to us, and we would use Derrick's chopper and fly them to our LZ. Then we would receive six prisoners from Tram, and where he got them, I don't want to know. Getting six of our men back for two of theirs makes sense to me, plus we could build the peace with Tram and maybe finish our tour standing up."

"Sounds easy, so how do we get the letter?" asked Jesse.

"From the regiment's commanding officer."

Ernie said, "He won't trust lowly Special Forces guys. We need someone else to help us."

"I could plead the case with an intelligence officer at regiment who is a friend of Derrick's. He might offer a suggestion."

Jesse said, "He won't do anything. What are the odds? We might as well ask Wilberforce."

Slater noticed that Vico had not spoken. "Everything all right, Vico?"

"I like your plan, Slater. We will need Derrick's limo service."

Jesse laughed. "What are you talking about? His plan is dead. Are you bonkers?"

Ernie said, "Oh oh. Beware when Vico likes anything."

Vico looked at Slater. "I was just thinking how we could streamline it."

Jesse said, "Is your streamlining legal?"

Vico said, "Common, Jesse. Would I get you in any trouble? Let's go to headquarters, check it out, and see if Derrick's friend will help. If not, we can develop another plan."

* * *

Because of the friendship with Derrick Williamson over the past months, Slater felt comfortable in asking him for a favor. Derrick flew the team to the 187th Headquarters to meet with his friend, Lt. Kransky, who was assigned to the G-2 section, Regimental Intelligence.

"I may have an opportunity to get a release of six American prisoners if we trade the two Vietnamese prisoners. Can you help me?"

"Kransky laughed. "It's easier to enter Fort Knox. We don't get many prisoners, so these two have a high priority. We don't know who they are, but someone thinks they are important people from Hanoi. Who's arranging the exchange at your end?"

"Locals."

"They're tricking you. How long have you been here?"

"Three months."

"You're so gullible. Got your gold bar and now you want to win the war. Second lieutenants amaze me."

"Not worth the risk?"

"No one would approve it. Besides an interrogator, a Major Hawkins, from II Corps is coming tomorrow, and he'll figure out what to do with them. I'll do you a favor, though."

"What's that?"

"I won't mention our conversation to anyone, so you won't be embarrassed or harassed." He chuckled as Slater departed.

* * *

Slater met his team at the mess hall. "I didn't get anywhere. Too much red tape. They don't want to risk their careers. Derrick's friend thinks I'm loco, and an interrogator is coming tomorrow."

Ernie said, "So Vico, how's the streamlining idea now?"

Vico's face showed a greedy smile and he looked around. "Why don't we eliminate the red tape?"

What do you mean?" asked Slater. "No one can get them."

"I can. We'll follow Slater's plan but omit a few steps which will make our effort more efficient."

Slater said, "This doesn't sound good."

Ernie said, "Why would you take such a big chance? For what? You like going against rules and regulations?"

"I'm from New Jersey. It's part of our culture. No one follows rules. I grew up going against authority. I've been expelled from two schools, kicked out of movie theaters, been a permanent guest at the principal's office. Why follow the pack?"

"Those are small pranks," said Ernie.

"But they're fun. At Catholic school, I put the entire class on double detention because in their new dictionary I inserted a word between frontier and fudge."

"If you're caught, punishment will be much more than cleaning chalkboards," said Slater.

"Vico, you could get us serious jail time. Why pick on the army?" said Jesse.

"I love sticking it to Uncle Sam. He sent me here, didn't he? He owes me."

Everyone looked at each other and realized that no amount of arguing would sway Mr. New Jersey from his course of action. The group looked to Slater for final approval.

"So tell me your plan," said Slater, "for entertainment purposes only."

"First of all, why bother anyone to get a letter of authorization when we can write it ourselves and even sign it? Second, why doesn't another interrogator show up?"

"Are you planning what I think you are?"

Jesse said, "Don't listen. He's anxious to visit Fort Leavenworth."

Vico said, "I'll need Jesse, a typewriter, and four uniforms."

"What about me? Don't you need an officer?"

"They know you up here, so you can't do it. Besides, an officer will be present. I will be an officer without going to Officer Candidate School. Pretty efficient, eh?"

17

JULY 1969

Against Slater's better judgment, he let Vico run the show. "You wanted to be the leader, so here's your chance. Just don't muck it up."

"You have a lot of guts, amigo," said Jesse.

"And I'll need you as a guard."

Jesse shook his head declining the offer. "No, no. Not me. I like living with the Viet Cong. It's safer."

"You don't have to do anything except act like a prison guard."

"Why me?"

"Because you look imposing. No one will mess with you." Then he turned to Slater and Ernie. "Can you arrange for a chopper to be available at 2:30 AM to take us back?"

"Anything else, general?"

"Yeah, recon the area, so we'll avoid guards and get to the chopper pad."

Ernie said, "Do I salute you now?"

"Just bow down at my feet. Hey, this officer stuff works great."

"Just make the plan work," said Slater. "How about we meet at seven and go over all the details."

*　*　*

Vico went to the regiment's personnel section and looked for an enlisted man from New Jersey. None existed, but he found a Spec 4 from the Bronx. Putting on a New York accent, he convinced the good-natured fellow to let him use a typewriter.

Later he and Jesse went to the enlisted barracks and spoke to mama-sans who washed uniforms and cleaned the sleeping quarters. Vico paid them to get four old fatigues. He had the name, rank, and insignia removed from two and kept the 187th Regiment patch, names, and ranks on two others. Jesse lifted an M-16 that needed repair.

Slater and Ernie scouted the brig, which fortunately was located away from the main Quonset huts. They observed the placement of guards and surveyed paths to the helicopter base. Slater confirmed that Derrick would have a chopper ready.

After hearing Vico's plan, the group accepted it and even considered the ruse inspired. Yet Slater said, "It's still tricky, and we could do ten years in prison. Do you still want to proceed?"

*　*　*

At 2:05 AM, the team assembled and assumed their roles. Vico took a deep breath and strode into the brig with Jesse in tow. Dressed in unmarked fatigues with gray specks in his hair to look older, he went through the reinforced doors. Jesse also wore unmarked fatigues. He carried the borrowed M-16 which looked more official than his M-14.

"I'm Major Hawkins. Are the prisoners ready?" Vico said in a condescending manner as he approached the duty sergeant. Vico modified his New Jersey accent and combined it with a southern drawl to equal a perverse dialect that even linguists would not be able to fathom. To the sergeant, who was from North Dakota, southern accents all sounded the same. Vico's resembled that of South Newark.

"Ready for what, sir?" the sergeant asked.

"Interrogation. What else?"

"Are you the interrogator? I thought you were coming tomorrow."

"I arrived as soon as I could as a favor to your commanding officer," said Vico as Major Hawkins.

"Interrogation at this hour?"

"This is the best time. When they're tired, sleep deprivation works best." Jesse marveled at Vico's performance.

"I haven't received any orders, sir. Besides you don't have any rank on your fatigues. How do I know you are a major?"

"First of all, sergeant, if you knew anything about interrogators, you would know that we don't show rank or anything to prisoners. Keep them confused."

Jesse, not wanting Vico to assume all of the risk, said, "He's Major Hawkins all right. I'm his security."

"Didn't HQ inform you?" Vico turned from the sergeant and looked at Jesse. "They screwed up again. What did I tell you? I bust my ass to get here, and they forget to get things ready for me. What's the matter with this outfit?"

The sergeant found himself in a quandary. He faced an impatient major who came on orders from the commanding officer. Not wanting to upset the brass, the duty sergeant said meekly, "I need paperwork."

"Of course you need it. Good for you, son. Can't release prisoners without it."

He fished the paper that he typed earlier in the day from his pocket, unfolded it, and said, "Here it is, signed by the regiment commander, what's his name?" He looked at the bottom of the letter for the name.

The sergeant said, "Brigadier General Jarvis Brennan."

Vico looked at the signature. "Yep, that's him, see?" He shoved the letter into the sergeant's hand. He hoped the sergeant didn't recognize the general's script. Vico signed it hours ago. "Now where are the prisoners?"

Armed with orders, the sergeant brought out the two manacled prisoners.

Vico as Major Hawkins said, "Keys?"

"Oh, right, sir." The sergeant gave him the keys to the handcuffs.

"I need blindfolds too."

The sergeant produced old rags. "These will have to do. Where are you taking them?"

Vico winked at the sergeant, "A special place that I've prepared."

The sergeant didn't want further information. He hated torture. He turned his eyes away from the prisoners as Jesse steered them out of the Quonset hut.

"We'll have them back after breakfast or lunch depending on their performance." Vico gave another mischievous wink which repulsed the sergeant.

Outside in the night air, Vico and Jesse stiffened as they carefully scanned the area. With Jesse in front, Vico guided the terrified prisoners to a vacant spot beyond the brig and away from the command center. They met Slater who wore a Spec 4 uniform and addressed the prisoners in Vietnamese.

As Vico undid the shackles and blindfolds, Slater said in Vietnamese, "Uncle Tram has nuoc mam for you." The prisoners barely acknowledged the code words but wondered how these Americans knew Tram. "Be quiet and follow me."

Despite the code words, they didn't trust the Americans. They wondered if they would be tortured. Yet how did they know about Uncle Tram? Cooperation seemed the best option, so they complied with Slater's instructions.

After meandering around three Quonset huts, Slater ordered everyone to stop. The group stood in the shadows of the outside lights while the lieutenant went to the far side of a building and peered around the corner. Seeing that everything was clear, he signaled the others to come.

They rested while Slater waited for Ernie. Finally he showed up. Ernie wore a Sergeant First Class uniform and liked outranking Slater. "Our route is blocked by six guards smoking pot. We need to go the long way."

The group backtracked, went around the far side of the Brig, and doubled back toward the chopper pad where they would rendezvous with Derrick. Walking single file through a parking area between two-and-a-half-ton trucks, they continued on the path beyond two aluminum sheds. The group of six saw the helicopters under lights about one hundred yards ahead. They did not see any soldiers between them and their destination.

Walking two by two past dark Quonset huts, they reached an open area and heard a gruff voice say, "Halt."

Two guards stepped out of the darkness by a building's shadow. The light from a nearby tower shone on their faces.

Ernie saw that both guards were white. In Albuquerque he would act in a submissive manner when talking to this race. But tonight, he had to act differently. He saw that he was the only person to save his cohorts from a court martial. He didn't want Slater to be exposed, and Jesse and Vico without any insignia couldn't say anything.

Walking quickly to the front, he faced the sentries and asked them, "You gotta problem?"

"What are you doing at this hour?"

Relying on machismo from his Albuquerque adolescence, he said, "What does it look like we're doing?"

"No one is supposed to be here at this hour," said the first guard. He looked past Ernie and noticed the two Vietnamese. "What have we here? What are you doing with the enemy?"

Ernie improvised. "They're our allies, and don't give them a bad time. We can't mess with them."

"So who are they?"

"They're interpreters, and the Intelligence Section ordered us to escort them to Pleiku."

The guard said, "Where are your orders?"

"Who gets orders here? We're at headquarters."

"We need orders," said the second guard emphatically.

Ernie visualized how the army lawyers would charge him at his trial. He decided to put caution away and take the offensive.

"Are you new? I've done this before at four in the morning without experiencing any problems. But if you need something in writing, wake up the lieutenant colonel. He'll give you paperwork."

Ernie hoped his deflecting words would have an effect.

The two guards with a rank of private recognized that upsetting a high-ranking officer would not go well for them. They received the graveyard shift as punishment for agitating their sergeant and didn't need further trouble. Besides they couldn't go against this man who held the rank of sergeant. In their minds sergeants ran the army.

"You may pass. No sense in waking any brass. Who else would the Vietnamese be if not interpreters."

Ernie nodded and moved forward with the group leaving the guards in their wake. Five minutes later, the six approached the edge of the flight pad.

Slater said, "Stop here for a moment. I need to find the chopper." He smiled at Ernie. "Good job. I think you're officer material. Plenty of bluff and deception."

Ernie was still quaking from the confrontation.

Slater found the aircraft. "Derrick, sit in your seat, look straight ahead, and don't say anything."

Slater directed the group into the helicopter. Their own Special Forces fatigues were already put aboard hours ago. When all were secure, he said, "All right, Derrick, take us home."

He put on his night vision goggles, and they departed at 2:35 AM. Everything went smoothly, and Derrick dropped them at their Landing Zone.

After the Vietnamese were assisted off the helicopter, Slater said to his friend, "This flight did not happen. I will fill you in when I can. It's a Special Forces mission, top secret. Sorry for the mystery. I owe you."

Derrick said, "I don't know what I'm going to say to Kransky."

"Tell him to play dumb. It's a Special Forces priority. Tell him not to mention anything, and he won't get into any trouble."

Since Kransky could only look bad if he said anything, he would accept the advice. Slater knew the two guards would not reveal that they let six men pass. If they did, they would receive harsher punishment.

After the chopper departed, Slater's team led the two Vietnamese ex-prisoners on the well-worn path to Phan Lac. When they arrived, Tram was standing in front of his hut. He heard the helicopter land and got dressed to welcome his countrymen.

Slater said, "When do I get the Americans?"

"I'll let you know."

On the trip back to camp, Slater said to Vico, "Major Hawkins, I will never question your leadership abilities again. You got guts."

Vico said, "Bet Tram made a sucker out of you. We'll never see American prisoners."

18

JULY 1969

The next day, news about the escape reached II Corps. Senior officers were pinning blame on everyone inside and outside of the regiment.

When the real Major Hawkins arrived and found the prisoners missing, he railed against the incompetence of the 187th Regiment. According to the scuttlebutt, he departed in a rage on the next flight for Nha Trang without coordinating with the G-2.

Investigators came up with few leads. They focused on the forged letter and on the duty sergeant at the brig. Hearing that Major Hawkins had bad-mouthed the regiment gave Slater an idea. He decided to distract the investigation by starting a rumor.

He radioed his friend, Sergeant Boydston. "Herb, I just received the news about the prisoners."

"Man, we can't keep Charlie even when we have him locked up. Heads are going to roll."

"You know what someone told me? The escape was planned by the interrogators. They didn't want you guys to get all the credit. Can you believe that?"

He hoped Herb would inform his friends about this new twist.

* * *

For three days after turning over the Vietnamese prisoners to Tram, the team relaxed. Slater decided to delay a visit to Phan Lac; he would give Tram time to address the next phase of their relationship.

His troops feasted on plenty of warm coke and C rations. Each meal had three cans containing a meat item, fruit, dessert, and snack, which yielded 1,200 calories or 3,600 calories per day. Despite the nutrition planning, all soldiers lost weight.

Jesse had beefsteak, canned pears, and crackers. Ernie ate ham and lima beans, applesauce, and a chocolate bar. Vico bit into chicken and noodles, pound cake, and peanut butter and crackers. Slater consumed meatballs and beans in tomato sauce, fruit cocktail, and for dessert, cheese spread.

They slept, ate, and read. Jesse had improved his skills so that he read more easily. They continued to give book reports over dinner.

On the morning of the fourth day, Slater's warriors relaxed near the LZ as Jesse took his turn as lookout.

Toward the end of the watch, Jesse spotted a woman from the village walking toward the campsite. As she came nearer, he recognized Lien, Lan's mother. He alerted everyone, and Slater came out with Ernie and Vico behind. Lien walked with timid strides. Her head moved nervously from side to side, and she folded her hands, unfolded them, and then refolded them. When she eyed the Americans, her body became even more anxious. She stopped about ten yards away and said in Vietnamese to Slater, "Tram say come." She turned and left.

"Any bets?" said Vico.

"You stay here if you want," said Jesse. "I'm curious."

"Me too," said Ernie.

"Let's go, gentlemen," said Slater. "Major Hawkins, you can guard the camp if you wish."

Without any dawdling, they put on their gear and strode toward the village. Vico reluctantly joined them. When they arrived, the entire place was empty. The team tensed and would jump for cover at the slightest noise.

Tram walked out of his hut and said, "Go west two miles."

Slater's team had not reconnoitered the western zone. He worried that his team might not even find the location since the western part covered a large sector.

In Vietnamese Slater said, "I don't know the area. Where do I go?"

"I give you boy. He help."

"Where are your men? I only see women here?"

"They come when I need them," said Tram who turned and left.

Ten minutes later the Vietnamese boy, whom they captured with his girlfriend a month ago, arrived to serve as guide. The boy revealed little except his name was Nguyen but was called Thai. The group didn't trust Thai, but they held their doubts in check while keeping a tight grip on their rifles.

After forty minutes, Slater noticed huge patches of open space amidst the forest. Thai said the clearings resulted from bombs by big planes. He spoke the words in simple Vietnamese, so Slater could understand. He concluded that B-52s were the big planes. Instead of a moonscape appearance from the bombing, the soil appeared to have been plowed and raked; it looked primed for planting.

"What will you grow?"

"Don't know. One man want vegetables. Another want to do nothing. Tram want coffee."

Slater thought coffee was grown in South America. When he heard that the villagers might plant it, he was surprised. He knew nothing about the coffee plant. Maybe he and Tram could talk about it, anything to develop a deeper relationship.

In the distance the group noticed six men lying down. His team couldn't determine if they were Americans or Vietnamese. Could they be a work crew? Farmers? Prisoners? As the group walked toward the men, they recognized tattered fatigues and dense beards that could not be grown by Vietnamese. The prisoners sat up in slow motion when they saw Slater's team. No one spoke.

"Go now. You take," said Thai and departed into the trees before Slater could say anything.

Slater kept his eyes on the haggard men.

"Are you prisoners too?" asked one soldier with ragged jungle fatigues showing a fragment of his sergeant's insignia.

"We're here to take you back to camp. You're free," said Slater.

"You got food, American food, man?" said another soldier who acted dazed.

"I have candy bars," said Jesse and passed them around.

The former prisoners grabbed them and started eating paper and all without giving any thanks.

"Are you guys able to walk?" asked Slater.

"Not too well but we'll make it," said the sergeant. Seeing Ernie with a radio he added, "Can you call in a chopper?"

"As soon as we get to our LZ," said Ernie.

The six men got up slowly and trudged down the path toward the camp. They were thin and had little energy. Their crazed behavior compelled Slater's men to be wary. Looking into their eyes told them the feral nature of these former captives. Slater's group trusted Thai more than this pack. Slater couldn't help but wonder what these men had endured. Did they start out unbalanced?

Nearing the LZ, Ernie radioed for a chopper. Twenty-five minutes later, they heard the sound of rotor blades and a familiar voice came over the radio.

"Anyone want a free ride?"

Slater was relieved. Derrick would collect and transport everyone to Regimental Headquarters. The helicopter dropped to the team's LZ, and the men headed toward the side doors.

Most of the six ex-prisoners climbed aboard, but two hesitated. They were afraid of the big blades, and the loud noise disoriented them. When Jesse and Ernie tried to coax them, they pulled back. With the assistance of the Lurp's sergeant, somehow the last two forced themselves inside but did not want anyone to touch them.

Slater was afraid they might jump when the chopper lifted off, but they settled down when Derrick passed out snacks and soda.

Ten minutes later, the chopper landed. Derrick had previously alerted Lt. Kransky about the cargo, so men from the Intelligence Section guided the former prisoners to the medical tent.

"Thanks, Derrick," said Slater as he watched the spectacle. "What a strange group."

"Would you go on a long-range patrol if you had all your marbles?" said Derrick.

"Point made."

"You don't need to give me any explanations about that night run a few days ago. I see the results."

"You made it possible."

"By the way, a big story just came in. Did you hear? We put a man on the moon," said Derrick.

Slater quieted upon hearing the news. Ever since President Kennedy challenged NASA to achieve this feat, the entire country was entranced with the possibility. Flash Gordon would become a reality. Slater was even caught up in the frenzy back in Iowa but not now. Stuck in the highlands of a small nation in Southeast Asia trying to survive gave him pause.

"I realize it is a great technical accomplishment, but right now I'm not impressed. We can't even solve Vietnam, and it should be easier. Our politicians can do calculus but can't add."

Derrick was surprised at the reaction, but he had seen plenty of cynicism especially among the draftees.

Derrick and Slater wandered to the Officers Club to talk the night away, eat semi-real food, and sleep on a cot. The others went to their club and drank until they reached a comatose stage.

Slater thought that Regimental Intelligence analysts might talk to him and his crew about the rescue, but no one recognized their noble deed of freeing American prisoners. He thought his team merited a medal, but intelligence officers understood that Slater's crew stumbled on the lost patrol and therefore did not deserve a commendation. The Intelligence Section instead concentrated on debriefing the LRRP.

Other members of G-2 directed their efforts to solve the kidnapping of the two Vietnamese captives from their own brig. They did not have any clues outside of a forged letter. Since Vico signed the general's name with his left hand, not with his right, the signature would not provide any leads.

Three choppers departed during the early hours of that same night for a medevac operation, so Derrick's flight was included with that mission, and he was not suspected.

Intelligence wondered why no one witnessed two Americans and two Vietnamese escaping from the brig. G-2 was beginning to believe the rumor that Major Hawkins somehow had a hand in the escape.

* * *

II Corps Briefing: July 28, 1969

Combat activity remained low according to Major Hardy. Few field reports were submitted, so he kept the briefing short.

Major Laurel said, "The 187th Regiment infiltrated a VC border camp and rescued six American prisoners who braved torture for months. They reported enemy soldiers killed, 11; wounded, 26. No casualties occurred to the American forces.

19

AUGUST 1969

The next day, Slater's team returned to their camp courtesy of Derrick's shuttle service. They settled into lethargy in the languid afternoon and spoke about the rescue. Spirits were high but in the back of their minds loomed the possibility of a court martial for impersonating an officer and abducting two prisoners. They wondered if Slater would incur a harsher punishment for an officer impersonating an enlisted man.

Slater questioned if Tram would make peace now that each side experienced a prisoner exchange. He concluded that his group would force the issue and proceed to Phan Lac the next morning.

When they entered the village, the women observed them first, and the children ran up waving their middle fingers accompanied by giggles. Lan went to Jesse and gave him a big smile which Jesse returned. The women stayed away, but one old woman looked at the lieutenant and said, "Dinky dow." She shook her head and shrugged her shoulders.

Vico said, "Nothing seems to have changed."

"Give it time," said Slater.

The woman that Slater found enchanting came out of her hut. She retained her chilly attitude. His curiosity would not be denied. He had to know her.

"Good morning, miss. What is your name?"

She ignored him and continued across his path into another hut. Slater kept his eyes on her and did not notice that Tram ventured from a nearby hut.

He approached the Americans and stood in front of Slater. "Her name is Binh. She hate Americans."

"So she hates me?"

"You are American. Americans bombed her village and killed her parents. Eight months ago in a battle, Americans killed her boyfriend."

"I don't blame her then. I just wanted to be friends."

"Do you have something to tell me?" asked Tram acting in a distant manner.

Slater said, "We returned the prisoners to you, and you did the same for us. Can we build on this cooperation? Can we have peace?"

"You crazy American. Why peace? America want kill us."

"War is not good for any side."

"What about 187th Regiment and B Company and First Platoon?"

Slater was surprised that Tram identified the unit designations.

"You Special Forces. I hate Special Forces."

"Why?"

"Wilberforce bad man."

"What did he do to you?"

"He killed children, my nieces, in village near Pleiku."

Slater had no use for Wilberforce either but decided to keep the focus on the present and not the past deeds of a demented colonel. Slater said, "You help us. We help you."

Tram heard the words and doubted that he could gain anything from the Americans except misery. "You have nothing I want."

Slater grasping for a way to connect and remembering what Thai mentioned about the empty fields said, "Maybe we can help with coffee plants." He paused. "I am a farmer too."

Tram almost spun around. "You know coffee?"

For the first time, he revealed a dent in his armor.

"No, but I can find out. If you want to plant coffee, we can help."

Tram looked at Slater in a different light. Maybe this American could help his village realize a dream of prosperity.

Being a farmer was all Tram aspired to, yet he grew up in war. After the victory over Japan in World War II, his parents fought the French in the First Indochina War to gain freedom for Vietnam. France was defeated in 1954, and Tram at seventeen emerged from the victory battle tested.

When the United States assumed France's imperialistic role, Tram continued to fight in what they called the Second Indochina War or known in the West as the Vietnam Conflict. In 1968, he was thirty-one, held a rank of colonel in the Viet Cong, led a large force of VC, and controlled a vast network of spies as well as being highly regarded in Hanoi for his leadership qualities.

Tragedy struck him in a similar fashion as Binh. South Vietnam units killed his parents in 1959, and B-52 bombs killed Tram's wife and two children in the village three years ago. After their deaths, he tired of fighting, tired of life.

The TET Offensive cemented his change. Launched on January 30, 1968, the North Vietnamese Army and Viet Cong soldiers engineered a massive surprise attack in one hundred cities across South Vietnam. Tram led units in an unsuccessful battle against the provincial capital of Kon Tum.

The North Vietnamese's plan was to use the Viet Cong as the vanguard in the majority of the attacks. Despite initial triumphs, the Communist forces were beaten back and the Viet Cong in leading the assaults suffered massive casualties.

Discouraged by the losses, Tram engaged in fewer missions while retreating to his village of Phan Lac with the intent of becoming a farmer.

Hearing this American mention coffee struck an ironical note. Tram found it odd that he would seek aid from Americans, his sworn enemy. He invited Slater to sit outside the hut and offered tea to the others while they rested nearby. The children played near Jesse and Ernie. Vico did not appreciate screaming kids and sat away from them and leaned against a tree. The kids ignored him.

The village women wondered why Tram served tea to these mindless invaders.

One woman said, "Tram no longer has a working brain when he talks to Americans."

A second woman said, "He must have a big idea how to eliminate them."

A third woman said, "No, he's dinky dow too." They smiled.

Slater was surprised that he captured Tram's attention and enjoyed drinking tea with him. His next problem: where could he find information about coffee?

After finishing his tea, Tram got up and said, "Come."

Slater followed. During the jaunt, he broke the silence and asked, "Why do so many people in your country have the name Nguyen?"

Tram chuckled. "Many stories. The Nguyen Dynasty started in 1803. The emperor made everyone change name to his."

One half mile later, they came to a massive clearing. Tram said, "This is it."

Slater remembered the place where he picked up the six American prisoners.

Tram said, "I worked these fields for months to prepare for coffee. I want no more war. Only time to farm."

"Why is coffee so important to you? Why not other crops?"

Tram said, "Climate and soils here are best for coffee. My uncle worked for French coffee company years ago and said coffee had great potential in Vietnam. My uncle was a smart man."

* * *

The team left Tram at his hut and returned to the LZ. As they sauntered along the trail, Slater updated them about the village leader's commitment to coffee.

Vico said, "You don't know anything about that crop, Slater."

"You're right, Vico. I don't even like coffee, but if Tram does, that's enough for me."

"You'll get us in trouble when Tram finds out that you're a fake."

"Maybe."

"You said you were a farmer. Did your dad teach you about planting coffee?"

"He didn't teach me much. All he wanted was a farmhand at no cost."

"At least you had a father," said Vico.

"Sometimes it's better not to have one," said Jesse.

Ernie added, "If you have one, hide the alcohol."

At their camp digesting another unglamorous meal of C rations, Slater saw that coffee provided the opening he needed. He had to contact Bruce at II Corps Headquarters. He'd know where to look for a coffee expert.

20

AUGUST 1969

After a few days, Slater hitched a ride on a passing helicopter. He went to Regimental Headquarters to use the phone and called his friend, 1Lt. Bruce Hendrickson.

"Hey, Slater. Are you still alive out there?" He recognized Bruce's saliva drizzle every time he pronounced the letter "s."

"I need to talk to an agricultural expert about coffee. Does the embassy have anyone like that in Saigon?"

"We have a guy here at II Corps from USAID, you know Agency for International Development. His name is Ross Wexler. He could stand some activity. No one uses him since he's not military." After giving him Ross's phone number, Bruce said, "I'm short, Buddy. My DEROS is next week, and I'm out of this Southeast Asian spa. Hang in there."

*   *   *

Ross Wexler received few phone calls. No one was interested in helping villages because the VC infiltrated them. They were too dangerous. Only Ross saw the potential in providing help. He did not like being idle. He wanted to make a difference, take positive steps, and watch the progress in the field. From Seattle with a Stanford degree, above average in height with a slight build, brown hair, rosy cheeks, an engaging smile, and a deliberate manner of speaking, he possessed an idealism that many twenty-six-year-olds carried.

He served in Saigon for five months before being transferred to II Corps Headquarters two months ago. He didn't miss South Vietnam's capital, the land of advisors: white men working in air-conditioned buildings. His zeal for helping indigenous people with their projects was subverted by the mountains of reports required to obtain approval and dispense aid.

After seven months in-country, he experienced pangs of doubt about his mission. He tried to exact reforms against a cumbersome bureaucracy on the American side and corruption on the duplicitous South Vietnamese side. He tried to take the "long view" but couldn't overcome the feeling of hopelessness as America tried to convince the Vietnam people about the merits of democracy. Each day he questioned his country's effort to support the South Vietnamese government.

Ross kept himself busy nine to ten hours per day by studying Vietnamese and teaching English in downtown Nha Trang. Eddie Doyle's live-in, Thien, was one of his students.

When Ross arrived at his office on the first day, the adjutant, called G-1 at II Corps, a full bird colonel, sent him a memo. He wanted a report on all of his projects. When they spoke, which was seldom, the G-1 showed his bias against the Vietnamese: "They are corrupt, dishonest, and tricky. They use the black market for their own greed."

Because Ross rarely spoke to the high-ranking officer, he submitted notes about his projects. He didn't have many AID opportunities, so his memos were few.

When the phone rang, Ross answered it on the first sound. "Hello. This is Ross Wexler."

Slater introduced himself and explained his assignment as a Special Forces outpost operating near a Vietnamese village. "Could AID evaluate the merits of growing coffee? They don't need any money."

After writing down the name of the lieutenant and the name of the village, Ross said, "You're with Special Forces?" Then he realized what he just heard. "You mean they don't want money? They're prepared to buy the seed themselves?" Ross could not believe what he heard.

"I need to find out about coffee plants. Can they grow here? And how do I buy the seeds for them? They probably could use information about growing, nurturing, and harvesting the plants. Can you obtain any material?"

This conversation was music to Ross's ears. He didn't have to prepare any reports, just advise. He would use all of his resources to get Slater the data he needed.

Slater hung up grateful that he had acquired an advocate.

A few days later, Ross wrote a memo to the adjutant about his newest project. The colonel was not impressed with the likelihood of it amounting to anything. He forwarded the note as a courtesy to Colonel Wilberforce since Ross was coordinating with a Special Forces unit.

The report rested in Wilberforce's in-basket for days until he returned from military meetings in Saigon. The envelope went untouched since no one dared to open it without permission.

When Wilberforce read the contents, one emotion emerged: rage. He believed the project would help the Viet Cong, and Special Forces should not be involved in this traitorous activity. He directed his fury against 2Lt. Marshall. The colonel ordered his aide to arrange travel to the 187th Regiment.

For this upcoming trip, he made sure to glide around the Phan Lac area in a helicopter. He needed to accumulate hours to earn an Air Medal. Originally the award was designated to honor meritorious service in combat air assaults, but in Vietnam where medals were bestowed liberally, one had to show hours of airtime. Flying around the mountains near the 187th Regiment's zone of control would add to his total. Because he was good at rounding numbers, Wilberforce's airtime was usually inflated by a factor of three.

After rereading the memo, he suspected that Slater and his band of heretics switched sides and joined the enemy. No other explanation emerged because the VC hadn't killed them. The more he thought about the Viet Cong and these outcasts, the more vengeful he became.

21

American soldiers were paid in dollars which posed problems in the Vietnamese market. Because the dollar was strong and coveted, officials in Washington wanted to prevent the destabilization of the local currency, the piaster, so they took two actions. First, they set the bank rates between the dollar and piaster and second, kept greenbacks out of the country by issuing Military Payment Certificates. MPCs looked like monopoly money but in fact were backed by the United States government.

The U.S. government made it illegal for the locals to possess MPCs, but the merchants accepted them anyway and used them to buy hard-to-get items on the black market. The Viet Cong amassed MPCs to buy weapons. They played the black market with cunning against the naive American soldiers.

To deter black marketers and reduce hoarding, MPC banknotes were converted every twelve or thirteen months into new MPCs making the old notes worthless. The conversion occurred over one day known as C-day, and the date was kept confidential. Soldiers would be restricted to the base in order to exchange the new MPC and prevent them from assisting the locals to convert their holdings.

*   *   *

Tram had a problem. He had $40,000 in MPCs. He acquired them through his operation in Nha Trang's black market. He needed the funds to buy coffee seeds and other items, but he could not spend them outside of the country.

He feared that C-day was approaching and didn't want to lose his stash. Tram needed Slater's cooperation to buy coffee seeds and other items by using his MPCs.

*   *   *

Five days after the phone call to Ross, a chopper appeared for an unscheduled landing at the Phan Lac LZ. Slater's group saw a man jump off the craft and walk toward them. He was dressed in civilian clothes, tan pants and sports shirt. Ross decided to visit the area despite being discouraged by everyone at II Corps. They said the village was too dangerous.

After the pleasantries, Ross and Slater headed for the village. Tram via his sources already knew Wexler would arrive. He greeted the group and immediately took them to the west zone. Upon completion of the tour, they adjourned to Tram's hut for tea.

"Are you coffee expert?"

With Slater translating, Ross said, "I have read books and spoken to agriculture experts in Saigon and in other countries."

"Can coffee grow here and make money?"

"Your land is perfect for growing coffee."

Tram smiled. "Where can I buy seeds?"

"Usually USAID gives or loans money for seeds. It can take five months or more to get approvals."

"I no want your money or wait five months. I pay with cash."

Ross said, "The buyers only accept U.S. dollars not piasters. You need the South Vietnam government's approval to convert to dollars."

"I have US dollars. I give to lieutenant. He buy with it." Tram eagerly hoped the USAID man would accept his idea.

Ross was surprised. "You have MPCs?"

"I have MPCs."

Slater looked at Ross. "I'll open an account with his MPCs and buy seeds. Will that be agreeable?"

Ross said, "It has to be. It's illegal for a local to open a dollar account at a foreign bank."

"How much money do you have?" asked Slater.

"Forty thousand dollars."

"What?" Ross was also shocked when Slater gave the translation.

"Not enough?" said Tram when he saw their reaction.

Slater said to Ross, "Can you help for the sake of this project?"

The USAID man shrugged his shoulders. He could justify to his friend, the bank manager, that this project met USAID guidelines and that Slater would oversee the program. "Let's go to Nha Trang."

Slater asked Tram, "Do you trust me?"

"Yes, for now. If you steal, I kill all you."

Slater wondered if he translated the word "trust" properly.

Slater managed to bundle and stuff all of the MPC bills that Tram gave him into a knapsack. Vico volunteered to carry it, but Slater said his team was needed at Phan Lac. When Slater and Ross landed at the Nha Trang airport, they went directly to the Bank of America branch on the army base.

The jeep ride took ten minutes, and Slater kept his arms wrapped around the stuffed backpack until he entered the bank

Quonset hut. The air conditioners had little effect on the muggy air. Ross and Slater perspired as they prepared to meet with the bank manager, Virgil Petrosi. He was the only American employee and served as an operations supervisor rather than the typical branch manager. Twelve Vietnamese women staffed the branch.

Bank of America, in ten locations throughout Vietnam, served the soldiers. Checking accounts paid ten percent interest.

Virgil was twenty-eight, had short black hair, the build of a soccer player, and affable. He was popular among the expatriates and enjoyed the opportunity of an international assignment. He and Ross were friends.

"Virgil, I need your help," said Ross.

"Name it."

"Don't agree until you have heard my request." Virgil tensed. "I am involved in a new farm operation near Pleiku. I told you about the project."

"I remember. You thought it was a good deal."

"I just returned with Lieutenant Marshall who as a member of Special Forces is overseeing the venture. We have a large deposit to make that will pay for coffee seeds and equipment. I may need you to provide assistance to vouch for our financial strength."

"How much?"

Slater put the backpack on the table. "Forty thousand."

Virgil's eyes popped and his jaw dropped. "This isn't drug money, is it?"

"Of course not. It was all put together by legitimate businessmen in Pleiku when they were told that USAID was involved." Slater didn't mind white lies since the truth that it came from black market dealings would not push the project forward.

Ross knew this deposit looked dodgy but hoped his credibility could weather any fallout within the bank.

He said, "The owners directed the funds be placed in Slater's account so they can avoid Saigon's tedious paperwork and delays. I agreed to it. Slater has full check writing authority."

Virgil took a breath. "I'm surprised at the amount."

Ross needed to get Petrosi on board. "Virgil, Lieutenant Marshall and I are approaching seed companies, and I may need you to validate that funds are available for the purchase. Any problem with me giving them your name and number?"

Virgil agreed but wondered how he was going to explain on his report that this large deposit did not come from gambling or drugs. Saying USAID was involved should placate them, but he still worried.

Ross and Slater left the bank and went to the USAID office at II Corps Headquarters. Ross phoned his counterpart in Saigon about buying top quality coffee seeds. The agriculture expert instructed them to buy Arabica beans.

He said, "Don't buy Robusta. Poor quality, poor taste, more caffeine. On the plus side, Robusta is cheaper and matures after two years as opposed to Arabica which takes longer. But Arabica does better even in bad times. Larger demand."

The order was placed to a company in Brazil. Ross went through an American firm to acquire tools, planters, and other items. The Saigon man estimated that arrival in Nha Trang would take one month or so.

Slater made out the checks which approximated eleven thousand dollars and then returned to Phan Lac. He didn't stick around and visit Special Forces to coordinate with higher headquarters as one normally did. He wanted no part of his chain of command.

The next day after returning to Phan Lac, he informed Tram about spending eleven thousand dollars. Somehow Slater suspected the village chief knew that fact, probably from one of the Vietnamese women in the bank.

"What do I do with the rest?"

"Keep the money until I need it." Tram was pleased. He succeeded in getting MPCs converted to dollars residing in a checking account of an American citizen. No one from Vietnam could confiscate his funds. He had real capital for the future.

He decided to become a capitalist but wouldn't inform his Communist brethren.

22

I n Colonel Wilberforce's mind, anyone who disagreed with him was a turncoat. While scheming to devise an appropriate punishment for Lieutenant Marshall, Wilberforce kept repeating, "My vengeance will be done."

Sergeant Doyle made the arrangements for his CO to fly to Pleiku. He would take three personal guards as security and then proceed to the 187th Regiment.

That night a message from Thien found its way to Tram in Phan Lac.

After landing in Pleiku, Wilberforce grabbed a waiting Huey and flew to Regimental Headquarters. He met with its commanding officer, Brigadier General Jarvis Brennan, and warned about Marshall's lack of military bearing and inaccurate intelligence. The general who had served as CO for four months was not aware of a Special Forces listening post in his theater.

After the brief meeting, Brennan called for a chopper and ordered the commander of Company B, Captain Delaney Gray, to give Wilberforce a tour. Gray selected Lt. Derrick Williamson to serve as pilot for this VIP. The three guards manned the gunner positions next to the door.

Once airborne, Captain Gray reeled off a typical military briefing in unemotional bullet points. He demonstrated proper protocol seeking to gather favor from a superior officer. He spoke in a dogmatic and robotic timbre and expounded about how he had reconned the territory and reduced enemy activity with their search and destroy operations.

Colonel Wilberforce accepted the point by point summary as gospel since it was given in the proper military format. Why should an Academy graduate lie? The fact that search and destroy activity had not occurred for over three months was not mentioned. Wilberforce preferred form over substance especially if it bordered on officious.

They flew past the Phan Lac LZ and stayed close to the upper canopy to avoid any snipers.

When asked about Marshall, Captain Gray said, "He and his men helped stop a surprise attack against Company B's First Platoon months ago. He also freed six American POWs."

Wilberforce did not want to hear any positive commentary about Marshall whom he considered an embarrassment to Special Forces. The colonel ceased the conversation and looked straight ahead.

Derrick noticed a puff of smoke in the distance. "Looks like trouble. I'll fly around it."

Wilberforce also sighted it. "Do we have men there?"

"No sir," said Captain Gray.

"Any recon patrols?"

"No, sir. Not our units."

Wilberforce thought the billow of smoke was similar to those emitted by his special operations. "Let's check it out."

Derrick said, "Sir, I strongly urge that we leave. This area is VC controlled, and we are vulnerable to an attack."

"Nonsense. The smoke is asking for help." Wilberforce didn't admit his true feelings. He hoped that by saving

Americans, he might earn a Silver Star, an award lacking on his uniform.

Derrick turned to Gray. "Captain, we are not aware of any American presence here. Assault helicopter groups are operating elsewhere. Please explain our risk to the colonel."

Derrick did not avoid danger when saving American lives, but in this situation his instincts told him that flying closer was unwise.

The VC knew chopper procedures and how to entice them with the proper smoke colors, purple for medevac, green for pickup.

Captain Gray respected Derrick's judgment but decided not to contravene the colonel. He did not want Wilberforce to think he was weak or hesitant in a war zone. In the back of his mind, he too was thinking Silver Star.

"We'll approach the smoke cautiously. Derrick, be prepared to withdraw quickly."

Wilberforce would not be denied. "Lieutenant, go toward the smoke. I won't pussyfoot around when our troops are in trouble."

Derrick did not appreciate this blustery colonel but had no choice unless he wanted a court martial for disobeying an order. He guided his craft toward the smoke. As it descended, purple smoke became visible.

"See. I told you our troops need help." Wilberforce was smiling at his foresight. Derrick remained cautious.

The chopper went toward a clearing and everyone saw four men dressed in American army fatigues. They slung their rifles around their shoulders and carried a wounded man on a stretcher covered in bloody bandages around his face and neck. Three men with M-16s protected them on the side. They all wore sunglasses.

"Saving our troops will make this a great day," said Wilberforce.

Derrick said, "They don't walk like Americans." Captain Gray looked more closely.

"Son, get this chopper down right now. Gunners, get ready to bring them on board."

Derrick landed the Huey. The side doors were already open, so the seven soldiers with their comrade on the stretcher went to the near side. They stopped just in front of the doors and took aim with their M-16s at the army personnel on the helicopter. They were VC disguised in U.S. Army fatigues and now held the Americans as prisoners of war. Even the wounded VC had a weapon and was smiling. Derrick looked at Wilberforce and then Captain Gray with disgust. The colonel became small, and Captain Gray couldn't look Derrick in the eye.

The VC motioned for everyone to exit. Derrick turned off the engine.

On the ground out of earshot of the others, he nudged Gray. "What an ego. Does he think he's Patton?"

Captain Gray said, "If we ever get out of this mess, you will get a commendation for military brilliance."

The eight laughed at their captives. After covering the helicopter with branches, they marched the prisoners toward Phan Lac which was miles away.

Wilberforce did not speak. He was too mortified. He fell for an elementary school trick. He blamed Lieutenant Marshall for causing him to come out in this god forsaken land. The colonel planned on heaping more disciplinary measures against Marshall and his miscreants if he ever got out of this fiasco.

After two hours of walking in the hot sun without water, the U.S. troops were dragging. The VC drank water and were alert. They halted and indicated that the prisoners could sit. During the rest, the VC isolated Wilberforce. He sat on a rock alone while the remaining Americans sat on the ground thirty yards ahead.

The guards ignored the Special Forces CO and concentrated on the other five. After ten minutes, Wilberforce decided he could escape, so he left the clearing and slipped into the forest behind him.

Gray noticed the break. "Derrick, Wilberforce is bolting. Where does he think he's going?"

"He's in no shape to hike let alone flee in this terrain. Look, the guards see him but don't care."

"Maybe they don't realize he's a colonel," said Gray.

"They do realize it. Maybe they have a separate plan for him."

At that moment, the guards directed them to move out and indicated no more talking.

23

SEPTEMBER 1969

Earlier, 1Lt. Clancy Kreuger, who replaced Dale Whitney as First Platoon leader, received an order from Captain Gray. Kreuger contacted Ernie on the radio and forwarded the message.

"The brass wants you to remain at your camp until further orders."

"No one cares about us, so why would anybody order us to stay here?"

"I have no idea, but be on the alert for friendlies."

Slater's troops for once accepted the order. They relaxed and pored over a pile of worn paperbacks that had come with recent supplies.

After hearing a chopper pass by, Ernie said, "I wonder if a VIP from Saigon is touring the place. Maybe the 187th's CO didn't want us to upset his show. What's the general's name?"

"General Brennan," said Jesse.

"Doesn't he have a weird first name?"

"Jarvis," answered Vico.

"What kind of name is Jarvis?" asked Ernie.

"Must be from the deep south or New England," said Vico. "No one in Jersey would admit to it." They all laughed.

Ernie said, "By the way, shouldn't we be getting pay?"

"I got paid at the Signal battalion monthly," said Jesse. "Slater, you should check it out."

"It's your duty to contact the adjutant or Wilberforce and take care of your men's welfare," said Vico half kidding but clearly frustrated.

"Don't waste the call," said Ernie. "They don't even know we're in Special Forces."

Vico said, "Slater, when did you receive your commission?"

"June 1968."

"And when did you become active?"

"November 1968."

"In two months you'll be a first lieutenant. I don't know if I can handle a senior officer in our presence."

Jesse said, "What do you mean?"

Ernie said, "All second lieutenants are promoted to first lieu-tenant after one year even if they are dolts."

"Gee, I wonder what the odds are as to second lieutenants being dolts," said Vico. "You should check on our promotions too."

Jesse added, "And check on when we get our CIBs."

Slater said, "You want a Combat Infantry Badge?"

If we've been in enemy territory or on patrol for thirty days, we get one," said Vico.

"For someone who hates the military, you know quite a bit about the regulations," said Jesse.

Before Ernie could add to the grousing, they heard noises from the LZ and saw Thai. "Now what?"

Thai was becoming more relaxed with this motley group. He walked up to their campsite and said to Slater in Vietnamese, "Tram need see you. Come. Bring your fake bullets."

Ernie said, "We can't. We've been ordered to stay here."

Slater said, "Tram outranks General Abrahms. Let's go."

Ernie said, "Who's Abrahms?"

"Commander of all troops in Vietnam," said Jesse.

The four arrived at the village with rifles and magazines filled with blanks. They saw that Tram had a broad grin.

"I help you. Okay?"

Tram couldn't hide his glee. He was ecstatic. He had tricked Wilberforce and captured a bad man, someone who had killed his friends. He was only interested in Wilberforce and had no use for the others. He would release them to Slater and not worry about the situation any further.

"I have prisoners. Follow Thai." With that, Tram returned to his hut with a spring to his step.

Thai said, "Follow me."

Slater translated and said, "I've heard 'Follow Me' before."

"Yeah, the motto of the infantry school at Fort Benning. Did Thai go through basic there?" asked Vico.

The group headed out.

After a one-hour march, Thai motioned for everyone to halt behind a group of trees and rock outcroppings.

He said to Slater, "Stay here. Be quiet."

Slater repeated the message to his men. They waited not knowing what to expect. They couldn't see anything from their hiding place and felt like sitting ducks.

Ernie whispered, "What is Tram up to?"

Unknown to Slater, Tram received intelligence through his grapevine about Wilberforce's trip. He directed his troops to capture the helicopter, let Wilberforce escape, and take the others to a certain junction. Then wait for Thai.

* * *

Thai appeared at the designated site and finalized the plan with the Vietnamese soldiers who were still dressed in American uniforms.

In a clearing near large boulders surrounded by forest, Derrick, Captain Gray, and the three Special Forces men sat on the ground and rested while their captors watched over them. Ropes were wrapped around each soldier's neck, so no one could escape without dragging the others with him. All five were tired and thirsty.

Gray tried to remain alert to any openings for a counterattack or escape. Since the VC had eight armed guards, a counterattack seemed unrealistic, and an escape seemed equally improbable. He didn't know where they were going, but they seemed to be headed toward Phan Lac.

Gray spoke softly. "Can any of you loosen the rope around your neck?"

They shook their heads.

"I don't see how we can escape."

One of the Special Forces men said, "Seems strange to be guarded by men wearing U.S. Army uniforms."

Derrick said, "We need an earthquake or a flash flood to get out of here."

After ten minutes had elapsed, Gray noticed that a new person was speaking with the guards. "We have a visitor."

The prisoners stared at the new guy who was wearing pajamas. They didn't know that his name was Thai.

"I wonder what they're talking about? Are they going to shoot us?"

Then the visitor left. The guards drifted from the prisoners toward the trees and waited.

* * *

After speaking with the VC, Thai returned to Slater. The noise from birds and insects filled the air, yet Thai motioned that everyone be quiet and follow him. They thought, "Why all the mystery?"

For ten minutes, Thai led them from the outcropping to the backside of boulders. Each step in the weeds made a crunch, and Thai gestured to go slow and keep the sound down.

Vico said, "What the hell is going on?"

Slater spoke softly, "Thai is following Tram's instructions. Tram knows what he's doing."

While Slater spoke the words, he questioned his faith in the village leader and wondered if this expedition posed any danger to them.

Jesse whispered, "Do you trust him?"

Slater said with false confidence, "Of course." He hoped his instincts proved correct.

Thai positioned them at the rear of the large boulder. On the other side were the American prisoners.

Thai whispered to Slater, "I go on top. When I wave hand, go around big rock and fire rifles. Okay?"

"Is it safe?"

"It is easy."

The enlisted soldiers still had misgivings and didn't like being ordered by Thai. They had serious reservations about advancing without knowing who or what was on the other side. Are they headed into a trap? Should they retreat and say the hell with it? This problem did not come up in infantry training. They remained riveted on Slater to check his level of self-assurance.

He saw the uncertainty in his men and indicated that he would go first. Vico waved his right arm in a broad sweep similar to a courteous escort allowing a debutante to go first.

Slater waited for Thai's sign and tried to put a courageous face to the task ahead.

Thai climbed to the top of the rocks and looked to the other side. He saw the VC guards. They nodded to each other; then the guards withdrew into the forest. Thai lingered for one minute while his fellow Vietnamese departed, and then motioned for the Americans to start firing.

Slater darted around the rocks followed by the others all blindly firing their clips filled with blanks. When they arrived on the other side, they found no enemy. They saw five Americans who had fallen to the ground to protect themselves. Jesse went to them.

Vico said, "I'll watch for Charlie."

Ernie and Slater flanked Vico in support.

"I don't see anybody," said Vico.

Slater smiled. "What's so funny?" asked Ernie.

"Tram set this up."

After Jesse untied the ropes, Slater recognized Derrick and Captain Gray but not the others. "What are you guys doing here? Never mind. Tell me later. Let's move."

* * *

After one hour into his escape, Colonel Erastus Wilberforce was exhausted, lost, and dehydrated. He fell to the ground and hyperventilated. He expected to die. He couldn't imagine any other alternative. Minutes after these thoughts flitted through his brain, five Vietnamese in black pajamas arrived and led him for another mile to a road and a small truck.

24

SEPTEMBER 3, 1969

Slater's men passed out water and snacks to Derrick, Gray, and the three guards. They took frequent rest breaks on the trek back to the LZ.

When the liquid and protein kicked in, the former prisoners showed more energy. Fifteen minutes from the destination, Ernie radioed the 187th and requested a pickup. Wilberforce's three guards remained silent for most of the trip. They wanted to get back to their base.

Captain Gray stayed in the rear to avoid talking to his reprehensible trainee. He was embarrassed at becoming a prisoner and then being rescued by a hippie lieutenant. He watched Slater and Derrick in front talking and laughing; he saw their mutual respect and friendship. Gray valued Derrick's flying skill, commitment, and bearing. How could he become friendly with this radical?

Gray needed to get out of his funk. He walked forward and spoke to Slater. "How'd you know where to find us?"

"I had my lookouts in place. We become more alert when a chopper comes into our space."

Gray didn't mention his order to keep Slater's team at their camp. Keeping Slater away from Wilberforce seemed wise since he did not like Marshall, a concept Gray understood. Yet Lt. Marshall had saved the First Platoon a few months ago, and his group just rescued him from Charlie. Did the jungle produce a secret potion that somehow transformed these renegades into competent soldiers?

Slater said, "By the way, sir, we scared the VC off with blanks. Can someone supply us with ammo? We have made repeated requests without any results."

"You still don't have bullets?" asked Gray. "Why won't Special Forces supply you? They must be in short supply especially since you have M-14s."

"The black market has M-14 ammunition," said Slater.

Ernie said, "Why would they have them and we don't?"

Slater said, "There is a Mafia within our military stealing millions. The troops in the field suffer by being without food, weapons, and medicine. Supplies get diverted at the port or at a distribution center."

"How do you know that?" asked Captain Gray.

"From your infantry training class. Your instructors in field exercises, lieutenants and sergeants back from Vietnam, told me. The profiteering is massive."

"You believe them?"

"Yes, sir, I do. I learned more from them than all of your majors and colonels put together. One lieutenant said they fought against a VC unit who was armed with M-16s. They even found a label on the rifles which designated delivery to his unit. American taxpayers were financing the enemy."

Vico said, "So that's why we don't get ammo?"

Jesse said, "Come to think of it, we didn't get all of our supplies either when I was in the Signal battalion."

Captain Gray dropped the subject of army corruption and kept trudging toward Slater's camp. Derrick mentioned to him that Wilberforce was on his chopper and also became a prisoner but escaped two hours ago.

Slater said, "He'll never make it. The place is crawling with VC."

"And he doesn't look to be in good shape either," said Derrick. "Funny, the guards let him go. Didn't even try to go after him."

Slater started to smile and then let out a soft laugh.

"What's so funny?" asked Derrick.

"Nothing. I'm just imagining Wilberforce running or rather waddling away, not knowing where to go."

Slater realized that Tram orchestrated the mission but kept this thought to himself.

After reaching the LZ and waiting for a few minutes, a Huey arrived. The three Special Forces men entered quickly without thanking Slater's crew. Derrick shook hands with everyone, and out of earshot of Gray, said, "I'm ready for another night mission if you need one."

"Derrick, we're even. In fact, I still owe you." Derrick went into the cab.

Gray thanked Slater's underlings and then faced the lieutenant. "You must have received excellent training at Benning. Good job, soldier."

Slater said, "Is this the time I'm supposed to salute you, sir?"

"I would faint if you saluted me. I'll look into getting you some real bullets, but everyone is low."

When the chopper returned to the base, Derrick led armed helicopters to search for Colonel Wilberforce and to recover his own aircraft. They accomplished the latter but not the former.

*　　*　　*

When Slater returned to the village, he asked Tram where Colonel Wilberforce went?

"He is bad man, has bad heart."

"Is he dead?"

"He is working on farm. If he heals his heart, he can go home."

Slater did not understand Tram's meaning. At least Wilberforce remained with the living.

* * *

The capture of the Special Forces commander was big news in Nha Trang. Most of the brass at II Corps expressed dismay that a high-ranking officer suffered, but no one had any fondness for the arrogant colonel.

* * *

II Corps Briefing: September 3, 1969

Major Laurel used his pointer to show the area of Wilberforce's capture which was ten miles from the actual site. "A LRRP is being organized to conduct a search and rescue. It will commence at 0700 tomorrow, isn't that right Major Hardy?"

Neither knew any details about anything, so he said, "This was yet another planned attack by Colonel Nguyen who mobilized a VC battalion to down Wilberforce's helicopter."

One officer in the briefing asked, "How about the crew? What happened to the others?"

Major Laurel said, "The pilot, a company commander, and three Special Forces men survived and made it back to the base."

"How did they escape and Colonel Wilberforce didn't?" asked a battalion intelligence officer.

Major Laurel couldn't answer. Instead his partner said, "Special Forces hasn't revealed that information at this moment."

To those high-ranking officers in attendance, that response meant that Special Forces didn't know anything or that the CIA was involved and something went awry. No one broached the subject further.

* * *

Slater and his crew barely knew what year it was let alone the month. They operated one day at a time and knew that DEROS was many months away. When Ernie received a call on the radio, he found out the date.

He came to Slater and said, "Ho Chi Minh died yesterday on September 2, 1969."

Slater got on the radio to Company Commander Gray. "Do not do anything to upset the Vietnamese. Cancel all military operations. The Vietnamese are mourning the death of Ho Chi Minh, and he is popular on both sides. You will only aggravate them if you attack soon after his death."

Gray said, "No operations are scheduled anyway. Now let me get back to important matters."

Slater and his men travelled to Phan Lac. He instructed his troops to be formal and mournful. When Tram came out of his hut, he looked sad.

Slater said, "I am very sorry for the death of Ho. He was a great man worthy of great respect."

The lieutenant bowed slightly and with his team exited the village.

25

OCTOBER-NOVEMBER, 1969

I n early October, Derrick's rotor chariot arrived at the LZ and deposited ten hemp sacks plus various tools and boxes. Each man carried one heavy bag and trekked to the village.

Binh looked up when Slater arrived and saw that the lieutenant's face beamed with a sense of achievement. He smiled at her, but she did not reciprocate. The crew dropped the bags in front of Tram's hut.

Tram came out, saw the items, and felt the coarse burlap mesh of the sack's exterior.

"I bring you the finest Arabica coffee seeds from Brazil," said Slater with pride.

"Arabica seeds? I want Robusta seeds. Robusta take two years to harvest. Arabica take five years. I no wait this long. I be dead in five years. You wasted my money."

Slater expected gratitude for all his efforts, and now the person that he wanted to impress was scolding him. Binh frowned too when she heard Tram's tone.

For the first time, Slater displayed anger at Tram and raised his voice.

"These are the best coffee beans in the world. They receive high prices on the international market because of their quality and fine taste. Robusta beans are easy to grow but taste sour. Buyers pay lower prices. You will never have problems selling in good or bad times because of the large demand for Arabica beans."

The argument did not soften Tram's attitude. He pouted, scrunched his face in frustration, and returned to his hut.

Vico said, "You sure know how to upset the Viet Cong. Any other ideas, Slater?"

Ernie said, "Knock it off."

"You have a talent for getting our enemy mad at us, and all we have are blanks."

Jesse said, "Let's move the rest of the stuff and get out of here."

After dumping the remainder of the shipment in the village, the troops returned to their camp with shoulders sagging, especially Slater's.

*   *   *

Three days later, Thai ambled down the path and approached the campsite. "Tram want to talk."

They followed Thai to the village.

When they reached Tram, he said, "I need people to plant seeds. Can you help?"

His outburst days before was apparently forgotten, and no one wanted to bring the subject up. Tram seemed to have accepted the situation, and so Slater forgot it too.

He was surprised at the request. Didn't Tram have enough men in the area to assist? But Slater answered in a positive spirit. "Of course. When do we start?"

Over the course of two weeks, the Americans joined ten Vietnamese men and five village women as everyone spread out over the fields. The Americans perspired in the hot sun except during the daily rains. The laborers buried each seed one and one half inches deep following the instructions from Ross Wexler.

During breaks, a few women circulated among the group and provided cups of tea and fruit for a snack. During each rest period, Binh came to Slater's area and offered drink and food. The Americans eagerly accepted. Her face still had its grim look, but hour by hour her expression softened because she saw how hard the Americans worked.

Slater was grateful for these rare moments when Binh acted in a civil manner. As she poured the tea into his cup, her shy eyes indicated that she wanted to say something, but her mouth wouldn't cooperate. He experienced the same challenge with the result that neither spoke.

At the end of the day, Tram walked among the tired workers and conveyed his thanks. When the soldiers left for their camp, the Vietnamese smiled and waved good-bye except for Binh. Everyone seemed happy at starting a coffee plantation.

On the third day, when the soldiers and villagers spread out to plant, Binh plopped down on the soil next to Slater and labored with the rest of the people. He was nervous with her being so close. He watched her movements out of the corner of his eye. Her hands were more nimble and more efficient than his. Her ability gave him an inroad to start a conversation.

He didn't open with a "good morning" or "how are you?" He finally looked at her and blurted out, "Your hands are good."

Binh saw his embarrassment. His manner mirrored her shyness. She didn't know how to accept his compliment.

"You have strong hands too." She couldn't think of anything else to say.

Both paused and kept their eyes down focusing on the coffee seeds. Then they looked up at the same time and tried to speak. They stopped and waited for the other to talk.

Finally Slater said, "Where are you from?"

In a timid voice she said, "Pleiku."

"How did you get to Phan Lac?"

"A friend brought me. I don't have mother or father any-more." She paused. She didn't elaborate about their deaths. "Tram help me. He treat me like family, so I stay here."

"I like Tram," said Slater, happy that Binh was finally talking to him.

"I no like Americans. With this coffee, I see Tram smile. Before, he not smile."

Slater understood that she changed her thinking about him because of Tram. Gradually she felt more comfortable although her shyness governed her behavior.

Responding to his questions, she told him about Pleiku, her schooling, the hard work that people in the village do, the reverence for Ho Chi Minh, and her desire for the war to end.

"And I no like Americans. Can't you go home?"

"I wish we could."

"Then go."

"If I could work out a way for us to go and leave you in peace, I would."

Binh smirked. "No one listens to a second lieutenant, is that right?"

She didn't mean it as a put-down, just a fact of life. Slater laughed. "Right. No one pays attention to a second lieuten-ant."

She returned to her work and did not talk again. That night in her hut, she wrestled with her conflicting thoughts. She liked the second lieutenant, but he was the enemy. Was he being nice to her to have sex? A previous encounter with American sol-diers told her not to trust him or any foreigner.

*　*　*

133

Each day working together in the fields, Slater would initiate a conversation. She would give a brief answer, always superficial. The differences between them were huge, so Slater tried to be polite and accommodating.

Binh seemed so innocent. When she was planting coffee seeds, Slater stole glimpses of her. She was beautiful. Her brown eyes with laser concentration expressed intensity as she worked. On one occasion, she looked up. He tried to maintain some poise, but Slater's composure melted. She returned to the work and remained aloof which frustrated him even more.

He knew they could never be a couple. The disparity was too pronounced. But the problem didn't stop him from fantasizing. What if he somehow surmounted the intractable cultural barriers? They could live together without any cares and just enjoy each other. He could stare at her face all day and enjoy the bliss of her smile.

Reality returned to his brain. "Come on, Slater. Rally. Just enjoy the fantasy and daily interactions. Those memories will last forever."

Slater found that talking to Binh and the other villagers improved his fluency. He gained new words and developed more confidence in speaking their language.

With each daily interaction, her resentment eroded. He was a person and not a soldier, and she wanted to know more about him.

On the eighth day, after the normal pleasantries, she asked, "Are you married?"

Slater shook his head and was surprised at her bold question. "No."

"Do you have a girlfriend?"

"No."

"Why not? Doesn't every man in America have girlfriend?"

When Slater blushed at the question, Binh became embarrassed and put her hand to her mouth. "Is my question wrong?"

Slater gave a gentle shrug. "Your question is fine. I'm not used to talking about girlfriends to a woman."

"I thought you would have many girlfriends."

"Why?"

"You are kind."

Slater changed the subject. "Do you have a boyfriend?"

Binh grinned and said, "You are right. It is difficult for me to talk about boyfriends with a man."

"Well, do you have one?"

"Not now. I'm not looking for one." She became sad and resumed the planting.

They did not bring up the subject again.

26

After the planting was complete, plenty of unopened bags remained. Tram promised the extra seeds would be used in new meadows when they were cleared.

One week later on a visit to the village, Slater walked with Tram to inspect the fields. Tram started the conversation.

"I see you and Binh talk." He turned and stared at Slater. "Are you friends?"

"What do you mean?"

"She is beautiful girl. You are away from home. No be with girl for long time. I see how American men act."

Slater looked surprised and hurt at Tram's insinuation. "I was only talking with her. Is that wrong?"

Tram said, "Last time Americans here, they tried have sex with her. They were mean. They were animals."

"What happened to them?" asked Slater already knowing the answer.

"We stopped them from hurting Binh. That's all."

"Did you kill them?"

"They attack Binh first. We save her. Later other Americans come and destroy our village."

So that's why the previous listening post was ambushed.

Tram said, "Be careful. Too many differences. And you are enemy."

"I don't want to do anything impolite. After the war, I hope we can remain friends."

"I worry about Binh."

"Do you want me to stop talking to her?"

"No, you say you friends. Okay, but only friends."

* * *

When Slater returned to camp, Ernie said, "How was the inspection?"

"Tram is pleased with the progress."

Vico asked, "Did you ask Tram for Binh's hand?"

Ernie and Jesse laughed. The three could see their leader's infatuation with Binh but had not spoken about it until now.

Slater said, "I sure like her, but there's no way. I enjoy talking with someone intelligent for a change."

Vico grinned at the put-down.

Slater said, "With the coffee planted and with us being on friendly terms with the village, we don't have anything to do except relax and inspect the coffee until we DEROS."

Jesse said, "So we'll have more time to read."

"Good thing. We received a new batch of paperbacks," said Ernie.

Jesse said, "Sorry, Vico, we didn't get any picture books this time." They chuckled.

Since they did not have recreation facilities, reading broke the monotony and became the principal activity. Each man kept a book in the side pocket of his fatigues to read in spare moments when the group went to the village or returned to the

First Platoon. Outside of trips to Phan Lac, the only patrols they took entailed trips to the latrine or to their LZ to smooth out its surface and make it a better landing field.

The group devoured books such as the sweeping sagas of James Michener's "Hawaii" and "The Source" and William Manchester's "American Caesar," a General McArthur biography. Agatha Christie mysteries and books about history and current events were popular too. The story analysis and critique at dinner went for one or two hours.

Slater named their group, the Deros Book Club. In addition to the entertainment and education, they gained an improved vocabulary. They were surprised when Vico used the term "pedantic" to describe the writing style of one author.

Jesse and Ernie gained more confidence in speaking since they couldn't avoid their turn to talk in the roundtable discussion.

* * *

In November, Ross paid a visit to see the coffee fields. They approximated sixty hectares in size. A hectare was one hundred meters by one hundred meters which equaled two and one half acres.

Ross was pleased at seeing the growth. With Slater translating, Ross told Tram how smart he was to purchase Arabica seeds. Tram eyed Slater with suspicion since his translation supported his side of the argument.

When Ross touted the benefits of Arabica, Tram relaxed his skepticism and even smiled. Ross impressed the Vietnamese leader with his knowledge and sincerity.

Slater thanked Ross as they returned to the camp and waited for a helicopter.

"Tram likes you. He listens to you. When will you come again?"

"Tram doesn't need me anymore. The seeds need to grow. Besides I have a new project outside Da Lat that will keep me busy for a while."

"You're the most positive force in this country, and you've given me credibility with Tram. It's taken me months to reach him. You did it in two meetings."

"Look me up when you visit Nha Trang. We can update Virgil Petrosi about the project funded by Tram's drug money."

They laughed, shook hands, and then Ross parted. Slater watched him clamber aboard Derrick's chopper. One last wave, a big grin, and he was gone.

*   *   *

II Corps Briefing: November 20, 1969

Major Hardy reviewed recent enemy activity for the general and colonels in the first session and then turned to another subject. His expression became more serious.

"We have received intelligence from captured documents that the North Vietnamese Army will make a major thrust into II Corps. We aren't sure of the exact location but suspect it is north of the 187th Regiment. The attack may occur in two months."

Responding to the questions, Major Hardy said, "We don't know anything more except that all units in the area will take the appropriate steps for preparation. All Intelligence Sections will coordinate with our G-2."

*   *   *

One week later, Slater received a letter from Bank of America, the first letter he received from anyone since he arrived.

Dear Slater,

Sorry to be the bearer of bad news, but Ross was ambushed and killed at Da Lat while helping the Province Chief with an infrastructure proposal. Everyone in Nha Trang loved him. Ross thought his biggest success in Vietnam was your coffee project.

Sincerely,

Virgil Petrosi

Slater didn't talk or read for two days. He became sad and angry at the same time and once in awhile mumbled, "What a waste."

Two days later, he went to the village and told Tram about Ross's slaying. Tram looked shocked. His eyes lowered, and he returned to his hut. Slater knew Tram's feelings were sincere but thought he had a tinge of shame since obviously the Viet Cong did the killing.

27

NOVEMBER 1969

Intelligence about an impending NVA attack was not communicated to Slater and his centurions. They continued their normal activity of staying close to the village and watching the coffee plants. On each visit Slater managed to see Binh and talk about nothing important. At least she tolerated his presence.

He saw less and less of Tram. On occasions when they were together, the conversations were short and dismissive. Slater saw the worry on the village leader's face and wondered if his Viet Cong comrades were planning a raid.

Slater cancelled the book discussions that evening and shared his concerns.

"Something's up. Tram looks awful. Won't even talk to me."

"Everyone else acts normal," said Ernie.

"Tram hasn't seen the coffee plants in a long time."

"This is serious then," said Jesse. "He worships those fields."

Slater said, "So what do we do?"

"Ask him," said Vico.

"He won't talk to me."

"Get in his face. Force him to talk to you."

Jesse said, "Like they do in New Jersey." They all laughed.

Vico said, "Ask him if the VC are planning an attack."

After they broke up, Jesse realized that he missed the Deros Book Club meeting. Books had taken on a new importance in his life.

When Jesse awoke during the night and viewed the stars, he reflected on his tour in Vietnam. He had spent months with two white guys and a Mexican American, and nothing bad had happened. In fact, his lieutenant had encouraged him to improve. No one at home ever complimented him or guided him.

* * *

At midmorning the next day, Jesse accompanied Slater to the village. Ernie's stomach acted up, so Vico stayed with him at the camp. Slater and Jesse each carried a canteen and a book and left their weapons at the camp. No need for arms at Phan Lac.

Walking side by side on the path, Jesse asked, "Do you know what you want to do after you get out?"

"Probably work in some business."

"You at least have a college education. I didn't graduate from high school."

"Jesse, you can get a GED. Many companies prefer someone with army experience. I'll help you."

Jesse didn't think employers liked vets who camped in Viet Cong jungles.

Two minutes later, they rounded the bend that led to the village. Emerging from the trees in plain view of the huts, they stopped and saw three men talking to Binh and three other women. Slater and Jesse carefully hid behind some shrubbery.

Jesse said, "These guys are wearing uniforms. Who are they?"

"They might be North Vietnamese. The women seemed scared. Let's get closer."

The two moved to the left where the trees were dense and provided cover. They came to the first hut and had to navigate past the piled bamboo. Slater peered around the corner and focused on the three men with AK-47s slung over their shoulders. He couldn't hear them but saw that the women froze in fear of these strangers.

The three uniformed men included two young boys and one older man. He seemed to have a rank of sergeant and did all the talking. He was looking at Binh, leering at her with stained teeth which resulted from chewing betel nut. Slater resented anyone talking to Binh.

He turned to Jesse and whispered, "I think they are NVA. And where is Tram?"

Jesse whispered back, "He's probably inspecting the coffee."

When Slater poked around the corner again, he overheard Binh saying that all the village men were gone.

Slater thought to himself, "Bad answer."

The older man seemed pleased. He ogled Binh, gave his comrades a wink, and then grabbed her upper arm. She shrieked as he led her to the nearest hut. She tried to run away, but then he pushed her through the entrance.

As she stumbled inside, the older man ripped her clothes and forced her down on the mat. She screamed as the soldier undid his pants and landed on top of her. She fought until he hit her in the face.

Witnessing the proceedings from the edge of the hut, Slater pulled back. "I've got to help her."

"You're not armed, and two other NVA with rifles are out front."

"I have a pocketknife."

"That little thing? It can't even open an envelope."

"I can't let her suffer."

Jesse felt Binh's problem was not theirs. "We could get killed."

"You don't have to come."

Slater peered around the corner of the hut and saw that the two other NVA had their backs to him about twenty yards away.

The three Vietnamese women were crying and screaming. Slater stepped out and gestured to the women to occupy the men. They were surprised to see him and understood what they needed to do. Using their fists they pounded with weak force on the chests of the two teenagers who laughed at their pitiful punches and continued to face the women.

Slater slipped past them to a hut on the right side next to Binh's. Jesse shrugged in frustration and ran after his lieutenant.

28

November 1969

E ach hut had one doorway in the front. The walls were covered with thatched siding, each side measuring six feet in
height. Fortunately the palm fronds at the bottom of the walls
were not tied to anything, so one could crawl under them.

Slater crept to the back of Binh's hut out of sight from the
other NVA. He didn't have to be quiet since her shrieks filled
the air.

Binh continued to resist even with the pain from the slaps
she received. She freed her fist and hit him in the stomach. He
ignored the light blow, held both wrists, and looked down at her
in carnal lust. His bad breath and dirty teeth repulsed her as she
strained to free her arms.

Filled with rage and a sense of urgency, Slater slipped under
the fronds behind the NVA just as he hit her. She screamed more
loudly. Slater had never been in a fight before, so he didn't know
what to do except follow his instincts. When the NVA raised his
arm for the next blow, Slater came from behind and lunged at his
enemy with his small knife in his right hand as the left hand went
over the enemy's mouth.

Despite his stabbing the NVA in the neck and chest, the
wounds didn't weaken his foe. Jesse was correct about the knife's

ineffectiveness, so Slater struggled and Binh screeched. Slater was bigger and seemingly had control, but the NVA had fight in him. Slater was concerned that the rapist might yell for help, so he kept one hand over the man's mouth, but the NVA wiggled out of his grasp.

* * *

Jesse adopted a rule he learned in LA to let fights play out. Getting involved led to consequences. He didn't feel any loyalty to any one person except his sister. Since no one helped him in his youth, he remained aloof.

He couldn't see why Slater would risk his life for another person, especially a foreigner. But in the highlands, Jesse changed his rule. He admitted that the four Americans had become a team, not a team of men who wore the same uniform. They became brothers.

Jesse heard the commotion and knew Slater could use help. He hesitated no longer and dove under the thatched walls.

Surfacing inside, Jesse saw Slater stabbing his adversary. Blood was shooting everywhere. When the NVA turned his body and tried to strike, Jesse leaped and wrapped both hands around NVA's neck. Slater continued to jab his knife, and Jesse choked the NVA until life escaped the body.

Slater pushed the rapist off Binh and whispered to Jesse in a kidding manner, "Thanks, man. I of course had everything under total control." Jesse nodded and accepted the compliment. Both men knew Jesse saved the day.

Convulsing in tears and smeared in blood that had also spurt over the two Americans, Binh clutched her torn shirt and covered herself.

Jesse said, "Now what do we do?"

Binh knew. She gathered herself, stood up, kicked the dead soldier, and went to the back of the hut. She opened a box and pulled out a rectangular object.

Jesse said softly, "It's a Claymore. What the hell is she doing with that?"

A Claymore mine fires seven hundred small steel balls up to a range of fifty yards when someone trips the wire.

Binh signaled the Americans to drag the corpse underneath the hut's back side and down the gentle slope. Slater, splattered in blood, knew no one could see them from the main part of the village and grabbed the dead man's wrists. Jesse joined him and together they yanked him under the fronds to a clump of trees and leaned his body upright against the trunk. Jesse set the Claymore and aimed it. Binh knew the drill about arming and firing the mine. She took the string from Jesse and waved them back to her hut.

When they went inside, she screamed as though being chased. The two younger soldiers were probably laughing at their leader's escapade.

When ready, she gave a final wail and then pulled the string from a protected spot. The explosion fricasseed the deceased soldier as the body toppled from its upright position. Binh rushed into the dead zone, lay down next to the corpse, and pretended to have suffered the same fate.

The two soldiers and three women dashed to the hillside. The women cried at seeing Binh all bloody. The men gaped at their fallen countryman when they saw that his dismembered body had a huge whole in it. The women, shaking with sobs, kicked the two NVA on the shins.

The shock of the event and the thrashing from the three women caused the soldiers to panic, and they stampeded from the area.

After they fled, Binh opened her eyes to the surprise of her friends. She stood up and they hugged. Slater and Jesse came out and watched the scene.

Binh walked to Jesse covering herself by clutching the torn clothing in her hand, looked at him with tears in her eyes, and said simply in accented English, "Thank you." Slater must have taught her the words during time in the coffee fields. Jesse was touched.

Torrents of emotions streamed through her as she approached Slater. She had misjudged this American who had rescued her from the evil soldier. She projected onto Slater her anger against the troops who had killed her boyfriend and against the Americans who tried to rape her. She was wrong and felt guilty about her behavior.

"I not be kind to you, yet you save me. You are great man." Then she burst into sobs and ran into her hut.

After hearing the detonation, Tram ran from the coffee fields and reached the village out of breath. Fifteen minutes later, Ernie and Vico arrived carrying rifles. Slater updated them while the women attended to Binh. Jesse and Vico buried the mutilated body. A shaken Tram gathered Slater and his men.

"We talk."

Slater and the others saw Tram's depressed expression.

"What about?"

"Many soldiers will come to valley." Tram halted, trying to gain composure, and the Americans saw a deeper sadness.

Slater didn't know what to say and let Tram continue.

"I cannot honor peace."

After translating to his stunned comrades, Slater said, "Why not?"

"We are friends. You helped with coffee. You saved Binh's life. I grateful to you, but you need to leave."

Slater suspected that the three-man scouting party portended bad news.

Tram remained silent and looked at Slater with red eyes. "My coffee will be destroyed."

As Slater translated, Ernie said, "Looks like the NVA is planning to attack the regiment."

The Americans saw the obvious: no more comfortable life in the highlands. Reaching DEROS now looked daunting.

Slater said to Tram, "When will the NVA come?"

"In three or four weeks, maybe longer. They will come north, two valleys beyond. America will bomb everywhere and destroy the village and our coffee."

"Are the NVA talking with Colonel Nguyen?"

"He advised them to avoid this area because the village has no importance. I don't like North Vietnamese. They don't like Viet Cong. They fear our power and influence in the South. That's why they ordered Viet Cong to lead dangerous missions during TET and not North Vietnamese, missions that ended in killings of our men. And today they try to rape my niece. I don't forgive them."

"Are you and Colonel Nguyen in any danger?"

"No, they need us, but we don't want to fight with them. We fight to keep American army away from our village and out of our country." He stopped and looked at Slater's soldiers. "The peace between us is over. You must go. If you stay, they will kill you."

On the way back to camp, Ernie said, "What's the big deal about TET?"

Slater said, "My ROTC instructors told the class about it. In January 1968, days before TET or their lunar new year holiday, the North Vietnamese and Viet Cong launched a massive attack throughout South Vietnam at over one hundred cities. It caught everyone by surprise, and we almost got clobbered. They even occupied a part of our embassy for a few hours. Good decisions by our commanders turned the momentum in our favor. We inflicted massive casualties mainly against the Viet Cong who led the assaults. Afterward they resented the North Vietnamese for the bloodbath."

Jesse said, "I remember that TET was a defeat for us."

"TET was technically a victory, but it shocked the American public. General Westmoreland kept asking the government for more men to finish the job since we were winning. After TET, the people back home lost confidence. The protests increased in 1968, so the real victor was North Vietnam."

29

NOVEMBER-DECEMBER 1969

As they walked to their camp, all remained silent. Their thoughts returned to the attempted rape and the news of the impending attack. Their assignment near Phan Lac had ended.

Slater replayed the scene where he and Jesse killed the NVA. Slater didn't remember the face, only the body odor, blood, and brown-stained teeth. He was upset because he didn't feel any guilt.

He nudged Jesse and said in a low voice, "Why did you help me?"

"I couldn't let you go in there alone with your little knife. You might have stabbed yourself."

Slater smiled full of gratitude. "Thanks. I thought I could handle it. If you hadn't showed up, more than my ego would have been wounded."

Jesse accepted the recognition.

Slater then asked, "Do you feel bad or guilty about killing him?"

"He shouldn't have gone after your girl. Had it coming." Jesse walked a few more paces and said, "I'm sleepin' fine tonight."

Slater thought about it, and said, "Me too."

* * *

II Corps Briefing: December 19, 1969

Major Hardy stepped to the podium with his trusty stick.

"Our patrols have not spotted any enemy movement. It seems they have disappeared, and we as yet have no explanation. Major Laurel, however, has received intelligence from I Corps."

Major Laurel commented, "Air recon has noted increased activity along the Ho Chi Minh Trail both in terms of troops and materiel." He pointed to the eastern part of Laos and the northeastern corner of Cambodia called the parrot's beak.

"New enemy documents indicate that an offensive will probably occur in four to six weeks against Kon Tum."

Kon Tum was a large city and the capital of Kon Tum Province, twenty-nine miles north of Pleiku, thirty-four miles east of the Cambodian border.

"Since the 4th Infantry Division controls the area, G-2 put them under alert as well as the 187th Regiment who control territory south of Kon Tum to Pleiku."

Major Laurel continued. "Our Intelligence Section expects that the NVA will make a diversionary attack near the 187th Regiment."

Major Laurel went to the large map, borrowed the pointer from Major Hardy, and said, "Along the western side of the Regiment's perimeter run three valleys: the Huong Loc, the northernmost valley where the NVA will make their diversion; the Tay Son Valley, the middle valley, where a small strike force may try to mislead our commanders; and finally the Dong Giang, the southernmost valley. We don't anticipate any activity there due to the distance from the Huong Loc."

Everyone except the general scribbled copious notes about the three valleys and their geography.

Major Laurel finished. "We have informed the 4th Infantry Division that they are the main target and directed the 187th Regiment to be ready in support."

* * *

Over dinner, Slater informed his group about Tram's comments.

"The NVA will attack two valleys north of here, but I sense and Tram agrees that they may try to come south to our valley and attack the First Platoon. If they are successful, they can attack the rear of Company B. From the back, Company B is not well protected. If the NVA advanced through Company B and poured more men into the area, the Second Battalion could be vulnerable."

Vico said, "Does Gray see how screwed he is?"

"I don't think so. Tram knows that wherever the NVA strike, army commanders will alert air support and artillery to blast everything back to the Stone Age. That means Phan Lac and the coffee fields will be rocketed. Since we're in the middle of it, we should pull back, and stay with the First Platoon."

Vico said, "I like that idea."

The others agreed. Ernie said, "We can't do anything more here."

"Especially with blanks," said Jesse.

Slater said, "Let's return to Company B and share the news.

* * *

The meeting with Company B's leaders did not progress as Slater had hoped. Captain Gray showed that he didn't trust any second lieutenant especially one named Slater Marshall. Gray didn't notice that Slater's fatigues had become faded with a frayed collar.

"How long have you been on active duty?" Gray shouted.

"Almost fourteen months, sir."

The answer caught Gray by surprise since second lewies were promoted to first lieutenant after twelve months. "Fourteen months? Either Special Forces didn't promote you because of your ineptitude or their adjutant is incompetent which is highly implausible."

Slater ignored the disparing remark.

"What's so important that you've called this meeting?"

Slater regaled them about an imminent attack in Huong Loc and Tay Son, just one half mile away.

"I expect the NVA will send a force to the Dong Giang against the First Platoon. If they overrun the perimeter, Company B would be exposed. If they overwhelm Company B, Second Battalion Headquarters could suffer."

"The NVA would need a large force to penetrate our defenses," said Gray in a defiant posture.

"How did you obtain this information?" asked Lt. Kreuger. He had been in country for four months, and his fatigues were not as faded as Slater's.

"Through my contacts at the village and sighting an NVA scouting party."

Kreuger believed Slater; Gray did not. The CO said, "Your sources lied to you. G-2 has uncovered irrefutable intelligence that the NVA will attack Kon Tum, a long way from here. A small diversionary attack may occur at the Huong Loc. We're in a safe position. The NVA would never strike against the 187th. We have too much firepower and can call in air support quickly."

"And the scouting party?" asked Slater.

"To lure us away from the main target," said Gray.

"My source is reliable. The 187th will be attacked, and if the NVA sweeps through the Dong Giang, your platoons will be threatened."

Captain Gray did not need to listen to the rants of a marginal performer. Gray had received a proper intelligence briefing from his battalion commander, who in turn received an extensive report that morning from the regimental G-2, the Intelligence Section. The information was verified against documents, interrogations, and aerial surveillance.

Captain Gray said, "I put my faith in the army's conclusions and to suggest otherwise reflected naivete. And besides orders are orders, and my duty is to obey my superiors."

Slater didn't like the put-down especially since he was trying to protect Company B.

Gray spoke to his platoon leaders and said, "No way can the inexperienced 2Lt. Marshall, located in a remote part of the highlands, know the deployment of the North Vietnamese Army nor the positioning of U.S. forces to counter the attack."

Lt. Kreuger, as First Platoon leader, was worried about his unit and said, "But just in case, shouldn't we adopt a contingency plan? What if his source is right?"

"2Lt. Marshall is a rookie. He is arrogant to think that his small group knows more than the entire army intelligence network in II Corps."

Slater persevered. "Sir, I can appreciate your point, but I've attended a II Corps briefing, and I wouldn't trust any information they provide."

"What's wrong with it?" asked the lieutenant of the Third Platoon.

"It comes from men in the field who brag about their unit's effectiveness, so they inflate their totals or make them up. Check with others in the field. They'll confirm."

Captain Gray lost patience. "I've heard enough. This meeting is over."

He walked away, and the four platoon leaders felt compelled to join him. Lt. Kreuger, still concerned about his vulnerability, passed Slater and said in a low voice, "Let's talk again. You may be right."

Slater said, "Commanders should suspect any intelligence when it becomes irrefutable."

* * *

Rejoining his men, Slater said, "So much for our news flashes. Captain Gray didn't accept our information or conclusions. And he thinks I'm an idiot."

"You must have ticked him off big time in Benning," said Jesse.

"They don't teach street smarts at the Academy," said Vico.

Slater said, "Let's move our gear to the First."

When they reached the tents, Slater noticed that rock music normally played on the enlisted men's tape recorders was replaced by the sound of jet airplanes.

When he saw Sergeant Boydston, Slater said, "What happened to the rock and roll?"

Herb greeted the lieutenant and said, "A corporal received this tape of B-52s, so we're trying it out. He also has sounds of trains and cars. Maybe Charlie will get scared and leave." They both smiled. Herb added, "We'll have Steppenwolf shortly."

Slater said, "We're getting kicked out of Phan Lac. Can we hook up with you guys for a while?"

"You lasted longer than I thought. It's fine with me if Kreuger and Captain Gray approve."

Slater winced at hearing the company commander's name again. He can't seem to shake Gray out of his life.

Slater said, "Did you hear about the NVA attack?"

Herb got serious and nodded. "We won't be affected. It's way up in Kon Tum."

"Don't count on it," said Jesse. The army's got it all wrong. They may be headin' this way."

Herb tensed. "Don't say that, man. I'm getting short and don't need no send-off from the NVA."

30

JANUARY 1970

Tram loved his coffee fields and envisioned the prosperity his clan would receive from the harvests. Fearing their destruction unsettled him. He had come a long way only to have his dream dashed by the NVA.

As a young child, he grew up with a wartime mentality as his country fought Japan, France, South Vietnam, and finally the United States. While supporting his parents' zeal for Ho Chi Minh and for Vietnam's independence, he served in the army to earn their approval. His goal of being a farmer was forgotten. He distinguished himself as a fierce insurgent who earned rapid promotions due to his leadership skills.

Following his parents' deaths, he continued the fight hoping they would grant approval of him from the afterlife, but the success he achieved was never enough in his own mind.

After TET, he saw the futility of being in constant warfare and slowly weaned himself away from the many battles. He took a few troops and travelled to Phan Lac, the village of his ancestors, and started a new life. This upcoming NVA attack seemed like another TET which would disrupt his plans. The North Vietnamese had never supported him yet expected him to sacrifice for their cause.

He couldn't ignore the irony: Americans provided the coffee plants and his own countrymen from the North would smash them. Why couldn't they attack Hue or Da Nang or even Saigon? Why assault an out-of-the-way valley in a rural district?

He didn't know what to do or how to stop the attack. He didn't want to talk to the village folk or the Americans. He rebuffed Slater's attempts to engage in conversation. He did reveal that the attack would come sooner than the army expected.

*   *   *

A few days later, the four Americans worried as they dealt with their own anxieties about the upcoming battle. Slater needed to provide an update, so the team jumped on a chopper and went to Company B. Maybe this time someone would listen.

By directive, he had to report to the company commander. That meant Captain Gray. He couldn't speak with platoon leaders because they couldn't do anything without approval from their immediate superior.

Every time he approached Gray, Slater got the same result: the captain would chew him out and ignore his comments. Slater wondered why did he keep flailing himself against this impasse? But he had to try. He wanted to help the men especially those in the First Platoon.

With trepidation he went to the command post and reached Captain Gray who had his back to the second lieutenant.

"Sir, can we talk?"

Gray turned around and stared at this junior officer as though he had leprosy.

"Sir, I would feel irresponsible if I didn't give you current information."

The captain acted disinterested and said, "What is it, Lieutenant?"

"The attack will occur very soon. Our presence in Phan Lac puts our team at great risk. I still believe that some NVA units will come down the Dong Giang Valley, so I request that our team be brought in to help with the defense. Can we be billeted with the First Platoon?"

Captain Gray faced Slater and erupted as he did one year ago.

"Lieutenant, are you shirking your duty? Are you deserting your post just because you feel unsafe? We all feel unsafe. This is a war zone. Your mission is to provide information about the enemy."

"But you don't accept my information, don't even use my information." Slater saw the CO's arteries bulge as they did in Fort Benning, and he had not even mentioned Eugene McCarthy.

"You're a coward. No wonder Special Forces didn't promote you. First sign of battle, you bolt with your tail between your legs."

Ernie, Jesse, and Vico sat on the ground a few tents away and heard Gray's voice reverberate. They did not enjoy seeing their leader pummeled by someone with an emotional disorder.

"Ever since you went into active duty, you have criticized the army, protested the war, and acted righteous. You never participated with any group, just stood at the side, and sniped at everyone.

"Why don't you become the officer I know you can be? Don't hide behind the veil of an anti-war moron. You're not an outsider any more. You're in it, so like it or not, be a soldier. Do your duty. Take an active stance and help your fellow soldiers. They do their duties without any smart-ass remarks. Pull your head out of your ass, be a leader."

Gray's body pulsated as he finished. Then he added, "Dismissed."

Slater was furious as he left Company B. He had served his post well, protected the First Platoon from VC. He and his team saved the captain when he was captured. What an ingrate.

For some reason, Gray's upbraiding had more effect in Vietnam than in Fort Benning. A subtle message tried to get through, and the term "outsider" stuck. Slater had been an outsider all his life, in school, in ROTC training, and in Vietnam. His parents treated him as an outsider on the farm. He got punished less if he remained silent. The direct approach didn't work for him at school either.

These thoughts caromed through his head as he moved away from the command post. When he passed his men, no one said anything. Noticing his tormented face, they got up and followed not wanting to upset him further. After the chopper ride back to the camp, they continued in silence allowing their leader to process Gray's tirade.

Slater sat for fifteen minutes dazed by the abusive words and pondered the significance of the captain's message. He thought about his past, his experiences, his life in Iowa, and his hero, Dietrich Bonhoeffer whose courage was beyond doubt. What a great man.

Bonhoeffer didn't cringe when confronting danger. He maintained his beliefs and tried to protect those in Germany against a tyrannical dictator. Bonhoeffer was thrust into adversity and accepted it.

Coming out of the trance, Slater spoke to his troops but sounded as though he was talking to himself.

"We have been outcasts. The army treats us as outcasts, and we consider ourselves outcasts. We deserve better. They put us in VC territory and gave us blanks. No one thought we'd live, but we lasted nine months. Tram doesn't like the war either but doesn't know how to avoid this upcoming battle where many soldiers on both sides will die. So he broke our peace, an honorable decision which allows us to seek safety within the regiment."

Slater looked intently at his men. They had become so close in sharing all the hardships of this assignment. "I won't let him break the peace."

31

JANUARY 1970

" Let it go, Slater. Tram broke the treaty. We need to protect ourselves now," said Ernie.

"We're going to stay in this together somehow."

Jesse said, "Slater, calm down, man. The heat is getting to you. We can't do anything? Our time is over."

Jesse shook his head trying to figure out if any logic remained in the lieutenant's brain cells.

Slater said, "Tram knows the plan and how we can stop it. He said that the NVA will have a small force if they come this far."

Ernie said, "So what if they come this far? We don't have any weapons."

Slater said, "Hell, we're too far away from the main units anyway." He paused. "They probably won't show up here."

"But you think they might," said Ernie.

"What can we do? We have blanks," said Jesse.

Slater said, "We can surprise them. Keep them out of the valley, away from the village, and far from the First Platoon."

Ernie raised the level of his voice and said, "But how?"

Vico said in a calm manner, "In a fight, lots of bullets are fired but few soldiers are wounded especially at night or early morning. The NVA won't know we're shooting blanks."

Jesse got mad at Vico. "You don't know that. How many fire-fights have you been in? We only have four M-14s and a pocket-knife. They have mortars, AK-47s, and real bullets."

Ernie also tore into Vico. "I thought you hated the army. People in New Jersey will disown you if they heard you followed orders and chose to fight."

"Don't say anything against New Jersey, man. They have hearts of gold and do the right thing."

Slater interrupted. "First, let's make a plan and see if we can do anything. Maybe we can't, but the First Platoon is exposed, and we're supposed to provide support. Besides if anyone doesn't want to participate, that's okay."

Ernie and Jesse looked at each other and released a big sigh. Ernie said, "If one guy stays, we all stay."

Vico said, "Very military, Ernie."

"Shut up."

Slater stood up, grabbed his gear, and said, "Let's go."

"Go where?"

"To Phan Lac. Let's fix the treaty."

Slater strode at a brisk pace. When he entered the village, Binh, Lien, and one other woman stood in the center staring at them. Did they know he was coming? Slater and his men stopped in front of the women. Binh did a little bow to Jesse and spoke to Slater.

"Tram said you leave. Will I not see you anymore?"

Slater was so consumed with the NVA attack and Captain Gray that he forgot about Binh. He calmed himself realizing that their relationship had changed. Barriers had been dismantled. They could be friends.

"We aren't going, and right now I need to see Tram."

She smiled, happy that they were staying, and watched the Americans walk to the entrance of Tram's hut. Slater left his crew at the front while he went to the doorway and rapped on the frame.

Tram came out, and they conversed. In the beginning, their communication progressed in a polite fashion. Then Slater raised his voice and would not let Tram interrupt. Soon both quarreled, and Tram's face turned red.

Vico said, "I don't think it's wise to annoy the Viet Cong when we're in their camp, or is it just me?"

"One word from Tram, and we're fertilizer for the coffee plants," said Ernie.

A few more moments passed. Tram and Slater settled down, and the conversation became civil again. The Americans noticed that Tram lost his depression and began to smile. Then he spoke to Slater. Afterward Slater turned and said to his troops, "Tram has something to show us."

Tram stepped to the field behind his hut and motioned for the Americans to follow. He ventured into the forest, stopped, and pointed to a hole in the ground covered by foliage. Slater and team looked inside and saw an arsenal: M-16s, empty magazine clips, AK-47s with bullets, Claymore mines, and two anti-tank launchers.

Tram said, "I have no M-16 bullets, just guns."

Slater smiled. "I have bullets for them, sort of."

"What a haul. The VC has M-16s, and we don't," said Vico.

Jesse said, "Slater, what's going on? What did you say to Tram?"

"He and I have reinstated the peace. I don't want Americans killed; he doesn't want Vietnamese killed nor his coffee plantation destroyed. He knows the NVA strategy and how they will attack." Slater paused. "So all we do is foil their plan, and they will retreat. They don't get exposed to the army's firepower, and the Americans won't be exposed to the weapons from North Vietnam. Tram said the attack might happen within one week just before dawn."

"How does he know their plan?" asked Vico.

"He meets with an advance party of North Vietnamese every evening. They value Tram's spy network located in most American bases. Tram sets up phone lines and squads of runners to inform about troop movement. The NVA relies on this information."

"So Tram is a big wheel, eh?" said Ernie.

"Will Tram report our movements?" asked Jessie.

"Coffee trumps Hanoi at the moment, and Tram will keep us safe because he needs us to protect his crop," said Vico.

Ernie said, "So what's the plan?"

"The North Vietnamese will assault the 187th at the northernmost valley called Huong Loc. Tram discouraged them from the other valleys, and away from Phan Lac. But he believes that the North Vietnamese might start a fight in Tay Son and maybe a small force might come into the Dong Giang."

"So what do we do with our measly four men?" asked Vico.

"We stop their advance."

"You're not making much sense," said Ernie.

"Will a large force come down the Dong Giang Valley?" asked Jessie.

"Just a small one."

"And their objective is the First Platoon?" said Ernie.

Slater said, "If we can surprise them as they enter, we have a chance of disrupting their movement. They won't expect an ambush which blows their cover, so they will return to the main body."

"So how do we surprise them? We don't have any men but lots of blanks."

"You just gave the answer, Ernie."

"What'd I say?"

"We'll set up a perimeter with Tram's M-16s loaded with our blanks. We have three boxes of M-16 blanks courtesy of Colonel Wilberforce. Since the NVA doesn't expect any soldiers in the valley, we will fire when they enter and surprise them."

Jesse said, "Four men aren't much. We don't have enough men."

Ernie said, "We can rig rifles on bamboo, spread them out and fire with strings attached to the triggers, like a horizontal Gatling gun. The enemy will think they are facing a large force."

"Where will Colonel Nguyen's men be?" asked Jesse.

"He's not part of this operation according to Tram. They only serve as runners for communication."

Ernie said, "What if more men than you think come down Dong Giang?"

"Then we're screwed. We run like hell to the First Platoon."

Jesse said, "Why should we risk our lives? Nobody cares about us."

Vico said, "Let me answer this one. Because if we don't, the First Platoon will be overrun. Then the NVA will encircle Company B and occupy a key position against the Second Battalion. The Dong Giang is crucial, yet the brass don't see it."

Jesse said, "You should have been an officer, and then I wouldn't have to listen to you."

Ernie said, "Slater, we're not in charge of the regiment. We're only four lowly soldiers with blanks."

"I can't sit back."

Jesse said, "Did Gray's harangue change your mind?" Everyone was astonished at Jesse's use of the big word.

Ernie said, "When did you learn that one?"

"I've been waiting to use it for some time. Cool, ain't it?" Jesse became serious, looked at Slater, and said, "Did Gray get to you?"

"He made me realize a few things. This battle will cause the death of many soldiers on both sides and especially the men in the First Platoon. We can do something about it. No one else can."

"So what? Even if we stop them this time, they'll start another battle within the week," said Ernie.

"Maybe they won't. Maybe next time will be a minor skirmish rather than an outright surprise attack. Besides according to Tram, only a force smaller than a platoon might come in our direction."

No one said anything. They trusted Tram since his goal was to save his coffee. Their goal was to live. Slater doubted that things would work out as easily as Tram estimated, but every option Slater considered was bad, so this plan was worth a try.

32

JANUARY 1970

B efore scouting for a strategic ambush site in the Dong
Giang, Slater asked Tram, "Why will our plan work? They
have many men and can surround us."

"North Vietnamese are good planners. They set a precise
schedule for movement and specific details for attack, but their
plans have no flexibility. Their leaders not adjust if obstacles
arise.

"American planners offer few details and charge in. Their
plans are flexible, and their leaders adjust. If we surprise the
NVA, they won't know what to do and might retreat."

Slater picked up an important word. "You said they might.
You mean they might not retreat?"

"It is only a guess," said Tram as he raised his eyebrows and
gave a kidding grin.

Slater was not amused.

* * *

That afternoon, Tram and Slater's team surveyed the Dong
Giang Valley. It had a narrow opening from the foothills in
the west and widened as it advanced eastward toward the First

Platoon's perimeter. Soldiers leaving the base of the slope would be bunched together until they entered the valley.

Slater asked Tram, "What time will the attack start?"

"Around 5:00 or 6:00 in the morning, before sunrise."

"Where do we set up the rifles?" asked Ernie. "This is a large area."

Unfortunately the dry valley floor was relatively flat and offered few protective undulations. The land fanned out from the hills with minimal contours until one reached the forest in the direction of Phan Lac. The group wanted a small embankment that could protect them near the valley entrance and still be near the trees in the rear. Fleeing into the trees became a priority just in case their plan didn't work.

As the troops and Tram spread out to locate a suitable patch of ground, Jesse said, "We have the advantage because we know the territory. It will be new to the NVA, and they will be less aggressive in the dark."

Vico said, "We could set up the ambush by some dunes then fall back to a secondary spot before we retreat to the tree line."

Ernie said, "I like that idea."

After scouring the valley for twenty minutes, Tram found an acceptable swell in the ground which would act as an earthen rampart and provide cover from rifle fire. The Americans approved.

Slater spoke to Tram about their setup and asked, "You sure that the noise from our M-16s will stop them?"

"I think so. How you protect yourself if they come after you?"

"We move back into the trees. After that, I don't have an answer."

Tram said, "I have answer."

He retraced his steps away from the valley, past the trees, and into a meadow that was carpeted with scruffy vegetation. He strode to a place that had bushes and boulders. Squeezing between a cluster of rocks and waist high shrubs, he pointed to a spot invisible from the field.

Vico said, "What's in there?"

Tram waved for the soldiers to come, and then he disappeared.

"Where'd he go?" asked Ernie.

"Let's go, gentlemen," said Slater. "I bet the VC dug caves, tunnels, and shelters around the village."

They followed Tram and entered the cave. Each was amazed at the huge cavity in the earth.

Tram said, "We come when airplanes bomb."

"We could hide eight or ten people in here," said Jesse. "This will be our escape if we are overrun."

When Slater exited the large hole, he noticed a small knoll thirty yards beyond. He said to the group, "We may need to use this mound for cover if we escape to the First."

Leading them out of the cave, Tram could see the relief on their faces. He showed them other holes and dugouts just in case they needed shelter.

Slater said, "We need to tie the M-16s together and load our blanks into the magazines.

Tram said, "I bring help for you."

An hour later, Binh and Lien walked through the trees to assist with loading the magazines. Slater was happy at seeing Binh again. She spoke more freely since he saved her from the ugly toothed NVA, but he couldn't seem to get any private time with her. Everyone focused on preparing for the attack. Binh and Slater managed to converse while the Americans cleaned the rifles and she and Lien loaded the clips.

Other Vietnamese women brought twine from the village and gave it to Ernie. He and Jesse bound the M-16s to the bamboo stalks supplied by Tram and tied the twine around the individual triggers.

Vico said, "What about the AK-47s? Their magazines have real bullets. We could use them."

Slater asked Tram who replied, "You keep M-16s. We keep AK-47s."

A look of disappointment crossed Vico's face until Tram asked Binh to bring a large sack.

Ernie checked the contents.

Vico asked, "What's in there?"

Tram said through Slater's translation, "Guns with bullets."

"Does he mean pistols?" asked Jesse.

"Eleven handguns," said Ernie as he emptied the mini-arsenal plus boxes of bullets on Vico's lap.

He salivated at possessing so many weapons. "Now we're in business."

Jesse took one from Vico. "It's U.S. Army issue."

Ernie said, "Slater, you screwed up in asking our Supply Section for weapons. We should have requisitioned them from the VC."

Later the four Americans fired three shots from each handgun to get the feel and conserve ammunition.

At the end of the day, Tram came to Slater and said, "I not be with you during attack. I be with the NVA."

33

JANUARY 10-13, 1970

S later was upset that Tram would stay with the North Vietnam Army and not be at the village to assist. Was he betraying them?

Tram saw Slater's disappointment and added, "I give information to them, but it not be helpful. I send Thai to you about NVA."

Slater relaxed and understood. Of course Tram needed to be with the North Vietnamese. They would suspect an ambush or a surprise if he didn't join them. They relied on his intelligence that served them successfully in the past. Slater concluded that Tram would steer the NVA away from his coffee fields which meant away from his team.

Tram informed the village about his plan against the NVA and Slater's part in it. Many of the women thought the scheme would not work. Too many NVA. But they were duty bound to help Tram.

Binh worried about Slater and was angry for not opening to him earlier. Since the village was preparing for the coming fight, little time existed for them to talk.

After two days of groundwork, everyone was prepared. Ernie bolted five M-16s onto two parallel eight-foot pieces of bamboo and called each "a cluster." He and Vico fashioned six of these contraptions or thirty rifles. Twine was tied to the triggers and joined together so one man could fire all five rifles at different intervals. The Americans understood the timing to fall back if the ambush didn't work.

Binh wanted to help Slater and said to him that she and Lien would remain in the back to reload the magazines with M-16 blanks.

Slater raised his voice which stunned Binh. "I don't want you near us. It is too dangerous."

She thought he would appreciate her assistance. "I want to help. We be careful."

He looked at her with soft eyes and touched her arm. "I don't want you to get hurt."

She understood his concern and nodded. Slater took it that she accepted his decision. Binh nodded indicating that she only heard his words. She would make her own decision.

*　*　*

II Corps Briefing: January 12, 1970

Major Laurel said, "Intelligence from G-2 estimates that the North Vietnamese Army will attack Kon Tum in seven to ten days. Aerial surveillance continues to show activity on the Ho Chi Minh Trail. Most enemy documents disclose Kon Tum as the target. Two documents refer to a target near Pleiku along one valley, but G-2 concludes that these forces will act only to fool us.

*　*　*

Later in the day, Ernie fired up the radio and gave it to Slater who spoke to Captain Gray. "Sir, our sources say that the attack may come in one of the three valleys within a day or so and start around five a.m., probably at the Huong Loc."

"Lieutenant, you've been duped. Headquarters just confirmed that the enemy has targeted Kon Tum, many miles from here, and the attack will occur next week or so. If the NVA shows up in our area, it will be a diversion. I have my orders, and like a good officer, I obey them. You could adopt the same policy. What kind of listening post are you?"

"Sir, Kon Tum is the diversion. We are vulnerable."

"So someone from the Adjutant General Corps knows more than the army's extensive network of intelligence gathering? Now you see why we kept you out of the Infantry Branch."

"I thought commanders insisted on flexibility and had backup plans. Don't discount me just because you think my soldiering stinks."

"Marshall, you are over your head. My orders come from experienced officers not some butter bar."

Nothing he could say would penetrate Gray's impervious brain.

Somewhere between the beginning of the CO's sentence and butter bar, Slater's self-restraint collapsed. He raised his voice. "Don't you remember the chopper ride with Wilberforce? Where would you be if a butter bar hadn't saved your ass?"

Ernie didn't hear Gray's side of the conversation, but he cringed when Slater made that remark. Gray didn't like it either and hung up.

"Slater, you're not trying for a career as a diplomat, are you?"

"You think I overstepped?"

"And then some. He doesn't want to be reminded of his blunder."

"Maybe I overreacted. I just don't know how to reach him. He's been on my tail since Fort Benning. I feel for his men. His company is exposed."

Slater radioed the First Platoon leader, Lt. Clancy Kreuger, and related his concerns and his conversation with Gray. "Just be ready. We'll try to surprise them if they come down the Dong Giang. If you hear gun shots, expect the North Vietnamese and aim your mortars."

"Our mortar section was transferred to the Fourth Platoon. They expect to engage the NVA at the Tay Son. All we have are rifles."

* * *

At 5:35 AM the following morning, about fifty-five minutes before dawn, a small NVA force fired their mortars and rockets against elements of the U.S. 4th Infantry Division in Kon Tum. The commanders concluded that the assault had begun although they thought the attack was supposed to happen in one week. They were primed for action and called in air support.

Three Douglas AC-47 airplanes, the military version of the DC-3, took off from Pleiku Air Base and flew toward Kon Tum. This two-propeller aircraft called "Spooky" or "Puff the Magic Dragon" was modified to support ground troops from three thousand feet at night. It had three mini-guns that fired one hundred rounds per second. Every fifth round was a tracer bullet, so soldiers in the field saw a glowing red line coming from the plane to the target. With rapid firing the sound of the gun was a roar. One couldn't hear individual bullets being shot.

Helicopters could be employed during the night to complement Spooky, but only if the pilots had night vision goggles. The 187th had only two pair that worked. The first pair went to one gunship; the other pair was used by the commander's pilot.

* * *

Thai ran into Phan Lac and found Slater's team asleep. He awakened them and said, "Attack start in Kon Tum. More attack at Huong Loc and Tay Son soon." Then he left.

Slater had four hours of sleep. It was enough. He awakened his team. They had a job to do. The night was quiet except for the scampering of feet around the village. Thai apparently had informed everyone.

All the worry about the impending battle was pushed aside. No more waiting. The moment had arrived. Slater would go and fight and risk his life. His stomach tightened, but strangely he moved with ease; his muscles were loose.

He was confident in his team's role after nine months in a war zone and much more confident in his abilities than when he first arrived. He would take the necessary action for his crew, for Tram, for the village, and for the First Platoon.

The Americans grabbed their weapons and departed for the Dong Giang Valley. Upon arrival at the ambush site, they burrowed the M-16 clusters into the embankment, arranged the strings on the triggers, and waited. Ernie turned the volume down on the radio but was still able to send and receive calls. Everyone wore two loaded sidearms snagged from Tram's weapons bag. They looked to Slater to give them the go-ahead order when the enemy showed up.

All four waited and had time to experience their own thoughts about the coming battle. Will fate allow them to remain here after the battle or take them to an unknown destination?

The line of sight from their emplacement flowed to the valley entrance. If they had real bullets and machine guns, they could inflict serious damage.

34

JANUARY 13, 1970

I n the course of military operations, North Vietnam adopted a strategy of "one slow, four quick" when they formulated an attack. The "one slow" meant that they took plenty of time to gather intelligence, gauge the enemy's weaknesses, and move men and materiel on an unseen basis, so the Americans could not anticipate. The plan often took six or more months.

The "four quick" phases took on the element of surprise which they believed gave them the advantage. The first stage: move men quickly into the target areas. They would advance in small units to a collecting point to avoid being spotted.

The second stage consisted of the surprise attack against the weakest position. They would employ sappers or commandos who would use grenades, explosives, or mines to clear the area of obstacles such as barbed wire so their infantry could accelerate to the targets. Their theory was to overwhelm the vulnerable points and destroy the flanks so the main force could move in and overpower.

The third stage occurred when the NVA released their reserves to consolidate and deliver a victory. They wanted to hit the enemy with everything they had before it could call up its reserves.

After the battle neared its end, the NVA followed the fourth stage: quick clearance which meant rapid withdrawal including taking the dead, wounded, and weaponry with them. This phase would make it difficult for the U.S. to determine how many combatants were killed or even participated.

If the U.S. decided to counterattack, the NVA would set up ambushes.

This strategy succeeded especially during the start of the 1968 TET Offensive.

* * *

Against the 187th Regiment, the North Vietnamese planners orchestrated the deployment of one brigade, more than four thousand soldiers. Their strategy resembled the teachings of Sun Tzu in his "Art of War" written in the sixth century BC. He said that a wise commander took measures to have his enemy react to the wrong circumstances.

At 2:00 AM, they started the movement by stealth to their final staging areas. Sunrise occurred at 6:30 AM, so they planned the diversionary attack after 5:00 AM using the darkness to hide.

When the NVA launched mortars and rockets at the bases in Kon Tum, the American commanding officers and their troops were prepared. The operations officer called all of the air support in the region to aid the 4th Division.

Extra support was not available to the 187th Regiment since a squadron in Cam Ranh Bay two months ago had stood down and transferred home per Nixon's troop reduction program started in 1969. Other planes in the Nha Trang Air Base were withheld in order to protect the II Corps Headquarters.

The NVA planners, on information supplied by Tram, counted on the delay of air support for their assault against the 187th Regiment.

When the sun neared the horizon at 5:30 AM, a subdued twilight bathed the sky which allowed the NVA some visibility prior to sunrise one hour later. Both sides were able to make out vague profiles of people, trees, and buildings.

After the fake attacks against the 4th Division, the NVA's major thrust began at the Huong Loc Valley against the First Battalion, 187th Regiment. The NVA avoided the Third Battalion; they would divide and conquer with half of their brigade or two thousand men, outnumbering the strength of the First Battalion.

The Second Battalion to which Captain Gray's Company B belonged was held in reserve in the Tay Son, a long distance away.

The First Battalion manned defensive positions in a key point along the Huong Loc. Once the NVA engaged, the U.S. battalion commander realized he confronted a larger force than G-2 forecast.

He thought, "If this is the diversionary force, the 4th Division is in big trouble."

He called for air support. When it wasn't available, he radioed the commander of the Third Battalion for aid. They were hunkered in defensive positions and not able to mount an offensive quickly. Calls to Regimental Headquarters did not produce any resources.

Regimental G-3, the operations head, requested that the 4th Division release two Spookies to assist against the enemy's attacks. The 4th Division's commanding officer recalled that an NVA diversion was expected against the 187th Regiment. He feared that his area of operations as the main target could receive a further onslaught from additional enemy soldiers. He accordingly denied the request.

Brigadier General Brennan, commanding officer of the 187th, felt hamstrung that he couldn't get air support or mobilize more men. The enemy occupied positions that inhibited any coordinated action by his various battalions.

He couldn't remain cooped up relying on radio reports to monitor the battle's progress. He needed to get out and use his tactical skills and direct his troops from the air. The sky's beginning light would allow enough visibility, and his pilot had night vision goggles.

He quickly grabbed three support staff and two gunners and headed for his helicopter.

* * *

Promotions to top jobs in United States Army combat units were based on merit, not someone's uncle or contacts. Skills demonstrated in previous assignments, accomplishment in the classroom, and monitoring of performance generally produced superior selections for advancement. Such was the case in the infantry branch starting with platoon leader, to company commander, battalion leader, all the way to division head.

The proficiency of the First Battalion's commanding officer, a lieutenant colonel, would be tested in this battle.

He quickly realized that he needed to improvise or suffer dire consequences against an enemy who hit his unit's weak points with superior numbers.

When the command post of C Company was being overrun by sappers, he took immediate action fearing that his other two companies would be imperiled if C Company was routed.

After conferring with the other two company commanders, he commandeered four machine gun squads from their normal deployment and placed them at vital locations to concentrate their fire. While this repositioning exposed his command to strikes elsewhere, he took the gamble based on his tactical expertise and intuition. He could fill gaps later if necessary, but if he didn't act now, he would not have enough resources to withstand the assault.

In the background, the battalion staff heard a radio call requesting medevac to save eight severely wounded soldiers including the executive officer.

The lieutenant colonel, who also heard the message, hustled the units into place and ordered the enfilade to commence. This tactic of gunfire directed from a flanking position along the enemy battle line mowed down the onrushing North Vietnamese. The enemy couldn't counter the walls of lead streaming across the open ground.

Receiving this unexpected firepower, the NVA pulled back but continued the fighting. The radio operator in a panic yelled again into his mike for a medevac chopper.

"Help us. We have serious wounded."

The battalion CO said, "One is coming but give it protection."

"Yes, sir."

Concurrent with the ongoing enfilade and a flurry of rifle exchanges from both sides, Derrick, against his better judgment, plunged his flying ambulance into the fray. He knew that his helicopter made an excellent target, but in his mind, American troops needed help. He employed his considerable skills to land his craft amidst a spray of enemy bullets on a darkened LZ near the command post.

The mortar squad fired at NVA positions which temporarily reduced the concentration of gunfire. The wounded were loaded quickly as the cracking and explosions from all weaponry hurt eardrums.

With everyone secure and incoming bullets rattling the cab, Derrick lifted off, spun 180 degrees, and accelerated away.

The First Battalion's machine gun units spewed out an impenetrable wall of lead, so the NVA retreated and waited for their other battalion to enter the Tay Son Valley, south of their position. Once this detachment attacked and set up another front, the main force would re-engage and bring more confusion to the 187th.

By the time Brigadier General Brennan and crew became airborne, the battle had subsided. The main force had withdrawn, and an NVA battalion of seven hundred marched undetected toward the Tay Son Valley. Brennan couldn't advise his commanders where to deploy because he couldn't see any troop movement or rifle flashes.

35

January 13, 1970

The late night early morning temperature approximated seventy-four degrees. The sounds of insects broke the tedium. The sun was approaching the horizon as it dispatched the night into dawn. While lying on the cool earth with their clusters primed for the clash, Slater's group heard faint gunfire. They knew the 187th was engaged.

Slater was nervous but confident that the element of surprise favored his side. His troops would fire blanks, and the NVA would run if they came this way. No need for heroics or hand to hand combat.

Vico trained his eyes on the entrance to the valley, which remained in the shadows, trying to spot the intruders. Within ten minutes, he heard a faint murmur. As it grew more loudly, he thought it resembled muffled rushing water. His eyes detected a slight movement in the distance, but nothing emerged. Were his senses playing tricks on him since no water existed in the area?

Then the sounds intensified and vague shapes coalesced against the semi-dark sky. The movement headed right for him. Just as Vico was about to alert his comrades, he heard the flapping of wings and saw that that a flock of birds flew out of the trees. They scared him.

Jesse said, "See anything?"

Vico took a deep breath and muttered, "Nothing yet." But he sweated while looking at the phantom outlines.

Five minutes later, a rustling surfaced which seemed like wheat thrashing. As he stared at the valley entrance, the shadows sharpened. His eyes this time did not deceive him. The outlines of soldiers approached the valley.

Vico assumed a sober readiness and spoke with confidence. "This is it. They're here."

"Get ready to fire," said Slater.

Jesse slid next to his set of rifles behind the thick dirt wall, Vico grabbed his twine, Ernie moved with his radio to a place near the trees, and Slater crawled to his station behind his cluster.

They looked to Slater who whispered, "Wait until they become visible." Everyone held his breath in anticipation of the order.

The two enemy platoons filed down a path trying to be quiet. Their silhouettes advanced onto the valley floor and toward the direction of the First Platoon.

Slater saw the profiles. "They must have close to one hundred men. Didn't Tram say a small force would come down here?"

Jesse said, "Maybe we should leave."

"Too late now, but we can still scare them off whether they are a large or small force," said Slater.

As he waited for them to come farther into the valley, his stomach churned. After a pause, he glanced at his men and said, "Fire."

They pulled the twine at different intervals, five triggers per cluster. Slater hoped that the noise and sparks from the rifle bursts, spread out over a wide swath, would terrify his adversaries.

All fell to the ground and fired back. The AK-47 bullets screamed into the embankment. When a lull occurred, Slater's group ejected the empty magazines, loaded the spare clips, and continued the salvos. After four minutes of exchanges, the NVA retreated. The Americans continued their barrage until Slater ordered everyone to cease fire.

He imagined Tram smiling at the prospect of his village being spared.

During the quiet, Lien and Binh burst from the trees, went to the clusters, and picked up the empty magazines. Slater was furious.

"Get out of here."

Binh said, "We help."

"It's too dangerous."

"We be fast."

Before Slater could say another word, the women had gathered all of the spent clips and retreated to the trees where they reloaded them with M-16 blanks.

The team admired their success and shook each person's hand.

* * *

At the Huong Loc Valley, General Brennan's pilot scanned the area and noticed the exchange of fire on the southern boundary.

He said, "Activity at the far quadrant by the Dong Giang, Sir."

"No one is supposed to be there. Get closer," said General Brennan.

The chopper hastened toward the third valley.

Slater's group heard a whirling rumble in the sky as the spinning of helicopter blades came closer. The Americans treated the aircraft as a trespasser into their domain and a threat to their scheme. An irate Slater reached Ernie and directed him to contact the pilot.

When he answered, Slater took the mike and yelled, "Get out of here. You are endangering us."

The pilot said, "This is brass from HQ, and they want to check out the situation."

"The situation will get worse if you come here. Move out. We pushed the enemy back but are not sure for how long. You are hurting our mission, and the enemy could rocket you."

"We are checking the battlefield and will be gone shortly."

"Don't you understand English? Bug out."

Overhearing the radio exchange, General Brennan was shocked that a grunt would disrespect the pilot with such brashness.

On the ground, Slater bristled that some bureaucratic field grade type was upsetting their program. He could not tolerate stupidity especially since he and Tram had orchestrated this battle so precisely.

"I say again. I am ordering you away from here. You are risking our lives." Furious, he clicked off the radio and looked at his men. "Who do they think they are?"

After Slater transmitted, an NVA soldier launched a rocket. It grazed the rear of the chopper, not a direct hit, but the explosion damaged the tail rotor and impaired the craft's ability to maneuver. It spun around three times, and the pilot initiated emergency procedures and started the autorotation of the blades. This measure gave him room to navigate toward the meadow that he spotted behind a grove of trees. He flew over Slater's location in a wobbly trajectory and guided the chopper onto the flat ground. It landed with a thud causing metal and rotors to collide across the vacant field and a blaze started in the engine area.

Seeing the crash brought instant chaos to Slater's world. His triumph collapsed. He expected enemy troops to flock to the wreckage with weapons flaring. He also saw that the team needed to extricate the passengers from certain death.

In previous actions when Slater had acted as the fearless leader, each mission was mostly scripted for him like finding the lost LRRP or rescuing Gray and Derrick. With the chopper down, his ability to improvise would be acutely challenged. He needed to create a new strategy while facing onrushing NVA. He was furious with the men in the helicopter for putting him in this untenable position.

First decision, his men needed to fall back.

"Grab the clusters and take them to the mound." He yelled at Binh and Lien in Vietnamese to move with them.

The men gripped the clusters, ran from the embankment, and deposited them over a mound beyond the fallen craft. Lien and Binh escaped with them to bushes beyond the mound.

The flames from the chopper expanded and started to climb. Slater's group ran to the fuselage. The side doors were partially cracked, so they yanked them fully open. Vico entered first and guided one man at a time to waiting comrades at the door. He pulled the pilot out of the smoke and held on to his shirt collar as he dragged him to the door. Ernie and Slater helped them dismount to the ground.

Jesse saw one man caught on a mangled girder that jetted out from the structural canopy. He rushed in, disentangled it from the uniform, and nudged the man to the exit. The impact of the crash jarred the soldiers and caused them to stagger and fall as they attempted to run. Smoke inhalation brought coughing and disorientation.

Slater yelled, "Take them to the cave."

The four guided the six toward the rocks. Ernie led the first two, Slater secured the second two by the upper arms, and Vico picked up another. Jesse secured the last passenger who was older and had difficulty standing up. He put the man's arm around his shoulder and hurried toward the underground bunker.

Encouraged by the downing of the helicopter, an NVA squad fired mortars at it. Jesse heard the whistle of a descending shell.

Ernie yelled, "Incoming."

Everyone dropped to the ground. Jesse pushed his man down, and covered him with his body. The blast sounded like a loud "chonk" as it gouged the earth and rained dirt over everyone while shrapnel corkscrewed everywhere. Fragments burst near the cave, and many lodged into the bodies of all who were escaping. Jesse being in the rear absorbed the brunt of the lead in his left leg and back. He screamed in agony and lay on top of his man until Ernie came back and carried Jesse away. Vico followed Ernie and carted the older man to safety. Ernie who was also wounded lowered Jesse into the hole, and Vico handed his man down.

Despite the wound to his shoulder, Slater jumped into the cave and guided Jesse into a comfortable position. No one could see due to the darkness.

Slater asked Jesse, "You all right?"

"I'll make it as long as I don't move anything."

Slater was livid. His carefully constructed plan had become obsolete thanks to this errant helicopter and its crew. They were responsible for his men being wounded. As a lowly second lieutenant, he could control his anger. As a leader, he couldn't let this negligence slip by.

He knew some of the passengers outranked him since enlisted men didn't use aircraft during battles, but that knowledge didn't prevent him from releasing his temper. He launched a verbal attack that would make Captain Gray proud.

"What the hell are you doing here? We had everything under control. You were ordered out. Soldiers on the ground have priority. You risked the lives of my men for no purpose."

Ernie and Vico heard Slater's eruption from above and questioned if one of the six would object to the lambasting and tear into their leader.

Inside everyone was dumbfounded at the outburst. They didn't know this man or his rank, but no one interrupted. They knew they botched up. They crash-landed in the middle of VC territory. They expected assistance from their fellow Americans not a tongue-lashing.

Slater settled down and spoke with an edge to his voice. "You need to be quiet and watch over my man. The enemy will search for the crew and stay in the area. Any sound will bring them here. We'll try to scatter them and free you afterward. I will report your stupidity to the commanding officer." He then departed.

36

JANUARY 13, 1970

The men in the cave felt the sting from Slater's words but remained silent after he left. Blasts above ground and an occasional explosion changed their confusion to fear. The headquarters staff from the downed helicopter sat on the floor and wondered if they would be captured.

Jesse grimaced in pain. He felt blood trickle on his back and legs. He knew that his group's plan as conceived was not workable any longer. He had faith in his team but braced for the worst. He wanted to be with them in this difficult hour.

No one could make out any faces in the cave. Finally the man whose life Jesse saved whispered, "How are you doing, son?"

Jesse knew these men must be officers except for the gunners, so he spoke in a respectful tone. "I'm fine if I don't move. Every time I twitch a muscle, the edges of the shrapnel prick my insides."

"Thank you for saving my life. What's your name?"

"Jesse, sir."

"Call me Jarvis." Others in the cave were surprised that their commander allowed this enlisted man to call him by his first name. "Anyone who saves my life can call me Jarvis."

Jesse said, "Thank you, sir."

Jarvis said, "Who is that angry man who chewed us out?"

"He's Second Lieutenant Slater Marshall."

"A second lieutenant?"

"He's special, sir."

"He should have checked our ranks before mouthing off."

"He was too busy getting you out of the chopper and into the cave, sir."

Jarvis detested the humiliation of being shot down especially since he was the commander. He hated hiding in a cave without any light when a major battle loomed outside. He was the regimental leader and couldn't do anything about this fight except pray for their lives. He resented the way the second lieutenant castigated him.

"He should have showed more respect," was all that Jarvis could mutter.

Jesse could not let these comments go unattended. "Sir, Lt. Marshall asked you to leave. We had a plan to stop the NVA, and it was working. We warned G-2 and Company B about the attack, but they ignored us. Now we're all in danger."

"Are you with the 187th Regiment?"

"Special Forces, sir. A listening post, but no one listens to us."

Jarvis remembered words from Colonel Wilberforce about a Special Forces operation near Company B and recalled that he didn't have many complimentary words for this outfit. After being bawled out, Jarvis tended to agree with Wilberforce's assessment. The lieutenant showed no courtesy toward officers. On the other hand, if it weren't for this group, he'd be captured or killed.

Jesse could feel the tension in the officer's words. His whisper was getting louder. Jarvis said, "Maybe if your group communicated better."

"No one has supported us, yet we have proven our worth."

"The army has procedures and rules governing your assignment. You should obey them."

"We make our own rules out here, sir."

"What do you mean?"

"We can't rely on other units, sir."

"Have you faced combat?"

"Yes, sir, last May."

"That's a long time ago. Sounds to me as though you have taken it easy."

"You don't know anything about us." Jesse was getting angry and didn't care if these men were officers. "If you did, you wouldn't bad mouth us."

"So tell me, son."

Jesse quietly informed the group about their first action when they prevented a VC surprise attack against the First Platoon by making themselves targets. Then he described the freeing of Captain Gray and others when they were captured as well as freeing members of the Long Range Reconnaissance Patrol. Finally he expressed frustration that their intelligence was ignored about the current battle. Jesse omitted the part about stealing the regiment's prisoners.

"We succeeded despite being given blanks instead of bullets, limited supplies, and no cooperation from the 187th. And we had a plan to protect Company B until you came along."

Jesse stopped. He felt his pent-up anger rise and didn't like the attitude from the man next to him.

Jarvis paused too. He appreciated what Jesse had said and would question his subordinates about not receiving information from this listening post. Being issued blanks instead of bullets grated against Jarvis's sense of decency. Maybe the negative stories about Colonel Wilberforce were true.

The blare of gunfire and explosions brought silence to the cave. Each man conjured thoughts about their expected doom.

37

JANUARY 13, 1970

B efore dawn, one NVA battalion of approximately 600 men
broke away from the Huong Loc valley. Two companies
approximating 300 found the Tay Son. Their mission was to penetrate weaknesses in the 187th's western perimeter. This second
front would supposedly add confusion to the American defenses
and allow the main body to re-engage the entrenched American
First Battalion.

The other two companies of 300 men bypassed the second valley and proceeded to the Dong Giang. NVA strategists
saw how to score a victory against the undermanned Second
Battalion and especially the weakened First Platoon if they acted
quickly. The planners did not convey the changes to Tram.

As sunrise neared, the two companies could see more of
the landscape and continued to march toward the two platoons
who were supposed to be in the Dong Giang Valley. When they
viewed the downing of the helicopter, they advanced toward the
fiery wreckage.

The two platoons that retreated against Slater's initial rifle
blasts now regrouped and welcomed the increased manpower of
the additonal troops. Armed with new confidence, they headed
toward the valley and the crash site.

*　*　*

Tram stood with NVA forward observers and witnessed the rocket attack against the chopper and the influx of new soldiers into the Dong Giang Valley. This increased force was not part of the plan. Why wasn't he informed of any changes? When he confronted the NVA strategists, they professed ignorance as well. Tram was furious.

Meticulous plans to protect his village had been rendered irrelevant. He feared that if the U.S. Army called in the artillery, his village and coffee would be blown away. Tram didn't know that because the general's helicopter went down, the artillery was not authorized to fire. No one wanted to be responsible for the death of the commander.

NVA officers split up their forces. Two platoons were ordered to capture any survivors of the downed aircraft. The remaining soldiers of the other companies journeyed down the valley against the First Platoon.

Tram felt powerless. Phan Lac would be destroyed when the First Platoon fired its mortars in this direction. He sent Thai to warn Slater.

Upon hearing the message from Thai about the inflow of many NVA, Slater was shocked that his small area now had over 400 men. With limited time to maneuver, he directed Ernie and Vico to set up their M-16 clusters on the side of the mounds beyond the flaming aircraft.

He spoke to Thai hoping to add chaos to the enemy's side. "Tell Tram to warn the NVA that air support is coming."

Thai said, "NVA know that air support went to Kon Tum and some may fly to Huong Loc. Nothing left for Dong Giang."

"How did Tram know this information?"

"He know everything." Thai acted nervously. He knew the upcoming fight did not favor the lieutenant or the American platoon in the valley.

Slater saw the worry and became frantic as he evaluated options. He needed more troops and air support.

Thai said, "Sorry you no have more planes."

The comment jolted Slater's brain. He looked at Thai and said, "Do you know about Agent Orange?"

"Everyone know about Agent Orange and Napalm," said Thai.

"Tell Tram that air support is not here, but other airplanes are coming, and they carry Agent Orange. They will drop on Dong Giang. Also more American soldiers are coming to the ridge." Slater paused and pressed another idea into Thai's ears. "Tell Tram this is an army trap. The NVA will be slaughtered."

Thai didn't believe the American army was smart enough to prepare a trap in so little time, but he carried the message to Tram.

Slater looked at Vico. "Get me some Claymores. Maybe we can slow them down."

Vico liked the stratagem and acquired five anti-personnel mines from Tram's cache. He and Ernie raced into the valley and saw twice as many soldiers as before.

Vico returned to Slater. "The enemy has doubled or tripled. They have hundreds of men. This is a convention. We need to do something to save Jesse."

Slater said, "Set up the Claymores. I'll warn the First and Company B." He saw the worry on their faces and said, "Don't worry. We'll help Jesse."

Vico rejoined Ernie and placed the mines in the path of the oncoming NVA. Then they waited.

*　　*　　*

Slater hoped he could convince Captain Gray about the precarious plight of Company B. If Gray ignored the Dong Giang, the outcome to Slater and the First Platoon would be disastrous.

Slater got on the radio to Lt. Krueger. "Big problem. How many men do you have?"

"Fifty-one, why?"

"Is your middle name Custer? All of Little Big Horn is heading your way, about four hundred NVA. I'll call Gray. Oh, I want to talk to Boydston when I call back."

Gray answered when the radio operator said it was an emergency. His Second, Third, and Fourth platoons were not involved in any fighting, just held in reserve for the support of the second battalion.

"This is Captain Gray."

"Sir, four hundred enemy are headed for the First Platoon. If you moved to the ridge over the valley, you could save them."

"Who is this? Is this Marshall?"

"Yes sir, and you need to move now or they will massacre your men and attack your rear."

"You are exaggerating and afraid. Get control of yourself."

"Why are you so stubborn? I'm trying to save your men."

"My orders are to support the rest of the battalion at the Tay Son, and I obey orders, Lieutenant."

"Then you and your men will die while you follow orders. Check with the artillery forward observers. They'll give you a different story."

"You want me to risk my career based on the ranting of a second lieutenant?"

"You have ten minutes to get to the ridge. If I'm wrong, you can return. If I'm right, your company survives and you get a Silver Star."

"I don't take orders from a butter bar."

"You wanted my involvement, for me to act for the team. Dammit. I'm following your orders. The team needs you desperately. Move, captain. If you ever want to eat C rations again, move."

Slater hung up, shaking in anger, and thinking, "Do they teach cadets stupidity at the Academy?"

He called the First Platoon and was put through to Sergeant Herb Boydston. "Do you still have the airplane recording?"

"In my tent."

"Can you fire it up as loud as possible?"

"What for?"

"I want to entertain the NVA in the Dong Giang."

"I got it."

By this time, the troops in the Dong Giang meandered slowly around the foliage and rugged terrain while Ernie and Vico readied the cords for the mines. When various squads reached fifty yards from the Claymores, they pulled the strings at different intervals. Five exploded over a one minute period.

The bursts stopped the advance and confused the NVA leaders. Everyone recognized the sound of Claymores which has a sharp low blast with an echo. The NVA was concerned that the entire valley was booby-trapped. After minutes of delay, they looked to each other for guidance. Eventually they moved out with caution not wanting to trip any wires.

Ernie and Vico rejoined Slater and positioned the M-16 clusters on the mounds. They could see forty or more NVA surrounding the burning wreckage with more men coming. Once the enemy did not find any U.S. soldiers, Slater expected them to leave the site and fan out.

He was running out of options. Most of the magazines were empty, he had no air support, and a flood of North Vietnamese headed his way. Vico's and Ernie's eyes bulged as they viewed the swarm of North Vietnamese around the burning chopper. The immediate concern: get more loaded magazines.

38

JANUARY 13, 1970

S later said in a dejected voice, "We'll use the rest of the magazines and then retreat to one of Tram's caves. We'll rely on
our handguns if they come too close."

Lien and Binh came out of the trees and approached them
with the empty clips they gathered from the valley. They brought
a box of blanks that they kept nearby, sat down, and loaded the
magazines. Binh didn't look at Slater knowing he disapproved
of her taking risks. She finally raised her eyes and saw from the
smile on his face that he appreciated her help.

Even though the loaded magazines contained blanks, the
NVA had to treat rifle shots as real. Delaying the enemy became
Slater's priority. The effort would grant time for Gray's troops to
arrive if in fact Gray decided to move. Slater prayed that Gray
would come to his senses.

* * *

After talking to Slater and signing off the radio, Captain Gray
did not budge. He was paralyzed about what to do. He couldn't
follow the bluster of a panicked second lieutenant. Gray thought
that it was Lt. Marshall's first firefight and that he was scared.

He probably inflated the number of enemy from fifteen to four hundred. Being scared shouldn't justify the transfer of one or two platoons and ruin the integrity of battle formations set by higher headquarters.

Gray wondered if Lt. Marshall saw the big picture. He should respect the placement of troops in an organized fashion. Undermining the order of battle to protect his skin in the middle of a skirmish is not good soldiering.

When he saw the helicopter hit by a rocket and then heard gunfire and mortar explosions, Captain Gray conceded that the fighting was larger than a skirmish.

He radioed the First Platoon. "Krueger, what's happening over there?"

"Sir, our scouts just returned. They estimated that two or three hundred NVA entered the valley. Another two or three additional squads went toward the downed chopper. Marshall's right in the thick of it."

"Are you confident with those numbers?"

"We're big time outmanned, sir, and visibility is not good. It's dark and hazy."

Captain Gray realized that Krueger was spooked too.

"I'll be back to you."

Gray wanted to follow the regiment's plan. So far, events differed from the intelligence. Activity in the Second Battalion's zone had not occurred. No one was supposed to be in in the Dong Giang Valley, yet the enemy materialized with a large force. Gray agonized about his course of action.

Disobeying an order went against every sinew in his olive drab body. He couldn't reject the plans from superior officers. It violated his essence that went deep into his gut. On the other hand, protecting his men carried a great weight as his father preached during Gray's adolescence. As a third generation army officer, Gray wanted to keep the honor of his family intact. He felt the pressure to reconcile the two convictions. One had to prevail, and both vied for prominence: mission versus men, Academy versus father.

Doubts about Slater's military bearing influenced the company commander's judgment, but he had to admit that the rookie officer did free him from the VC. Gray wanted to support his commanders and support his men as one and the same decision, but at the moment these two concerns diverged. Then the light went on. He didn't care about the Silver Star. He cared about his men.

* * *

The NVA did not locate any survivors from the helicopter crash. As Slater predicted, they dispersed so that troops moved toward the valley and others headed toward Slater's position.

Having more loaded magazines gave confidence to Slater's crew despite being outnumbered. They saw the silhouettes against the flames and held onto the trigger strings as the shadows moved toward the mound.

Slater whispered, "Get ready." He waited twenty seconds and yelled, "Fire."

The flare of the M-16s startled the NVA. They ducked behind any cover they could find and retaliated. The Americans ceased firing when their magazines were expended. When they stopped, for some reason the NVA stopped.

A pause in the battle allowed Binh and Lien to crawl and grab the empty magazines while Slater's crew reloaded the full cartridge containers into the rifles.

Faced with a standoff, three intrepid North Vietnamese soldiers decided to skirt to their left and approach the Americans from the rear.

39

JANUARY 13, 1970

S later assessed his vulnerability. The NVA and burning chopper were in front of him, the Dong Giang Valley was situated to his right, and Phan Lac rested to the left. His only escape route to an underground cave was behind him.

If he, Binh, Lien, and his men retreated, they might make it to safety in a copse of medium sized trees and adjacent shrubbery, but the ten yards of open meadow was treacherous. The flames from the helicopter's wreckage provided ample light to make them easy targets.

As Slater contemplated his next fateful move, he heard bursts of rifle fire on his left from the direction of the village, opposite from the valley. The NVA who were getting ready to rush the mound also heard the rifles and recognized that the blasts came from AK-47s and not from M-16s. In their minds it meant that they were in the line of fire from their own units who had come another way toward the shimmering rubble of the lifeless helicopter.

With each burst, soldiers in front of the mound peeled off and fled the area to the safety of the valley. They did not want to be killed by their own troops. They would let this new unit of North Vietnamese tangle with the Americans.

Watching the enemy leave and seeing the sparks from AK-47s, Ernie said, "We're in trouble."

The sounds of cracking rifles came closer, and soon Slater's crew would become uncovered. He looked for the best route to pull back.

While loading magazines, Lien came to Slater and pointed to the rifle flashes. "No NVA. Only village women. They fire guns into air."

Slater grinned and inwardly thanked Tram for being so creative. He saved the day.

Since the NVA force withdrew, Slater's crew decided to hide in the nearby trees. Binh collected the spent magazines near the mound while the others dragged the clusters and hid them in the foliage.

Before Slater took his cluster into the trees, he noticed Binh alone on the mound. "Binh, get over here. Now." He then ducked into a spray of leaves.

Meanwhile, the three NVA fighters, who circled to the mound, were unaware of their comrades' bolting from the area. The three emerged from the rear and approached the back of the mound in tandem each separated by a short distance. The first soldier spotted Binh with the empty magazines. He assumed she was working with the American force.

Binh looked up and became petrified when she saw an NVA soldier aiming his rifle at her. Fearing for her life, she screamed in total terror.

The soldier saw her face and her beauty. He also saw her panic knowing she was about to die. They were alone, but he knew two other NVA soldiers would join him shortly. He didn't want his countrymen to think he was a coward, but for some reason he encountered paralysis of his finger and couldn't pull the trigger.

A rustle from the trees on his left distracted his concentration.

Binh heard the noise too, turned, and watched Slater, who heard her primal scream. He ran out with his pistol pointing at the NVA soldier. Both fired at each other. The NVA missed. Slater missed twice but the third bullet lodged into the hip and the fourth entered the abdomen.

The second soldier came into the clearing, fired at Slater and missed on the first shot, but hit him on the second. He fell. Vico who trailed Slater saw his lieutenant drop and unloaded his handgun on the second soldier.

The third NVA appeared from the shrubbery and fired two shots at Vico wounding him in the shoulder. The NVA didn't discharge another shot as Ernie ran between two bushes and pumped him full of bullets from his firearm.

The entire action took fifteen seconds. Binh felt relief at not being killed only to see Slater shot. When Ernie and Vico shot the other two, the danger ended. She went to Slater's side crying. Her American friend saved her life again and now he's hurt.

Ernie rushed to Vico who winced in pain from the searing wound.

"Thanks, man. I didn't see the third guy."

"I hope there isn't a fourth."

Binh held Slater's head. The pain centered in his right ribs as though a branding iron was pressed against his skin. He just lay there while his system absorbed the shock. He looked up and saw Binh.

With a clenched jaw tolerating the pain he said, "I'm okay. It's my side." Upon seeing that Slater wasn't dead, Binh managed to smile through her tears.

Ernie helped Vico up, and both went to Slater.

"We need to get out of here. Can you make it?" asked Ernie.

Slater said, "Let's head for a bunker."

As they were about to move, the group heard shots from the ridge. M-16s were blasting away.

* * *

Instead of moving just one platoon which was the conservative option, Gray ordered all three platoons to advance to the ridge above the Dong Giang and spread out. He had only fought against VC and not the North Vietnamese who used conventional warfare more often than guerilla tactics. Because he didn't know what to expect, he decided to deploy his full complement of soldiers.

In the twilight haze, Gray looked into the dark valley. He barely could make out any movement. Upon refocusing his eyes, he saw a horde of apparitions wearing pith-style jungle helmets. The canvas hats bobbed along the valley heading toward the First Platoon.

"There must be four hundred. That's almost one enemy battalion."

Gray's three platoons totaled 150. He was outmanned, and this fact alarmed him.

Three thoughts quickly came to mind. First, the NVA without any opposition would pulverize the First Platoon and probably wrack severe damage on his company if it had remained in place. Second, G-2 really screwed up. How could they miss a major force advancing in the Dong Giang? And third, he had been too harsh on Lt. Marshall when he cried wolf.

Gray radioed his platoon leaders. "Get ready to fire. Have your men slide a few feet along the ridge after they shoot. The NVA can't see and will aim at the sparks from the barrel."

When Company B started the fusillade, the NVA stopped and returned fire, 400 rifles against 150. The Americans kept their heads down and fired sporadically. They were cautious, so the NVA would not use the flash from the barrel as a target. No one side had favorable visibility or advantage. Since Gray's group enjoyed the protection from the crest, they were not exposed and could wait for sunrise to see their targets more clearly.

* * *

As Company B was firing, Thai, on orders from Tram, reached the NVA commanders and warned them about a trap.

"Planes with Agent Orange come. Tram say to leave valley."

The NVA leadership discounted Tram's message even though his information overall had been accurate. They wanted to exploit Company B's weakness and secure a victory. They didn't expect any airplanes to fly near the Dong Giang.

* * *

When Slater's team heard shots from the ridge, they couldn't believe their ears. They were saved at least temporarily. The three started to laugh and celebrate although Slater and Vico toned it down because it hurt to laugh.

"You convinced Gray," said Ernie showing his white teeth in a big smile.

"Imagine. A second lieutenant ordering a captain around."

"Don't press it, Vico. Gray probably realized how vulnerable Company B was."

Vico said, "Will the enemy come back this way?"

"Maybe we should head for the cave," said Ernie.

"I was expecting air support, but I don't hear anything," said Slater.

Two minutes later, they heard a faint noise in the distance.

Slater yelled, "The recording of B-52s is kicking in. Thank you, Sergeant Boydston."

At first, the sounds were muffled and hard to make out. The slight reverberation indicated that something large was coming. As Herb increased the volume, the noise pierced the sky.

"What a great recording." Slater wondered if the engine sounds would fool the enemy. Would they realize that B-52s didn't drop Agent Orange, only the propeller driven C-130 Transports.

*   *   *

When Captain Gray heard the jets, he was astounded. He knew B-52s were kept in air bases far away in Thailand, Philippines, and Guam, and took many hours of planning and flight time to get to Vietnam. How could these bombers arrive so quickly?

*   *   *

As the B-52 noise was building, Vico said, "What's happening, Slater?"

"The cavalry is here, and I hope the planes scare the North Vietnamese."

"Are they real?"

"They're Boydston's tapes. He's got the volume so loud, I hope his ear drums don't burst."

Ernie left the group and dashed behind vegetation near the valley's edge to view how the North Vietnamese reacted.

The plane recording worked; he saw the NVA stampede out of the Dong Giang. The leaders circulated the order to retreat. The withdrawing enemy fired their rifles at the ridge while running, so Company B's platoons continued to be cautious while discharging their weapons. Neither side shined in marksmanship.

Ernie thought, "Maybe the story Slater gave Tram about an army trap convinced the NVA to retreat."

*   *   *

The fleeing NVA feared the approaching airplanes. They did not want exposure to Agent Orange.

After the NVA exited the Dong Giang, Company B ceased firing, and Herb Boydston turned off the recording. The sun broke through the horizon emitting its first rays showing the now vacant valley. An eerie silence fell upon the battlefield.

* * *

Captain Gray reached his decision to move his remaining platoons based upon a number of reasons: the downed helicopter, the sounds of rifles and mortars from a large area of the valley, and the First Platoon's scouts. All factors persuaded him that his company could be overpowered, but Lt. Marshall's plea convinced him the most. He didn't selfishly request help for his group but for the well-being of the First Platoon and Company B.

Gray recognized that Marshall's notion was correct. If the First Platoon were penetrated, his company and battalion would be at a tactical disadvantage. Maybe his teachings at Benning were absorbed after all. Putting all factors together, he moved his men to the ridge.

Because the early morning light did not illumine the valley, no one could focus on anything clearly. Neither side inflicted serious damage aside from minimal wounding of the NVA. They scurried out of the valley despite an excessive amount of rounds discharged by Company B.

* * *

On the valley just north of the Dong Giang called Tay Son, the first two NVA companies proceeded with their part of the plan and attacked the Second Battalion. The North Vietnamese failed to penetrate the defenses of the entrenched forces. As such, the second front did not materialize. Without this diversion, the main force could not continue their thrust into the Huong Loc.

It never re-engaged and instead withdrew to their staging areas and waited for new orders. Units in the Tay Son and Dong Giang also retreated, and eventually all NVA departed for the safety of Cambodia.

40

JANUARY 13, 1970

At 6:35, the sun broke through the horizon shedding light over the countryside which showed that the battle, such as it was, had ended. A military historian at the War College would not select this encounter for a case study. The Americans based their strategy on false intelligence. The army prepared for an attack twenty miles away that didn't happen. A regimental commanding officer was shot down at the start of the campaign and never used his considerable skills although his battalion and company commanders excelled.

Air support bombed forests and agricultural fields in Kon Tum that did not contain any enemy. The flights cost a gargantuan amount in terms of money, materiel, and fuel but fortunately not in blood. Only the farmers and their families suffered if they happened to be near an explosion.

The NVA experienced its share of blunders too: being fooled by M-16s shooting blanks, fleeing from the mound near a burning helicopter based on a few Vietnamese women firing AK-47s, and soldiers disengaging from battle based on recordings of B-52s.

The failure on both sides didn't prevent the U.S. military from declaring a victory. The forces of democracy once again prevailed over the Communist aggressors. The American units falsely reported large numbers of enemy killed and wounded.

Various commanders and adjutants produced bushels of medals especially to officers for gallantry above and beyond the call of duty for fighting that lasted slightly more than one hour.

Final tally: both sides did not gain or lose territory, and both suffered few casualties.

* * *

Keeping his left hand over the wound on his right ribs helped Slater to handle the stinging in his side. He asked Ernie to help him stand. Binh suffered each time she saw Slater grimace when he moved but happy he was alive. He smiled at Binh acknowledging her concern. She giggled softly between the tears.

The other two were doing better. Vico endured his pain from the bullet in his shoulder, and Ernie coped with the shrapnel in his back from the earlier mortar round. They were grateful that they could move.

As they checked their hurts, Thai showed up. Binh updated him about the fighting and about the shooting of three NVA. Thai said that Tram will tell them when all North Vietnamese units have left. Thai then went to check on the fallen NVA soldiers.

Mindful that the enemy could return, which they often did after a retreat, Slater told Ernie, "Let's go to Tram's cave."

Slashing through the shrubs and finding the entrance, Slater called down, "Jesse, you all right?"

"Okay for now."

"Can you hold out for a while longer?"

"Sure, Slater."

"I think they're gone, but we're scouting the area just in case. I'll be back."

Slater did not talk to anyone else. After he was gone, General Brennan said, "He's an officer, right?"

"Right."

"You didn't call him sir."

"You said I could call you Jarvis, sir."

Quiet ensued.

* * *

When Tram entered the meadow, he spotted Slater holding his right side. He could see the others by the reflected light from the burning metal carcass but not Jesse.

"The North Vietnamese are gone. They won't return."

Slater smiled. "Thank you, Tram, for saving my life. You are a clever man."

"Thank you for saving many Vietnamese lives although they may not thank you right now."

"Can I call in the helicopters? We all need to see doctors."

"I have one man who is also wounded. Can you take him too?"

"Of course."

While Ernie radioed for a medevac chopper, Slater went to the cave's entrance.

"The enemy is gone. You can come out now." Slater turned on his flashlight so everyone could see.

In the darkness, Brennan said to Jesse, "Let me help you, son." When the group moved toward the opening above, the light beamed down and flashed on everyone's faces. The general looked at the man who saved his life and reacted in surprise. "You're black."

"Been that way all my life, sir."

Slater laughed but was startled when he noticed the one star on the collar of the man next to Jesse. His team had saved the life of the regimental commander.

General Brennan saw Slater's shock and said, "Lieutenant, I wouldn't make a habit of chewing out generals."

Ernie and the general guided Jesse to flat ground, laid him down, and waited for the chopper. Tram came over and was glad to see that Jesse was alive. Tram then recognized the rank of one star on Brennan's uniform.

Slater, still holding his ribs, introduced Tram. "General, this is the man who saved us."

Tram saluted and General Brennan returned it; then he eagerly shook Tram's hand. "Thank you."

Tram accepted the compliment and asked in a polite way translated by Slater, "Lieutenant said army take my man to doctor. Is that all right?"

When the general agreed, Tram motioned for Thai and another villager to carry the unconscious man and lay him down next to Jesse. Ernie brought Vico and eased him next to both men.

Tram looked at Slater and said, "Blood all over you."

Slater looked to the back of his shoulder and noticed the wounds from the shrapnel. He was so focused on the battle that he didn't realize how bloody he was. He looked at Ernie and spotted blood on his back.

"You all right?"

Ernie observed the red on his own fatigues. "Never better."

While waiting for the medevac helicopter, Slater said to the general, "We told a story that airplanes flew down the valley and dumped Agent Orange. We also said that the army is giving up its defense of the Dong Giang Valley due to the poison and massive defoliation. Can you include those stories in your report?"

"Why should they be included?"

"So the North Vietnamese will believe them and not come back. They have a way of finding out. Also say that Colonel Nguyen was killed."

Brigadier General Brennan looked at Slater with skepticism and said, "No one will believe it."

"If it's in the report, some people will."

"Aw, in one week no one will remember the battle anyway," said Brennan.

"It will make our day complete, sir."

When headquarters heard that the commanding officer was safe, they sent two helicopters. Brigadier General Brennan and his retinue made for the first one. Before boarding, Brennan looked at Ernie, Vico, Slater, Jesse, and finally Tram. He gave a smile and a brief flick with his right hand to his forehead, an informal salute, before disappearing into the cab.

As the wounded soldiers including the Vietnamese man were carefully loaded into the second chopper piloted by Derrick Williamson, Slater went to the place where Tram stood and asked, "The wounded man?"

"Yes?"

"North Vietnamese?"

Tram grinned. "Of course. Binh told me you shot him. He only one that live."

When Tram mentioned that Slater shot the NVA, he remembered that he fired his weapon at a man which was against a commandment. For some reason this incident differed from the killing of the NVA who tried to rape Binh. That man was evil and besides Jesse helped.

He could rationalize this confrontation as well. He was again protecting Binh, but this time he didn't consider his enemy evil. The man was fighting for a cause, and Slater shot him. He couldn't push away the guilt. His thoughts reverted to his Lutheran upbringing. He committed a sin and desperately wanted the wounded man to live.

As his crew prepared to depart, Slater gathered himself and went to Thai, Binh, and Lien and thanked them. He lingered in front of Binh and wanted to pour out his feelings but only a few words came. "I'm so glad you are safe."

Her eyes filled with emotion, but she couldn't speak any words. Slater received the message: "I'm glad you are safe too."

She saw his blood-soaked fatigues and worried about him. He looked tired and drained. He reluctantly pulled away and with Ernie moved toward the chopper. Slater looked at the outside of the bullet riddled, beat-up aircraft and shook his head in wonder.

He spotted Derrick in the pilot's seat and said, "Where'd you get this jalopy? It looks ready for the junkyard. Will it make it back to the hospital?"

"Maybe," said Derrick showing a slight grin.

"Where have you been? I've never seen so many holes."

"I had a tea party with Charles's cousins from the north." Both laughed.

Slater and comrades boarded, and Derrick flew them to the hospital.

41

JANUARY 14, 1970

One week after North Vietnam's forces retreated to Cambodia, Tram submitted his after-battle report via courier. He said the NVA achieved a significant victory. Their attack brought confusion to the American forces. On the negative side, the Americans' use of Agent Orange devastated the Dong Giang Valley, Phan Lac, and the southern perimeter of the 187th Regiment.

Because of the chemical's harmful effects, the American army will abandon the area. The NVA achieved its goal and ousted the unwelcome foreigner.

Tram added that he too would leave because of Agent Orange and would head south into Da Lat or Buon Ma Thuot, capital of Dak Lak province. Based on his report, the North Vietnamese generals ignored the valleys and stayed away from Phan Lac for the remainder of the war.

* * *

II Corps Briefing: January 14, 1970

With his pointer in hand, Major Hardy and his partner strolled to the podium and began.

"In the early hours of the morning, the 4th Infantry Division reported a large scale assault upon its forces in Kon Tum. With the aid of air support, four battalions fought off the surge. Preliminary estimates show no American casualties. Since the NVA remove their dead and wounded, enemy body count is not known but estimated at 730."

Major Laurel added, "A diversionary attack occurred in the Pleiku area against the 187th Regiment which they neutralized quickly. A fleet of aircraft dropped large quantities of Agent Orange thereby rendering the village and valleys hazardous.

"Company B, Second Battalion, managed to stop a sapper squad and in the process killed Colonel Nguyen. No Americans dead, twenty-one were wounded. Enemy count for this battle: 245 dead, unknown wounded but estimated at 400."

Major Hardy resumed his spiel. "Because of Agent Orange and the prescribed withdrawal of American troops by President Nixon, the 187th will stand down in two months and be repatriated."

Major Laurel said, "The North Vietnamese planned this operation for almost one year. They were defeated by the effectiveness of our intelligence operation and by the fighting spirit of the 4th and the 187th. Because it was such a large setback, I doubt if Hanoi will send troops to the area again."

42

JANUARY-FEBRUARY 1970

The five injured men were transported to the semi-mobile 94th Evacuation Hospital near Pleiku. Slater worried about the unconscious NVA since he hadn't moved on the medevac flight. When the chopper landed, each wounded American was greeted by a nurse or medic and taken for treatment. No one came for the Vietnamese.

Slater pushed the medic back and said, "The Vietnamese is hurt worse. Take him first."

The army medic, aged twenty-one and just recently arrived in country, saw the lieutenant covered in blood and was shocked at Slater's statement.

"Don't worry, sir. Someone will come."

"You don't understand. You have to take him now."

Not wanting to argue, the medic left and brought back a man who appeared to be a doctor.

He looked at the prone Vietnamese, approached Slater, and said, "He is worse, but you need treatment."

"I can wait. Please."

The doctor moved closer. "He's NVA."

Slater was nearing hysterics. "I know. I shot him and feel awful about it. Please help him."

"I'll take him. Go with the medic, and he'll clean you up and prepare you for another doctor."

"Thanks, Doc."

"Believe me, I understand. I've seen a lot in here."

* * *

The Vietnamese required extensive surgery, and after a three-hour operation, he was placed in intensive care. Jesse's and Vico's injuries required treatment over the next week. Slater's ribs sustained minor damage although he experienced a sharp pain every time he moved. The soreness from his shoulder where doctors extracted shrapnel bothered him as well. Both areas would be reduced to a dull ache in two weeks.

Ernie suffered light pains in his back where the doctors removed the metal fragments. He was released the next afternoon.

Since all but Ernie were bedridden, Slater said to him, "You're in charge. Your first task is to guard the Vietnamese. Make sure no one bothers him."

Two days later when the Vietnamese awoke, he saw an American staring at him and wondered if he would be tortured. One minute later, he saw the American leave and come back with another soldier.

The Vietnamese recognized the lieutenant as the person who shot him and whom he tried to kill. He expected ill treatment from his enemy. Instead he was shocked when the lieutenant spoke to him in Vietnamese.

"You're safe. I am a friend." Slater motioned to the first American whose name the Vietnamese discovered later was Ernie. "He will protect you."

The Vietnamese thought he had died on the battlefield and was more surprised to be in an American hospital. Why didn't these people kill him? He tried to kill them. He could hardly move and had no choice but to accept his predicament.

Into the fourth day of recovery, Brigadier General Jarvis Brennan caused a stir when he visited the hospital to check on his troops. At the end of his rounds, he called on the Special Forces entourage.

Ernie came to attention only to hear, "At ease."

Brennan went to Jesse's bed. "The doctors say you are making good progress. I am glad. Thanks for getting me out of the helicopter and saving me from the mortar."

Jesse continued being nervous at speaking to the general but couldn't resist a comment. "Even if I'm black, sir?"

Everyone appreciated the joke.

"I deserved that. And what's my name?"

Jesse smiled. "Okay, sir. Jarvis."

"If you need anything . . ."

"Thank you, sir, er, Jarvis."

Brennan introduced himself to Vico and Ernie. After shaking hands, he said, "Thanks for saving me and my men. I missed the battle, but it sounded loud, difficult, and full of suspense."

"And all we had were blanks," said Vico.

Ernie said, "We did get handguns from the village and they saved us."

"Amazing how you four withstood so many NVA. The report said you faced four hundred of them. Incredible performance."

Brennan passed the Vietnamese who was asleep. "I guess he's sedated, so please thank him too."

The general went to Slater's bed. "Any more words for me that you forgot to say in the cave?" He grinned.

"No, sir. I think I covered everything." Slater returned the smile.

"Are you going to report me to the regimental commander?"

"Upon further reflection, I'll let it slide this time. The general has enough paperwork." Slater gave another grin. He appreciated an officer who had a sense of humor.

"Lieutenant, great job. Captain Gray reported your incredible stand against so many of the enemy. He said you all deserved medals. After thirty years in this man's army, I can truthfully say that you made me proud."

"Thank you, sir."

"And to think you engaged the village to help. We don't often get locals to support us. You must have captured their hearts and minds."

"It was the opposite, sir. They captured mine."

"In any case, your group and the village saved my butt."

Bandages held Slater's right arm, so General Brennan extended his left hand, and Slater extended his left. As they shook hands in an unconventional manner, the general said, "Thank you, son."

Slater said, "Thank you, sir."

Over the next two days, members of Brennan's helicopter party dropped in to express their gratitude.

* * *

After eleven days of convalescence, only Ernie was fit. He helped everyone during the recovery and now aided in the exit to the hospital's chopper pad. Vico's left arm was in a sling, Jesse needed crutches, and Slater's torso was encased with light bandages. He moved his left arm easily but still had difficulty with the right. The North Vietnamese required a stretcher.

As Ernie got everyone on board, Vico said, "Ernie, you'd make a good nurse." They all agreed which embarrassed Ernie.

He told Slater but everyone overheard, "Jesse should have remained at the hospital. The doctors don't know he's gone."

Jesse said, "I'm not staying away from you guys."

"If you have any problems, we'll send you back on Derrick's chariot," said Slater, "so take it easy."

Ernie continued, "I was lucky to get the Vietnamese released. The army wanted to interrogate him."

After landing at the LZ, Derrick and Ernie helped everyone out. When the chopper departed, they organized the gear and prepared to carry the Vietnamese to the village.

Ernie lifted one end of the stretcher. Slater with his good left arm and Vico with his good right managed the other end. They carried the conscious NVA to the village as his eyes darted back and forth wondering what fate had planned for him. Jesse moved slowly but steadily with his crutches.

After setting the stretcher down in the village, the huts emptied as they welcomed the Americans. Binh leaped out of her hut. She was happy to see Slater standing up. They both gave each other broad smiles, and he answered her questions about his recuperation. Lan was ecstatic to visit with Jesse and sorry about his injuries. Lien used hand signals inquiring about Vico's health.

Tram walked from his hut and looked down at the NVA. He directed Thai and others to transfer him to the far hut especially prepared for his recovery.

He beckoned Binh to break from Slater and go to the hut. "Binh, you watch over this man and help him to heal."

When Binh saw the NVA's face, she gasped. He was the man who almost killed her and Slater, and now Tram wanted her to care for this beast? She became angry at Tram. Binh normally would never question the man who had done so much for her, but she couldn't accept this request.

"He tried to kill me and kill Slater. Let someone else care for him."

Tram said, "This is not a discussion. Take care of him."

"For how long?"

"Weeks, months, years."

Binh knew she had no choice. If Tram decided, then it was law. She went to the hut, looked inside, and saw that the NVA had a special place to sleep and a mat was placed at the other end where presumably she would sleep. She would accept Tram's decision but resent every moment.

43

For the next two weeks, Slater and company enjoyed the idleness to heal their wounds. They spent time at their campsite and at the village where Slater had long chats with Binh.

One day, she asked, "When you leave Vietnam?"

"About two months. Why?"

"I like our talks and wondered how much time we have."

Binh was happy when Slater visited but still hated being a nurse to the NVA.

"I mad at Tram. I no want to care for this man."

Slater surprised himself that he didn't feel anger toward the enemy. In fact Slater was pleased that the man was alive. "He fought for his side. It's war," said Slater.

"I no like war. I no like Americans to fight here or North Vietnamese."

Their discussions ended the same way: Binh being angry with her patient and Slater defending him. A psychiatrist would have a field day analyzing Slater's distorted reality, but something about the NVA triggered him. Something lingered inside, and Slater couldn't grasp it.

* * *

During the lazy days at camp, Slater read and thought about returning home. Where would be his next assignment and what would he do after the army? As often as these thoughts entered his brain, his mind reverted to the action in the Dong Giang Valley and especially to the shooting of the North Vietnamese. He relived the events, the firing of the clusters, the rescue of the general, and the hassles with Captain Gray that ultimately led to the retreat by the NVA.

Slater experienced continuing guilt at firing a weapon and almost killing a man. Ernie and Vico also suffered this distress. The tightness in their gut after taking a life remained with them every day. They rationalized their acts because if they didn't protect themselves, they would be dead. No one had any answers, and none of them slept well.

Lying in his sleeping bag, Slater replayed the scene in his head when he thought Binh would be shot. He retraced his movements as though he played a role in a film. No matter how many times the movie ran, the story remained the same: he heard her scream and rushed from the trees with fire in his eyes and a gun in his hand.

He saw the NVA aiming his rifle at her. And in the next frame Slater pulled the trigger. A second enemy came from behind and fired his weapon at Slater. He collapsed from the bullet and saw the second soldier drop from a shot fired behind him. Next he saw the third NVA go down. Slater saw the faces of the three soldiers as they fell. He couldn't erase the fright he saw in their eyes.

His memory played reruns each day and each night, and he felt the guilt, the strain, the wrongdoing. Would Dietrich Bonhoeffer excommunicate him?

When the four men visited Phan Lac, the villagers treated them as royalty. They drank tea with the Vietnamese and oversaw the growing of coffee plants.

Slater would steal time to see Binh. On each occasion he witnessed her growing depression. No amount of talk would overcome her mental state. The shooting of a North Vietnamese brought a double negative: it brought Slater guilt and Binh torment.

Despite her misery, she tended to the patient's wounds and nursed him on the road to improvement. The NVA was eating and drinking more and even greeted Slater with a warm voice and a friendly face. They only exchanged pleasantries, nothing serious.

Returning to camp, Slater couldn't shake the NVA's peaceful appearance when he saw him in the hut. For some reason it bothered him as though he'd seen the expression before. He saw two faces of the NVA: one near the mound which looked at him with hatred as he fired his rifle and the gentle one the man showed on his mat. Something about both faces nagged at Slater all night.

The next day, for breakfast the Americans drank warm Cokes, munched on chocolate bars, read, and bantered about their DEROS. Out of nowhere the wounded NVA's two faces appeared side by side in Slater's consciousness.

He left the others and walked to the LZ deep in contemplation. His mind repeated the memories of the early morning attack, but this time the film seemed more vivid. It showed him rushing out of the trees, seeing the North Vietnamese aiming his rifle at Binh. Same action as before, but the images were clearer.

Slater relaxed his thought process and ran the clip again, only this time his mind witnessed it in slow motion. He didn't rush but floated out of the trees and saw the North Vietnamese pointing his rifle at Binh. Slater stopped the show and did another rewind which repeated the NVA leveling his rifle at Binh.

The film stayed with the same scene as Slater slowed his movement. He focused on the NVA and saw that the he aimed his rifle for a long time. He could have shot Binh at any moment.

His face showed a gentle appearance, the same one Slater saw in the hut. Why didn't the soldier shoot Binh?

Returning to camp from the LZ, Slater said, "I'm going to Phan Lac."

Slater strode into the village, past Tram's hut, and headed to the one with the NVA. Binh heard a commotion and went outside. She smiled when Slater came toward her, but his stern appearance put her on alert. Something bothered him.

"How is he?" he said in a serious tone.

"He doing well. Talk more. He sleep many hours."

"Can I speak with him?"

Binh nodded and saw that Slater was determined.

He walked past her into the hut. The patient's mat was placed perpendicular to the entrance. The NVA turned his head and kept his eyes on the American. Slater sat down at the foot of the mat away from the entrance and faced the enemy soldier. The wounded man did not notice that Binh followed the lieutenant and remained out of sight behind his bedding.

Slater began by saying, "I shot you."

The patient said, "I know. I shot at you but missed. This was my first battle."

"I'm sorry I shot you."

"You protected the girl. I understand."

"I'm glad you are recovering."

"The doctor had an interpreter when he treated me. He knew I was North Vietnamese."

"He's a good man."

"Americans are strange. You shoot me. Then the doctor told me you said to take me first."

Binh's eyes widened at the NVA's news and looked at Slater with surprise.

"The doctor said if I went later, I would be dead. I don't understand Americans. We are the enemy."

"I don't understand either. My name is Slater."

"My name is Khanh." They didn't shake hands but their eyes did.

"And your last name is Nguyen?"

"No, my last name is Trung."

"Can I ask you a question about the time I shot you?"

"Yes."

"When I came out of the trees, you aimed your rifle at Binh. She is my friend. You hesitated and didn't shoot. When you saw me, you fired at me, no delay. You could have fired at her any time before I came. Why did you hesitate?"

Binh was astounded at the question and leaned forward to hear the answer.

Khanh paused and kept his eyes fixed on Slater. Friend or foe, Khanh liked him and was awed by his act of putting him first in the hospital. He would answer openly.

"I couldn't shoot her. She was so beautiful and seemed so innocent. I couldn't take that away from her. We are still Vietnamese. I wanted to shoot her because she worked for Americans, but I couldn't."

Upon hearing Khanh's admission, Binh looked at her patient in a different light. He wasn't a brutal soldier but a caring man. Her eyes softened. Then she gazed at Slater with gratitude for revealing the truth to her.

Khanh turned away, looked up at the ceiling, and said, "I have a question for you. Did you bring me here because I am going to die?"

Slater saw that Khanh was prepared for any answer and would accept one about his passing.

"No, you have to rest. The doctor gave me pills to help, and I told Binh when to give them to you."

"Are you telling me the truth?"

"Yes. But you must let your body heal. You have the best nurse in the world. Talk to her. Find out about her life, and tell her about yours. Tell her what you want to do when you are able to return home."

Khanh turned his face away from Slater and nodded slowly but did not smile. He felt humbled because fate had delivered him from death.

That night, Slater slept past sunrise and past breakfast.

44

Three weeks later as everyone was feeling stronger, Ernie received a call on the radio from Captain Gray.

"Tell Lt. Marshall that in two days all of you will return to Nha Trang. They will process the paperwork for your next assignment in the States."

Ernie could not believe what he heard. "Sir, can you say again?"

"I say again. Your group is going home."

* * *

Binh knelt next to Khanh's mat and gave him a sip of water. When she put the cup down, she heard activity in the village. Going outside, she saw Slater with children skipping next to him saying in English, "Hell-oo, Slay---der."

Slater went to Tram's hut, turned his head, and spotted Binh. His face conveyed the news that Tram was yet to receive. She put her two hands to her mouth, closed her eyes, and leaned against the hut.

After speaking with Tram, Slater walked to Khanh's hut to talk to Binh. Firing at the NVA in the Dong Giang Valley was easier.

She came to the doorway with a downcast expression. "When do you leave?"

Slater felt a lump in his throat and couldn't swallow. After a false start, he said, "In two days." He wanted to say more, but words escaped him. "I will miss you."

"I feel so sad like someone die in my family." She paused. "I want Americans to leave but not you."

He couldn't identify or comprehend any of his feelings that fluttered around his heart. She had been the only person to whom he could talk openly even with the language and culture barriers. The platonic bond they had established gave him joy. He wondered if their friendship could ever grow into a romantic one. He concluded that too many differences inhibited them and that in the end they just liked each other.

He tried to describe his emotions but nothing came out. His lips and throat moved, but he became tongue-tied. His eyes spoke for his mouth.

After his verbal paralysis, she let him off the hook. She looked into his eyes and said, "I know."

He did manage to release a few words. "Tomorrow my team will cook dinner for the village. Then we can talk."

She watched as he headed back to camp. When he went out of sight, she started to cry. Going inside the hut, she looked up and saw Khanh staring at her from his reclined position on the mat. "He's a special man."

Surprised that Khanh had overheard them, she said, "I will miss our talks."

"Do you love him?"

She thought Khanh rude to ask such a personal question.

Seeing her tighten, he apologized. "I don't mean to pry. You don't have to answer, but it seems you two have a special relationship."

Softened by his comment, she said, "Yes, I love him but only as a close friend. I have never been able to talk with a man and be accepted as he accepts me."

Khanh turned his head, looked upwards, and took a deep breath.

* * *

The next day, in an open area between the huts, the Americans hosted a farewell dinner for the people of Phan Lac. They built a makeshift grill and obtained provisions of meat, fixings, desserts, and sodas. Derrick managed to purloin the items from the commissary. The assistant manager, an army sergeant, allowed Derrick to dip into the inventory because he saved the life of the sergeant's brother in a medevac mission.

The dinner started at four in the afternoon. Ernie did the cooking and trained Vico to barbecue hamburgers, a task that required more time and patience than Ernie anticipated. Slater organized everything else and received help from Binh and Lien. Jesse felt stronger but still needed to rest. He enjoyed playing with Lan.

The soldiers wanted to dress nicely for the dinner, but their fatigues had grime suffused into each stitch. The green had faded to the color of a pale lime or light celery. But no one cared. The joy of being together took precedence over sartorial standards.

During the meal, Slater spoke Vietnamese, but the other Americans used body language, hand gestures, plus pigeon Vietnamese and French to communicate. The language barrier did not exist. It was replaced with laughter, camaraderie, and warmth. Even the North Vietnamese soldier in his weakened condition enjoyed the feast. He had two or three women serving him strange American food. He liked the hamburger best.

Binh sat next to him and helped with the serving. She felt better about caring for her patient and enjoyed the stories about his home in Hanoi. At times Slater sat next to her and talked about his country's customs at an informal dinner.

As the evening progressed, Slater resumed his seat next to Tram and said, "Thank you for the peace."

Tram smiled. "Peace is difficult, don't you think?"

"It should be easier."

"It will be now."

Slater asked, "What do you want me to do with the rest of the money in the bank account?"

"Keep it. I'll need more seeds and other items. You can purchase them for me."

They discussed logistics about mail, addresses, and keeping in touch. Then Slater said, "How's Colonel Wilberforce?"

"He's making slow progress in our labor camp. We may let him leave in six months." They both chuckled.

After dessert, Tram addressed the crowd. Slater translated for his men.

"For years we fight Americans, so they will leave our country. I was mad at Americans. I'm still mad at Americans, but these men showed me that America has people I like. I think these four must be part Vietnamese. They make peace without bullets, play with our children, help us with the coffee, and protect our village against both armies. They are our friends. I thank Colonel Wilberforce for sending them here.

"I know your army gives its soldiers medals for bravery. I don't have any medals, but instead I offer you this blue ribbon. It is a North Vietnamese ribbon and is given for bravery."

Tram smiled as he gave four ribbons to his allies and then sat down. Each American was touched and would make them into slide-on ribbons to put on their rack-builders which held the medals together on uniforms. So far this ribbon would be their fourth one. The other three are the U.S. defense medal one gets automatically, and two medals just for serving in Vietnam.

Regardless of the few they had, the Americans will hold Tram's in high esteem and wear it with pride. They hoped no one would inquire as to its origin.

After Tram's speech, Slater stood up, looked at the villagers, winked at Binh, and said in the best Vietnamese he could summon.

"I am honored to know Tram and this village. Thank you for your friendship. We have been here for ten months. We leave tomorrow morning on our trip back to our homes. Even though thousands of miles separate us, please know that we carry you in our hearts. I look forward to being with you in a better world. I wish peace for you and for Vietnam."

* * *

After the dinner, Slater and Ernie carried Khanh on the stretcher to his hut.

"Heal quickly, Khanh. I leave you in good hands."

"Thank you for my life and for my nurse."

Ernie, Vico, and Jesse cleaned the cooking area as best as young American men knew how. Binh and Slater walked away from her hut, stopped, and faced each other about one foot apart.

She looked at him with watery eyes, and when she blinked, tears streamed down her cheeks. She tried to be brave as Slater had been strong for her. He saved her from physical danger and brought her friendship, laughter, and exposure to a world beyond her country.

He wanted to hug her but felt his action would be misunderstood. How does one say good-bye forever? He stared at her face wanting it emblazoned on his brain so he could recall it with ease.

"I don't know what to say. Leaving you is sad."

She understood and put both hands out to him. He clasped them and held them frozen for one minute. She smiled, nodded, released the grip, and bowed her head as she returned to her hut.

* * *

The other three felt Slater's unhappiness and remained quiet as they returned to the LZ. Prior to arriving at their camp, they commented about the good time they had at the dinner, similar to good times associated with family reunions or at parties among close friends.

Early the following morning as they packed and waited for a helicopter, no one said anything. They had anticipated DEROS for months and months. With departure so close, all four felt depressed.

"I am sad to go," said Vico.

"Me too," said Ernie, "and yet I want to go home, but I want to stay too. Am I crazy?"

"I'll miss all of them especially Lan. And I don't have any pictures," said Jesse.

Slater didn't say anything. He just moped around while he rearranged his gear in his duffel bag. They expected Derrick's arrival around 9:30.

At 9:00, they heard sounds beyond the landing zone and looked up. All the villagers walked down to extend a final farewell. The Americans were moved by this gesture. Binh did not come with them.

Slater approached Tram and said, "I will miss you. You are a noble ally, Colonel Nguyen."

Tram reacted in amazement. "How did you know?"

"I saw you lead your men against the First Platoon last May. And who else could be Colonel Nguyen?" They laughed and then saluted each other.

"Thank you for telling your general that Colonel Nguyen was killed. The Americans won't be looking for him."

As they heard the sounds of rotors in the distance Tram said, "Binh asked me to say good-bye. Seeing you go is difficult for her. She said you would understand."

Slater looked down and said, "Thank you. It is difficult for me too."

As they shook hands, Slater heard sounds on the path. He turned and saw Binh running toward the LZ and toward him.

Out of breath, she calmed down, looked at the descending helicopter, and said, "Khanh told me to come. He said I would regret it if I did not." Her words came haltingly, and she labored to get them out. "I had to see you one last time. I had to show you that I am happy to know you and to thank you for everything."

She smiled, no tears. She looked directly into Slater's eyes. Then following Tram's advice that Americans appreciated a good handshake, she shook hands with Ernie, Jesse, and Vico saying "thank you" to each.

At 9:25, Derrick landed the helicopter and waved to everyone. They waved back. The children smiled and raised their middle fingers at the pilot. Derrick laughed.

The four loaded their gear on the aircraft, and three climbed in. Before going in, Slater bowed to Tram, waved to the villagers, and with his eyes welling up gave Binh a long affectionate look. He turned and stepped into the craft helped by Vico and Ernie.

All four peered out the open door of the Huey. They felt downcast but managed to smile. As the chopper slowly elevated, the children gathered around Tram, stood at attention, and with their leader, saluted. Binh could not hold back any longer and waved amidst a torrent of tears.

Water formed in the Americans' eyes, and they saluted back and held it until the LZ disappeared.

45

MARCH 1970

D errick saw the sadness in Slater's group as they boarded. He felt heavyhearted too. He would not be landing at the Phan Lac LZ again. He said, "Sorry for departing so quickly, but I have to arrive at Company B before ten."

"Why the rush? Can't we have a drink together?"

"Your team is supposed to leave as soon as possible." Special Forces is anxious to see you."

Slater said, "You look neat and clean. What's up?"

"An award ceremony is scheduled for ten. You won't believe this, but they're giving me a Silver Star for my rescue of soldiers in the Huong Loc."

"A Silver Star? Well done. You certainly saved my butt many times. You deserve a medal for helping us steal the two prisoners." They both grinned.

"Don't say anything about that mission. They might take this award away from me."

"Only if you give me your address, so I can look you up when I get out of the army."

As they approached the landing zone, Derrick said, "Thanks for showing me another side of this war. I'm not much for good-byes, but I wish you all the best."

"It's mutual."

"Company B owes you their lives," said Derrick.

"They don't even know we exist except a few in the First Platoon."

"They know. The clerk typist who prepared the general's report mentioned it to a friend, and word spread. First Platoon knows they would be dead ducks except for you guys."

Slater shrugged.

Derrick continued. "Even Captain Gray admitted his company was screwed if he hadn't moved to the valley."

"Think he'll tell me?"

"I doubt it."

Slater said, "I guess it's against military doctrine to give compliments, right?"

"The report said four GIs against four hundred enemy. You guys are heroes."

"You're hyping it too much."

"You haven't been at camp. If you showed up, you'd see."

"I'm going to miss you, Derrick."

"I'd love to stick around, but our unit is needed in Qui Nhon. I leave this afternoon."

When the helicopter rested its skids on the rocky earth, Derrick got out first. "Got to run." Then he pointed south. "The transit area is beyond the ceremony grounds. See you in the USA."

After they shook hands, Derrick gave a big smile and hustled toward the awards presentation.

All alone, the four men sorted out their gear.

Vico said, "Where's a luggage cart or skycap when you need them?"

Dirt kicked up with each stride and they proceeded to the other chopper pad. They moved slowly given Jesse's crutches and their lingering aches and pains. Their wounds hadn't healed completely.

* * *

Captain Gray scheduled the ceremony to honor the brave men in Company B. Brigadier General Brennan made an appearance to present the awards. He developed a special relationship with these soldiers and wanted to surprise Captain Gray with a Silver Star for his heroic actions. Gray's decision to leave his assigned post and do a reconnaissance in force to the edge of the valley saved the day and saved the general.

The company comprised four platoons approximating fifty men each. Each platoon faced forward where Captain Gray, Brigadier General Brennan, Derrick, and other honorees stood. Four squads in each platoon lined behind their first sergeant and lieutenant. Approximately two hundred men occupied the parade ground, as the sandy piece of clay was called.

* * *

As the four trudged forward, Slater said, "All right, men. Let's go past the ceremony as fast as possible. I don't want to give Captain Gray another chance to harass me."

Vico said, "We're not formally dressed. Our fatigues have too many layers of crud."

Ernie said, "Maybe we can blend in with the dirt. More of it is on us than under their feet."

They all laughed, a nervous laugh, since they wanted to avoid any hassles that could disrupt the formalities.

Slater carried his own bag over his good shoulder and grabbed Jesse's bag with his left hand since Jesse still needed crutches. Ernie carried Vico's bag and his own since Vico's left arm remained in a sling. They moved slowly wearing disheveled and very faded fatigues. The helipad where they needed to go would take fifteen minutes to reach. The distance seemed longer with the heavy gear. After five minutes in the hot sun, they were exhausted.

As they rounded a corner, they saw part of the parade ground with soldiers in formation. The path meandered five yards from the field. The First Platoon as it happened stood on the far right of Company B which was near the walkway.

Vico said, "Let's scramble past these guys."

"Amen," said Jesse. "They are wearing clean fatigues."

"Maybe the First Platoon will shield us from the company commander," said Ernie.

The four increased their pace slightly but given the wounds and gear, their efforts yielded little acceleration.

As they approached the assembled mass, Lieutenant Krueger noticed the stragglers and wondered why this motley group would interrupt the proceedings with Brigadier General Brennan in attendance. Then Krueger recognized Slater and grinned. He broke ranks and shook hands with all of them.

"Thanks guys, thanks, Slater. Bless you. Thanks for saving us."

Slater said, "Get back in line. Gray will get mad at you."

Krueger ignored the comment. "I owe you. We have many short timers who will be going home thanks to you guys."

The other soldiers in the platoon also recognized them and turned their attention away from the front to express their appreciation. Slater and his group were surprised at their gratitude.

Herb Boydston came up and smiled at Slater, then gave a thumbs up. He was wearing a bronze star pinned on his fatigues by General Brennan.

Slater looked at the medal and said, "Great job, Sergeant."

Herb shrugged as though it was nothing. "Can you believe it? I got me a bronze star for operating an open reel tape recorder."

"You earned it. How short are you? When do you go home?"

"Eight days. I am so short you can't see me."

"Where's home again?"

"Phoenix."

"They're blessed to have you. Be safe."

Herb said, "You take care and that's an order."

They saluted, and the Special Forces contingent continued down the trail hearing "thank you" "thank you, man" "thank you" as they passed the squads.

At the front of the company with Captain Gray at his side, General Brennan presented medals to three sergeants. He heard the commotion, looked up, and noticed the scraggly soldiers near the First Platoon. To him they appeared to disrespect the sanctity of the moment.

He turned to Captain Gray and said, "What's going on over there? Those men are a disgrace."

Gray looked over, identified Slater, and replied, "Sir, those four men saved you and this company."

"That pathetic group?" Brennan strained his eyes on the untidy bunch. He saw Jesse. Then he recognized the others. He turned to Captain Gray. "I'll take it from here." He faced the company and yelled, "Company. A--tten--tion."

The First Platoon fell into formation. The company stopped their fidgeting and braced at a crisp attention.

Ernie heard Brennan's voice and said, "Oh-oh. Let's get out of here."

As they attempted to move away, Brennan shouted, "Right face."

The entire company turned to the right with their bodies rigid and faced Slater and his warriors.

Brennan ordered, "Present arms." The company brought their right hands up in a mass salute.

Slater felt embarrassed. The four bedraggled men dropped the bags and helped Jesse as they stood in front of the company.

Seeing everyone salute them, Slater said, "Now what do I do?"

Vico said, "Tell us to stand at attention, sir."

"A--tten--tion." He paused. "Now what?"

Vico said, "Say 'present arms,' sir."

"Present arms." The four men returned the company's salute. Slater paused again. "What's with the 'sir' routine? I'm Slater."

Vico said, "We're in militaryville, sir."

Slater's men while holding their salute saw two hundred grinning soldiers, appreciative for the efforts of these unsung fighters.

Slater looked toward the front of the company and saw Derrick with his Silver Star. He beamed. Next to Derrick, Captain Gray with his Silver Star held a sharp salute that would make West Point proud. He kept his typical stern look but nodded his head. It was his way of honoring his former trainee.

Lt. Marshall swept his eyes to Brigadier General Jarvis Brennan who kept his arms at his side, his face impassive. When their eyes locked, the general's face relaxed, the edges of his mouth curled upwards, and he slowly raised his right hand to his right eyebrow to recognize this lowly second lieutenant and the troops who had saved his life.

Slater was feeling uncomfortable with this fanfare and said to his crew, "Now what?"

Jesse said, "Take it in, sir. They're digging us."

Slater turned slightly and glanced at his team. After ten months in Vietnam having to fight everyone for respect, they finally received credit that was overdue. He saw that Ernie held his body erect while a small tear escaped.

Jesse displayed pride. The sparkle in his eyes showed how seriously he treated this accolade. His salute was smart despite having to balance on his crutches with his left hand.

Vico's face morphed. Gone was the smart-alecky East Coast gunslinger. His eyes softened. He tilted his head up in dignity while the furrows in his brow disappeared as he absorbed the tribute.

Slater had to admit that he liked this validation. Even the salute from Captain Gray gave him a sense of accomplishment. Slater finally managed to please his nemesis.

A few more seconds elapsed, and he asked, "How do I end the salute?"

Vico said, "Say 'order arms,' sir."

Ernie said, "How do you know this stuff? Something must have stuck in your anti-military mind."

Slater said, "Order arms."

Vico said, "We can go."

Ernie said, "Vico, you're a prince."

"I should have been a protocol officer."

The four ragged soldiers picked up the bags and continued along the path.

The company held their salutes until the four went past the parade grounds. Brennan then said, "Order arms." He paused. "Left face." And the company resumed the ceremony.

After walking for two more minutes, Jesse said, "That was cool."

46

MARCH 1970

The flight on the rattling C-130 from Pleiku to Nha Trang was not passenger friendly. The web seats along the side were used for military transport and not regular passengers. They offered little comfort. The seat belts could not be buckled properly, and Jesse questioned their effectiveness if the plane came to a sudden stop on the runway.

Vico had a hard time getting comfortable with his injured arm, and Jesse squirmed the entire time to minimize the pain in his leg and back. Their gear was stowed near their seats.

After landing, the four took their time to deplane given the hurts and unwieldy duffel bags. An army truck driven by a Specialist Four greeted them.

"Going to Special Forces?"

"How'd you know?" asked Vico.

"I was told that two wounded men not wearing green berets needed help. My boss gave me a message for you: be in the adjutant's office at zero nine hundred tomorrow."

"Ernie said to Vico, "That's nine in the morning."

"Now I'll take you to your quarters."

Vico said, "Looks like we're in trouble again."

"Let's not react to anything they say. Let them chew us out, and then we can DEROS," said Jesse.

"Maybe they won't let us leave," said Ernie.

"Shall I return the blanks to them?" said Slater.

"Bad attitude. At least they gave us something to fill the magazine," said Jesse.

When the Spec 4 stopped at the enlisted quarters, Slater went with his troops.

"Lieutenant, I'll take you to the officer's quarters."

"That's all right. I'll be fine."

The driver didn't press the issue. He left the four alone and drove off.

Thirteen empty bunks were available at the far end of the Quonset hut. No one complained when a lieutenant decided to stay with his men in the enlisted digs. The top sergeant, an E-8, in charge of the facility was never there to object since he held squatters rights to a certain bar stool at the NCO Club. The Spec 4s and Private First Classes at the other end remained silent. They understood that based on their faded fatigues, the new arrivals earned flexibility from the rules. Besides they were preoccupied with smoking Vietnam Gold, high grade marijuana.

The next morning, after showering and eating breakfast, Slater and company strolled to the commanding officer's Quonset hut which contained the office of the adjutant. No one looked forward to seeing him. Maybe they could ask for sympathy since Jesse and Vico were wounded.

They took off their army caps, entered the office, and approached the desk sergeant whom they didn't recognize because the old one, Eddie Doyle, was transferred to the States, something about black market dealings.

Slater said, "We were told to report to the adjutant."

All four felt nervous until a major whom they had not seen before came out and introduced himself.

Slater said, "What happened to the old one? Did he DEROS?"

"You mean Major Pemberton?" The four nodded. "He was fragged about three months ago."

"Fragged?"

"You've been away from civilization, haven't you? Fragging is when a soldier, a friendly, tosses a fragmentation grenade into the quarters of a senior enlisted or an officer with the aim of killing him. It's become a big problem."

"Why do they do it?"

"Out of frustration, discrimination, or mistreatment."

"Then we're not surprised as it pertains to Major Pemberton," said Slater.

"We have no suspects. He was widely hated as you have concluded. But enough about him. Follow me."

The adjutant led them to a courtyard in back, and officers with the rank above captain filed in front of them and stood without expression. The adjutant stepped to the side. Being isolated, the four felt like they were defendants waiting for the court's verdict.

Slater wondered if Special Forces had their own form of Inquisition or was this gathering the firing squad?

The men came to attention as a colonel came through the door. He walked in front of them and said, "At ease."

Slater fell out of attention, but he wasn't at ease. The officer was slight of build, had leathery skin, and his ancestors came from Asia. Which country Slater couldn't determine.

"My name is Colonel Yamaguchi. I replaced Colonel Wilberforce."

He spoke in a straightforward cadence typical of all regular army officers. His voice did not modulate to any extent. Not a tinge of friendliness or a smile but no evidence of malice either, just another stoic army man. His name indicated his family came from Japan, and he spoke American English perfectly. No accent, so he wasn't from the South.

"My war college classmate was Brigadier General Jarvis Brennan. He informed me about your exploits."

With the mention of General Brennan, the Phan Lac four relaxed.

"I asked my staff to attend this presentation." He looked at his adjutant. "Everything ready?"

"Yes, sir."

"You can begin."

The adjutant took a piece of paper from his breast pocket and read: "For performance above and beyond the call of duty, for serving as a listening post in enemy territory and in combat readiness, each man is to receive a Combat Infantryman's Badge."

A sergeant major came from behind the crowd and passed out the precious silver and blue enamel badges to be worn above medals on the uniform's left breast.

The adjutant continued. "For saving the First Platoon, Company B, of the 187th Regiment against a Viet Cong attack, each man will receive an Army Commendation Medal with a V device for valor." He paused while the four had the award pinned on their uniforms by Colonel Yamaguchi.

"For rescuing a company commander, helicopter pilot, and crew held as prisoners by the ruthless Viet Cong, each is awarded the Bronze Star with a V device for valor."

Again each man had the medal pinned on his uniform by Colonel Yamaguchi. The four looked at each other in disbelief.

"For stopping an assault by the North Vietnamese Army against Company B and for saving the lives of a platoon plus six men of the regiment including the 187th's commanding officer, each man is awarded the Silver Star."

During a pause, Ernie asked, "How did they know?"

Jesse said, "I mentioned a few things to the general while we were in the cave."

"Way to go, Jesse," said Vico. The others nodded in approval.

"I bet you didn't mention everything," said Ernie. The group chuckled thinking about stealing the two prisoners from the brig.

"I skipped over that part."

"For being wounded in the last battle, each man is awarded the Purple Heart."

Slater thought the colonel would be tired at this point with all the medal pinnings, but he endured the distribution of awards in good spirits.

At the end, the colonel said, "You have brought great pride and distinction to Special Forces. Congratulations. And thank you for saving my friend, General Brennan."

He went down the line and shook hands with the award winners. He had a warm comment for Ernie and Jesse. When he reached Vico, he said, "Great job, soldier. Everyone is proud of your accomplishments."

Vico wanted to make his typical sarcastic remark. He looked at his mates who shook their heads ever so slightly in their feeble attempt to discourage a retort. For once, Vico agreed with them. Silence should prevail in this hallowed moment.

He looked at Colonel Yamaguchi and said with a straight face, "Thank you, sir." The other three gave a big exhale and looked to the heavens in gratitude.

The other staff officers in attendance followed the Special Forces commander. They gave the group a nod or "well done" as they passed. Slater's hand had never experienced so much shaking. The new CO received high marks from Slater and his crew.

After the ceremony ended, Colonel Yamaguchi ordered Slater's team and the adjutant to his office. Upon entering the drab office with eroded gray metal furniture, everyone sat down.

"As you probably concluded, Brigadier General Brennan informed me about your accomplishments and your bravery while saving his life. He was very impressed."

Slater and his men enjoyed basking in the glow of the CO's comments.

"General Brennan told me about your mission and your dealings with his regiment. He noted your cooperation with the First Platoon and your friendship with Lt. Williamson. He saw how you had access to choppers for unusual situations like medicine needs, transportation to Nha Trang, and use of the USAID representative.

"Your achievements more than offset the blemish on his command of two missing POWs. He noted that Lt. Williamson flew to headquarters on the day they were taken."

The glimmer of confidence gained from the CO's earlier compliments quickly vanished. They sat in stone silence fearing that their snatching of the enemy prisoners would be revealed.

"By any chance, did you know anything about this heinous act?"

The four answered together in an innocent manner. "Oh no. Of course not, sir."

"General Brennan didn't think you did."

Slater and his men breathed more easily but remained jittery on the inside.

"He wanted me to tell you that since the interrogator and brig sergeant had rotated back to the States and since no other witnesses were available, he was terminating the investigation."

The four looked at each other with relief. Slater caught Colonel Yamaguchi's smirk during the pause.

Changing the subject, the colonel said, "I am aware of your ill treatment by the army and by Special Forces. No R&Rs, no pay, no promotions, blank cartridges. It is embarrassing. I want to correct these blunders and honor your incredible achievements.

I have been authorized to promote all Spec 4s to E-6, Staff Sergeant."

Ernie, Vico, and Jesse looked at each other in amazement.

The CO continued. "For 2Lt. Marshall who should have been promoted to first lieutenant on the anniversary of his commission, I am instead promoting you to the rank of captain. All of you will receive the back pay owed to you plus interest and a bonus."

Getting a higher rank made everyone happy. Receiving money brought bigger grins.

Colonel Yamaguchi added, "Your next assignment will be at Fort Bragg, the home of Special Forces. You as a group are to develop a new course to show how to use locals as an asset and gain their loyalty.

"I have arranged for your departure from Cam Ranh Bay to return to the States. You will be transported to the base this afternoon. Again, congratulations on a job well done. That is all."

The group was stunned. They stood up, saluted, and marched out of the office. The adjutant arranged for two mama-sans to sew the sergeant stripes on khaki uniforms. He gave Slater the captain's bars to pin on his collar.

After lunch, a helicopter took them on a ten-minute flight to Cam Ranh Bay, a large air force facility and transportation depot where they would catch a plane for home. The only hitch occurred when the military required Slater to sleep in the officer's quarters and not with his men.

The next morning, they boarded the plane and sat together. When the aircraft lifted off, all the soldiers gave a resounding cheer.

Slater's goal was to return to the United States with all of his team. He accomplished it.

47

MARCH 1970

Many hours later, the planeload of tired soldiers landed at Seattle-Tacoma International Airport. No welcome home banners or greetings for returning servicemen were present. Slater and his lads went into the various airline counters to arrange the next leg on the journey to their hometowns.

To get their tickets, each serviceman had to show that he served in the military. That meant wearing the uniform on domestic flights. When Slater and company as well as all military personnel walked along the airport corridors, they stood out and were vulnerable to taunts and curses from hippies including vets from Vietnam who protested the war.

"Hey, baby killers. Go back. We don't want your kind here."

"How many people did you burn, hotshot."

"Christ will put you in eternal hell."

People nearby who supported the war or objected to the harangues against the soldiers remained silent. They uttered no words to thank the returning servicemen for their service.

Slater was against the war and did his best to make peace, but the protestors lumped him and his men into the pro-war category. Ignoring the jeers, they proceeded to a nearby food stand.

Slater said, "It feels strange being in the real world again. I served my country yet feel like a stranger here."

Jesse said, "I feel weird too, and everyone looks at me in this uniform as being creepy. Aside from my married sister, there's nothing at home for me. I want to heal my wounds in peace, and it's hard to do in my neighborhood."

Ernie said, "I'm looking forward to seeing my wife."

Vico and Jesse razzed Ernie. "Hey, hey, hey, you rascal."

Smiling, Ernie said, "I was getting tired of reading, you know. I just want to be a regular person again."

Vico piped in, "I got lots of people to see, lots of family to visit, lots of homemade pasta to eat."

Slater said, "I doubt if I'll stay long in Iowa. My father will put me to work and care less that I was in the army. Outside of seeing a friend, I won't stay long. I'll leave early for Bragg and get things ready for us."

Jesse said, "I'll join you as soon as I can."

Vico said, "I'll show up at the last possible moment. I want to use all of my vacation."

Ernie said, "My wife and I will drive back to North Carolina. I've never seen the South or East Coast."

They exchanged phone numbers and addresses and parted with the knowledge that they'd be reunited shortly.

* * *

Slater left the group and sauntered toward the departure gate to check in. He felt self-conscious amidst all the supposedly normal people. He didn't belong to anything normal anymore if in fact he ever belonged. He was deflowered by the war, and nothing could restore him to the time before he entered the service. The genie would not be put back into the bottle.

People looked at Slater and his fellow soldiers as though they were freaks with short hair, polished shoes, and vacant stares. Gone was the reverence the armed services enjoyed years ago.

Slater felt badly for the draftees. They had to join since no one could get jobs without the military obligation handled. They had love of country drummed into them by family, schools, churches, and now the army.

They came to Vietnam with high spirits to defend freedom. When the reality of Vietnam differed from the message proclaimed by America's leaders, many of the young rebelled. This rebellion remained inside for years after their discharge and after their return to civilian life. Exposure to killing and irrationality ruined whatever sanity remained.

Slater noticed the change in him as he interacted with people at the airport, even simple communications like "one order of fries, please" was awkward. Most of the people in the airport kept their distance.

It seemed as though he landed on Earth's double in a parallel universe. On the surface, things looked the same, but in reality nothing was right.

* * *

For his trip to Iowa, Slater boarded the plane and edged his way down the aisle. Finding his seat, he noticed that an anti-war hippie sat next to him. He had long hair, a red scarf around his head, unkempt beard, a skinny body, dirty jeans, and an old army jacket with a frayed sergeant's patch. He reeked of the aroma of hemp, and Slater wondered what extra thrills lay ahead on his journey home.

After sitting down, the man said in a calm voice, "Back from Nam?"

"Yeah."

"I came through Seattle too. No fun is it?" said the hippie.

"You served? When were you there?"

"Man, I left two months after TET. I didn't see any action. I worked at an air base loading bombs and chemicals. Now I protest. You see any action, man?"

"A little."

"A little is enough. Welcome home, but it doesn't seem like home, right?" Slater shook his head. "Where are your medals?"

Slater said, "I chose not to wear them. I'm back and that's the only award I want. Aren't you supposed to fill me with anti-war hype?"

Not missing a beat, the hippie said, "I'll start in around thirty-six thousand feet. I'm being nice before takeoff, man."

Slater smiled and extended his right hand. "My name is Slater Marshall."

"I'm John Radatz but they call me Sully."

"Why?"

"Because I do a mean Ed Sullivan imitation, man."

Both became quiet until after takeoff.

John continued. "Coming home used to be different for GIs, man. The units would arrive as a whole, get greeted by family and friends, and congratulated on serving the cause. Now soldiers come home alone, no placards, no family or friends. Just get to your destination on your own, man.

"People look at you in a strange way. Man, they expect you to be normal after killing and following the orders of deranged little Napoleons. It stinks, man. I'm against the war but not against the soldiers."

"You seem wise. How old are you?"

"In years, twenty-three, man. In life, about sixty."

"Why sixty?"

"I got problems. My body is aging too fast."

"What happened?"

"Cancer."

"Cancer. You're too young."

"The chemicals I loaded? Agent Orange. The military thought it was harmless. No precautions. No safety procedures, man."

"Any treatment for it?"

"Not from the VA. They deny it has any link, and there are thousands of us."

"Where are you going? Home?"

"No, I'm meeting friends. We hang out and smoke pot. It helps me cope."

They chatted for the entire flight.

John said, "Readjusting to America is difficult even for non-combatants. Just hang in there."

After the plane landed, Slater asked, "Can I help you with anything?"

"Thanks, man, but my friends are here. You take care, man."

They went out together, and as they parted, John saluted him, and Slater returned it.

48

1970-1973

S later cancelled most of his leave and showed up for duty two weeks early. He called everyone saying he would lay the groundwork. Jesse joined him one week later, and Ernie and his wife arrived five days after that. Vico arrived at the last moment in questionable sobriety to report for duty.

Stateside assignments had perks and a pecking order to which lifers adhered. Uniforms sparkled with polished brass, pressed creases in the pants, and unit patches. Medals, festooned on the left breast of the tunic, were called "fruit salad" and deeply respected. Officers and senior enlisted made sure their uniforms and fatigues were tailored and starched.

Slater could care less about the conventions of the post. He did not wear any patches, Combat Infantryman's Badge, or medals on his uniform beyond the required insignia that included a name tag. He gave in to convention and wore a green beret only when in khaki uniform or green dress jacket and felt awkward with it on his head. Out in the field, he used a cap with his fatigues.

When his group first reported, a major, who served in a staff capacity and frustrated because he had been passed over for promotion to lieutenant colonel, noticed Slater's bare uniform.

The major mistook this captain as a novice and in need of a reprimand.

"Where are your medals, captain?"

"I've elected not to wear them, sir."

The major guessed that Slater did not earn any and had not been to Vietnam where a soldier is given at least two.

"In this fort you are supposed to wear them. That's an order. Report to me tomorrow showing your medals."

"Yes, sir," said Slater. He glanced at the major's uniform which displayed four medals including a Bronze Star. This award is usually given to any officer just for being in Vietnam for one year regardless of the performance.

The next day, Slater walked up to the major at his desk and mocked him by saying, "Sir, reporting with medals, sir."

The major looked up and saw Slater's eight medals including the Silver Star, two medals with V devices, Purple Heart, a blue ribbon, and a Combat Infantryman's Badge. He he focused on the blue ribbon.

"What is the blue one?"

"A Vietnamese medal, sir."

"I know most of their awards but not that one."

"For Special Ops, sir."

"Oh."

The major never bothered Slater again.

* * *

One month into their assignment, Slater received a letter from Company B in Vietnam.

"Dear Captain Marshall, I thought you should know. Derrick Williamson was killed as he tried to save a wounded squad near Qui Nhon. Captain Gray."

Slater and crew took the rest of the day off and soaked their sorrows in alcohol. Thereafter, the memory of Derrick would visit Slater almost every day.

Eight months later, news circulated around Fort Bragg that a former commanding officer and prisoner of war, Colonel Erastus Wilberforce, wearing Vietnamese pajamas, was found flagging down a two-and-a-half ton truck near a Pleiku farm. He was sent to Fort Bragg for recovery. Slater never ran into him but heard that Wilberforce repaired a broken marriage, reconciled with his three estranged children, and retired from the military. He now worked to help Vietnam veterans' organizations.

* * *

Soldiers decompressing from a war zone experienced adjustment problems. Ernie, Jessie, and Slater had a hard time adapting to the "real world" as returning soldiers termed stateside. Only Vico remained unaffected. The others encountered nightmares, waking up in a sweat, recoiling at any loud noises, and ultimately questioning their sanity.

They didn't know what to call it. It wasn't depression, but doctors usually diagnosed it as such. Vico named their behavior as being in a funk. The condition didn't impair their performance of duty. They just needed time to repair their emotional batteries.

The group cringed every time they heard that someone was assigned for a second tour in Vietnam. Slater thought multiple assignments to a war zone were criminal. Too much stress on the person. Didn't anyone in charge see the repercussions? Couldn't army psychiatrists run some tests or write a paper?

It took the American Psychiatric Association until 1980 to recognize the ailment as Post Traumatic Stress Disorder or PTSD. Prior to this date, it was called "shell shock" or "war/combat neurosis," but most knew it as "battle fatigue."

Whatever the name, the problem had persisted for decades, maybe centuries. Doctors probed for answers, and they looked for malfunctions in the brain. Spiritual leaders suggested that war and killing went against the human software which is not physical but pervasive in every cell.

49

1973-1995

After Slater and his crew received Honorable Discharges, they went to Atlanta to make their fortunes. They had investigated many locations that would work for each person, and Atlanta won handily.

They took jobs in different industries to gain experience and acquire skills. Ernie worked for a commercial construction company eventually becoming a project superintendent in electrical and plumbing. Jesse, after completing various junior college classes in Fort Bragg, took a job with a local bank in its operations training program and advanced over the years. He found he was proficient in math and accounting.

Vico, to the surprise of many, hitched to a prominent real estate brokerage firm and earned his broker's license. No one thought a person with a Jersey accent could sell homes in Atlanta, but Vico made it work. He was pushy in a positive way enabling escrows to close by not tolerating delays. Buyers and sellers loved him.

Slater accepted a management trainee position with an international machinery company. Over seven years, he rose steadily assuming greater responsibilities.

Except for Ernie who was already married, the rest searched for mates, and the process took some time. On vacation to New

Jersey, Vico, thanks to a blind date set up by his friends, met a woman and developed a serious relationship. His soon-to-be wife didn't object to living in Atlanta as long as she was allowed home leave once or twice per year.

Jesse had difficulty adapting to North Carolina and meeting women. In fact, he gave up. The cultures between Los Angeles and Fort Bragg clashed. He was content to socialize with his Vietnam buddies, read, and take classes.

When he attended a retirement party for his master sergeant at the NCO Club, a black woman from Seattle looked into his eyes, batted her lashes, smiled, and it was all over. Her dad was the master sergeant who thanked his lucky stars that his daughter found someone as ambitious as Jesse. Jesse didn't bring up his anti-war attitude to the father. The daughter understood her husband's reasons for his unmilitary leaning.

The three friends evaluated Slater's dates at Fort Bragg and in Atlanta based on a point system of marriage eligibility. The conversations amused everyone, but his relationships did not produce a walk down the aisle. The three attributed Slater's lack of progress to his shyness with the opposite sex.

His moment came in Atlanta's busy airport. He was late and rushed to catch a flight. In his haste, he tripped over a piece of luggage and landed in front of a woman who was coming the opposite way. He looked up, and she looked down. Both laughed at his awkwardness. Without any words, he knew he found his special person.

Slater missed his flight so he could pursue this damsel over coffee at a nearby stand. They spoke on the phone every day but had to adjust their busy schedules to have their first date three days later.

*   *   *

Despite the career successes, the Phan Lac four missed working together and were anxious to try something new. After considerable study and analyzing growth sectors, they formed a home building company. It took time to organize the various projects to justify everyone quitting their jobs. When the operation finally coalesced, Slater served as president, Jesse as chief financial officer, Ernie as head of construction, and Vico as head of sales.

They seldom spoke about Vietnam but concentrated on the business. The families enjoyed their usual Sunday night get-togethers where talk about business was not allowed. When meeting other veterans, they avoided the subject of their wartime experiences. The wives knew very little about their husbands' military exploits because they didn't talk about them.

The memories of fallen comrades stayed with them as the years passed. Slater mourned Derrick and Ross. A few months after Derrick's death, an article and photo appeared in his hometown newspaper, the Palo Alto Times. Somehow Slater received a copy. He filed it away in a folder and looked at it periodically.

* * *

Iowa became a vague memory to Slater. His parents never phoned or wrote. He called home every Christmas and Easter for a brief conversation.

He was impressed with Iowa's Governor Robert Ray. In 1975 he opened the state to Vietnamese refugees. They settled in various towns and had an opportunity to obtain American citizenship.

In 1980, Slater's dad, after a full day of work, walked into the living room, sat on the couch, and died. Slater returned to comfort his mother. She had no desire to remain on the farm that had many horrible memories, so he arranged for her to live with her widowed cousin in Des Moines. Both cherished the reconnection and developed a mutual compatibility. Slater sold the farm to Albert Sun who was expanding the family's operation.

* * *

When the Vietnam Memorial opened in 1982, Slater said he wasn't interested in going. The others were surprised at his reaction but honored the decision even though they were curious about seeing it.

The home building firm succeeded beyond their expectations. They enjoyed meeting the challenges together and receiving awards for the quality homes they built.

They remained in contact with Tram and even hosted nieces and nephews for months at a time, so Tram's relatives could improve their education and speak fluent English.

Tram's coffee company flourished. Vietnam became the world's second largest producer of coffee behind Brazil, but most growers relied on the cheaper Robusta bean. Tram's high quality coffee from the Arabica beans guaranteed them strong profits and continuous sales even in lean times when Robusta growers suffered.

50

JANUARY 1996

I n 1996 after years of planning and anticipation, the four families, husbands, wives, and kids, flew to Vietnam for a reunion.
It was one year after the United States accorded diplomatic recognition to its previous foe. The home building company closed
its offices for three weeks over the New Year.

They landed in Hanoi and planned a two-day sightseeing tour
before heading south. On the first day, the tour bus arranged
by Tram took them to the Presidential Palace which was built
in 1906 for the French Governor General. The Communists
used the appealing colonial structure done in Italian Renaissance
architecture for state visits, but it was off-limits to the general
public. Only the botanical gardens were open.

The Americans were surprised when the bus stopped at
an entrance, and a soldier escorted them inside the impressive
building. They went up the grand stairway with its fancy balus-
trade to the second floor. From the landing they went into a large
room that was painted all white showing elaborate columns and
cornices with gold filigree on the sides.

Ten Vietnamese men and three women stood to receive them.
Slater thought he recognized one of the women but changed his
mind. He didn't know anyone in North Vietnam.

An older man approached Slater. He looked very distinguished wearing a dark blue suit with thin pinstripes, white shirt, and blue tie. He said in Vietnamese, "Welcome back to Vietnam. My name is Nguyen Quang. I am Deputy Prime Minister."

Slater translated emphasizing the man's important government position. They all felt honored but wondered why someone of this high position would attend this welcome meeting.

"I have a message for you." He paused, looked at the four ex-soldiers, and waited while Slater again translated.

The Deputy Prime Minister then said, "Uncle Tram has nuoc mam for you."

Slater did a double take at hearing the words. He relayed them to his fellow vets, and they too were stunned. The man was one of two prisoners Vico and Jesse stole from the brig. Slater alerted the wives and kids as to the revelation.

Then Mr. Quang spoke in English. "You all saved my life. My family and I thank you."

"You did well for yourself."

"My father pushed me into government work but said I needed to see the war in the south. I saw it too closely. I met Tram before I was captured. He and I have remained friends since. He told me to learn English, and I'm glad I followed his advice."

Mr. Quang then went to Jesse and Ernie and shook hands and thanked them. He stopped in front of Vico.

"Major Hawkins, you fooled them. Thank you." Vico smiled.

Mr. Quang added, "We're a Communist country, but I let Tram become a capitalist as long as I get a discounted price for his coffee." Everyone including the wives laughed. "Knowing you has softened my outlook toward Americans and helped me when I had to negotiate with your government representatives over economic and political issues. Thank you."

After the Deputy Prime Minister finished, another man came to Slater and said in Vietnamese. "Do you recognize me?"

He had short charcoal hair, happy eyes, a small mouth, and was bent at the waist.

Slater paused. The man looked familiar, but Slater remained uncertain. He said, "No, I can't recall." He looked at his team and asked, "Do you recognize him?"

The group concentrated. Ernie and Jesse shook their heads, and then Slater said, "Wait. I know. You're Khanh, the wounded North Vietnamese." They'd only seen him in bandages, not a suit.

Khanh grinned. "You have a good memory." Since Slater was rusty in Vietnamese, a female translator stepped forward.

"On the night of the attack, we came around to ambush you. I saw this Vietnamese woman. I thought she worked for the Americans. She looked at me, and I aimed my rifle at her. She was so scared. Then Slater came out of the bushes and shot me."

Slater said, "I apologized to you in the hut, but I still feel badly about it."

"Shooting me was the best thing. I was so full of hate. I wanted Americans out of my country. I was lying on the ground and thought I was going to die. My fellow North Vietnamese in the valley didn't see me and ran away. Normally we remove our dead and wounded from the battlefield.

"After they left, Thai spotted me and brought me to Tram. He entrusted my injured body to you four Americans. Everyone was wounded, and you included me to be treated. Ernie looked after me, so other Americans wouldn't torture me. Thank you for my life."

Ernie said, "Wow, what a story."

Khanh spoke more words and the translator said, "The story gets better."

"How can it get better?" asked Jesse.

"When I returned to Phan Lac, my nurse was Binh. She cringed when she saw me because I had aimed my rifle at her. She was angry at Tram who ordered her to care for me. Slater saved her life when he shot me. He also gave me a new life. As I healed, I got to know Binh. She is now my wife."

Khanh motioned for a woman to come forward. The American ex-soldiers recognized the older version of Binh. She still possessed her beauty and was smiling and crying at the same time as she approached the group.

Binh stepped toward Slater and looked into his face with warm and teary eyes. She grabbed both of his hands in hers. Slater remembered a similar hand clasp they had back in Phan Lac.

"Thank you for giving me a new life with my husband. When you spoke to Khanh, and he admitted that he couldn't shoot me, I saw him differently. You gave me a gift." Then she sobbed.

Slater was touched and didn't know what to do. He looked at his friends for guidance. He tried to utter a few words, but they didn't come out.

When she turned to meet the others, the American men weren't sure how to greet her, so they shook hands as she was crying and saying "thank you" at the same time. The wives knew what to do. They hugged her, and all of them wept together.

After the meeting, the Vietnamese gave the Americans the five-star tour of Hanoi and feted them with fancy dinners. Slater was surprised that his group would have a reunion with North Vietnamese.

He and Binh continued their talks after a long interruption, and included Khanh and Slater's wife. They exchanged many views and updated each other about their lives. Binh was delighted with Slater's wife and saw she and Slater were happy together.

When the group departed on the next leg of their journey, the American families gave sincere thanks to their gracious hosts. Binh and Slater hugged.

They flew to Pleiku and thought a bus ride would take hours to reach the rural locale of Phan Lac. They were surprised to find that modern highways greeted them. The trip took thirty minutes.

When the bus arrived at the Dong Giang Valley, the ex-Special Forces operatives didn't recognize anything from 1970. Coffee trees covered the landing zone and surrounding areas where they had patrolled. They saw many red berries on the trees and workers in the orchards. The driver said that the harvest season was December and January for Arabica beans.

The vehicle took them up a winding road to the village, and instead of huts they saw a large compound of houses and large buildings to handle the crop. Ripe coffee berries were spread on patios for drying.

"Looks like Tram succeeded as a businessman," said Vico.

The bus stopped at the office, and Tram and others ran out to welcome the visitors. He had streaky gray hair showing his fifty-nine years, but his smile reflected a youthful age. The families on both sides felt like long lost relatives. Even the American children blended with the Vietnamese youngsters. An adult Lan gave a present to Jesse.

Two days later after festive meals and talks, Tram gave them a tour of his coffee operation and described the process of harvesting, drying, washing, and preparing the seeds for the mill which his company also owned.

The visitors arrived at the main building, and Slater looked above the entrance and saw the English lettering.

Tram said, "I named it the Ross Wexler Building. His decision to buy those Arabica beans made our company prosperous. I'm sorry I got mad at you."

Slater remembered and said, "His killing upset me. He was a special person."

"He could have helped other Vietnamese villages," said the coffee plantation owner.

"Tram, You have an open mind. How did you develop it?"

"I got tired of fighting. When I received information in 1969 about four army bad boys coming to our area, I wanted to meet you."

"You knew we were coming?"

"Another cousin was a girlfriend of an army sergeant, and he liked to talk."

Slater smiled. "Not only did you know everything about the army, you are related to everyone in Vietnam."

"But it took Americans to get my business going, you and Ross."

The Americans stayed one week which was too short. Both sides made promises of visiting each other, and Tram offered jobs to the American children, so he could branch out in the United States. The good-byes were sad.

On the flight home, Slater told his army buddies, "This was a good trip, and I enjoyed seeing Tram again. I have avoided thinking about the war. All I know is that in 1969, I came here frightened and without friends. I got close to you three and became connected to the people of the village. This visit was healing."

The three comrades-in-arms didn't know what to say.

Slater quieted for a few minutes and then said, "Looks like I have one more journey."

They understood what their leader had to do. Slater had avoided paying respects to the memorial. Now he needed to confront the Wall.

51

APRIL 1996

B efore the reunion at Phan Lac, Slater avoided any discussion about the Vietnam Memorial. His emotions and
curiosity about the black granite walls shut down. When the
subject of the Vietnam War came up, his personality withdrew, and he changed the course of the conversation. Military
friends who saw the memorial said just standing in front of
it was a cathartic experience. Their comments didn't fuel any
interest in Slater.

Ernie, Vico, and Jesse accepted his decision. They wanted
to see it and did not share Slater's vehemence against it. They
planned to wait for an appropriate time, so they could see it
together, and now the moment arrived.

After they returned from the Phan Lac homecoming, Slater
organized the trip for the families to tour Washington, D.C. Two
months later they boarded a plane and headed north.

The men wanted to encounter the wall without wives and
children, so they sent their families to tour the Capitol. The wives
respected the decision. They knew the visit was a big step.

After parking the car, the men walked to the National Mall, an
open grassy area between the Capitol and the Lincoln Memorial
that contained monuments and statues.

270

The four veterans entered the grounds and were impressed with its scope. The black granite, V-shaped wall seemed enduring, even eternal. One end pointed to the Lincoln Memorial and the other to the Washington Monument. Names of the 58,272 deceased soldiers were etched into its face.

Slater wanted to honor Derrick and Ross. The others had high school friends in addition to Derrick to whom they wanted to pay their respects.

Jesse saw a booth manned by volunteers to assist with locating the names and asked one how to find their buddies. The volunteer pointed to books that disclosed the names and their placement in the stone. The four visitors leafed through the books that had laminated pages.

Slater looked up Wexler, didn't see the name, and went to the volunteer.

"Something's wrong. My friend is not listed."

"Was he in the military?"

"No, the U.S. government."

"This is for military only."

Slater felt cheated. Ross died serving his country and now wasn't accorded the reverence that others received. His anger welled up, but there was nothing he could do.

The others found their friends and went down the path to locate the names.

Slater returned to the book and found the name Derrick Williamson. Slater's finger raked across the page that showed where the name of his fallen friend was located: Panel 35W, Line 5.

As he was about to proceed, emotions engulfed him. He couldn't budge. His throat tightened, and his stomach twisted. Why was he so tense? He wasn't rushing a machine gun nest. He only wanted to pay tribute to Derrick. Slater's feelings intensified. Somehow he managed to hold them in check and ambled forward. Find Panel 35W.

On his way down the walkway comprised of unpolished granite slabs, a quiet governed, as though wind and car horns could not puncture the somberness and sanctity of this holy ground. Others milled around or just stared at the names on the black polished granite, mesmerized by a bewitching force that removed them from the secular.

Slater tried to distract his senses while he searched for Panel 35W. When he found it, his eyes went to the top line, then down to Line 5, then over to the name of his friend.

His senses would not be distracted any longer, and emotions overwhelmed him. Tears flowed, his lower lip quivered, his lungs heaved, and his body shook. With some effort he raised his hand and touched the name of the chopper pilot who did so much for him. He let his fingers brush across each letter in profound respect.

He could see Derrick looking at him with a crew cut, glowing eyes, and a big smile. Slater missed Derrick, missed seeing him at his home in Palo Alto, missed knowing him better in a sane world. Slater remained immobile. More tears meandered down his cheeks. Feelings surfaced from deep within, and he couldn't understand why his body trembled with such intensity.

His catatonic state wasn't even jarred when the arms of his comrades encircled him. They had been similarly moved with the names of their friends. They came to honor Derrick and support their lieutenant.

Minutes passed, then more minutes. Time stopped. People walked by. They understood. Finally the four broke the spell and inched backward. Derrick released them. Derrick healed them.

Slater looked at the name again and said in a sad voice, "See you, old friend. I'll be back."

52

POST MORTEM

Over three million American men and women were involved in the Vietnam conflict. It was not called a war because Congress hasn't declared one since 1941.

Of 115,000 Iowans who served, approximately 800 were casualties.

On April 19, 2005, thirty years after the end of the war, the Iowa House and Senate passed a resolution that thanked the Iowa Vietnam veterans for their service.

* * *

The Cold War contributed to the tension and even paranoia of the times. The military in the early sixties enjoyed more credibility as it was still basking in the victory and heroics of World War II that ended twenty years before.

On August 2, 1964, the naval destroyer, USS Maddox, twenty-eight miles from North Vietnam in international waters known as the Gulf of Tonkin, engaged in a small battle with three Vietnamese torpedo boats. Damage resulted to both sides.

On the morning of August 4, 1964, while cruising in heavy weather, the Maddox received radar, radio, and sonar signals

KENT HINCKLEY

indicating another North Vietnamese attack and reported it to higher headquarters. Taking evasive action, the ship fired on numerous radar targets. Afterward, the captain was unsure if the ship was attacked.

At 1:27 PM Washington time on the fourth, he reported that "freak weather effects" on the radar caused questions about the validity of the attack. He recommended "complete evaluation before any further action be taken."

The report from the ship's commander did not dampen the frenzy in Washington for action especially with an election in three months.

In fact, no attack occurred as reported by U.S. Navy pilot, James Stockdale, who witnessed the affair. Vice Admiral Stockdale was a highly decorated aviator whose awards included the Medal of Honor. In 1965 he was shot down over North Vietnam and became a POW for eight years.

On August 7, 1964, the Gulf of Tonkin Resolution was passed by the House of Representatives, 416-0, and 82-2 in the Senate. Dissenting, Senator Wayne Morse (Democrat, Oregon) opposed it on constitutional grounds. He tried to prevent the vote until Congress could review the USS Maddox's log. Senator Ernest Gruening (Democrat, Alaska) objected to "sending our American boys into combat in a war in which we have no business, which is not our war, into which we have been misguidedly drawn, which is steadily being escalated."

After the resolution was passed, the bombing of North Vietnam commenced.

In 1968, Senators Morse and Gruening were defeated in their bids for re-election. Morse's opponent criticized his anti-war position and his not supporting the United States of America in its effort to defend democracy.

274

Author's Note

An Indian parable tells of six blind men who touched a different part of an elephant in order to describe it to a seventh blind man. They came up with a range of answers. The moral relates to the existence of different realities and the respect for other truths. In similar fashion, my story describes only a part of Vietnam that I touched. The tale is fiction, but the time period corresponds to my tour in Nha Trang as a lieutenant.

While I was against the war, I salute all the men and women who didn't formulate the war policies yet answered their country's call. They did not receive the appreciation from this nation that they earned. I also honor their spouses, families, and friends who endured untold hardships.

The neglect of these valiant vets continues today. Many still haven't received their medical benefits that they are owed, especially for problems associated with Agent Orange and Post Traumatic Stress Disorder (PTSD). Even veterans from Afghanistan and Iraq have experienced ill treatment although some improvement has begun. If our country is to remain great, we need to care for our warriors and hold our politicians accountable.

I dedicate the book to three friends who died in the service of their country. I shaped two of them into the story.

My high school friend, Barry (Buck) Kingman, was an all-league football player at Palo Alto High School and a graduate of the University of California at Berkeley. Derrick Williamson was Buck's alter ego. Buck served in III Corps as a platoon leader for the highly distinguished and courageous scout pilots of the acclaimed 1st Squadron, 9th Cavalry Regiment, 1st Cavalry Division. Their mission was to spot the VC from a small helicopter. Each flight was dangerous. Buck received many decorations including a Bronze Star and a Silver Star. He was shot down doing reconnaissance on December 29, 1968. My emotions ramp up every time I visit the Vietnam Memorial and stand in front of Panel 35W, Line 5, to honor him.

My fraternity brother at Stanford, Fred (Rosey) Abramson, from Seattle, served as a model for Ross Wexler. Rosey worked for the United States Agency for International Development (USAID) in Vinh Long as advisor to the province chief in the southern part of Vietnam called the Delta Region or IV Corps. While assisting in a development program for a local village, he was ambushed and killed on January 6, 1968.

Another fraternity brother, Jim Cannon, a decorated navy lieutenant and pilot, had two assignments in Vietnam and flew many missions in North Vietnam. After being reassigned to the states, he flew an old F-8 Crusader from El Centro, California, to Miramar. The plane hit a turbulent mountain air wave near Ocotillo Wells which broke up the fuselage. He didn't have time to eject and was killed in the crash on August 26, 1970.

All three remain with me.

ACKNOWLEDGMENTS

The writer's world is blessed with generous people who assist authors in their growth. I extend my gratitude to other authors, "Writer's Digest," conferences, classes, San Diego Writers/Editors Guild, how-to books, bloggers, and webinars.

For background and research, my thanks go to Frank Fernicola, Dennis Burns, Carrie Kingman, Patty Sprigg, Le Tho, Cathy Thoung, Bruce Baum, Kerry Otterby, Kraig Kristofferson, Pete Pettigrew, and Ned Engle. You made everything easy for me.

I thank my brother, Dave, a marine, for his military stories and unfailing support of all my endeavors. His encouragement makes life's hurdles smaller.

My sister, Hilary, a writer herself, has been patient in educating me over the years. She critiqued my drafts, didn't pull any punches, and provided insightful comments. She knew how to reach the inner me. I can still hear her say, "Get into your Vietnam anger." Thanks, Hil. I couldn't have progressed without your help.

My copy editor, Linda Seeley, had to persevere through a minefield of spelling, grammar, and style miscues. Thank you for your assistance and expertise.

Michael Levin, a best-selling author, ghost writer (BusinessGhost.com), and contributor to the "Huffington Post," served as my writing guru. His guidance, acumen, and crucial suggestions advanced the quality of the story. I marvel at your many skills. Thank you, Michael.

My long-suffering English teachers, who, if they knew I wrote a novel, would be rolling their eyes. Thank you for your patience and dedication.

Our son, Bill, gave me many helpful recommendations. I didn't know he was talented at editing. He didn't let the ole man get away with anything. His aid with the finer points of Word made rewriting easier.

My wife, Sharon, has managed to smooth many of my rough edges in the course of our marriage. Through her talent as a watercolorist, photographer, author, and yoga teacher, she also showed me how I could access the right side of my brain and pursue creative endeavors. Thanks for the continuing adventure.